THE DOWNWARD SPIRAL

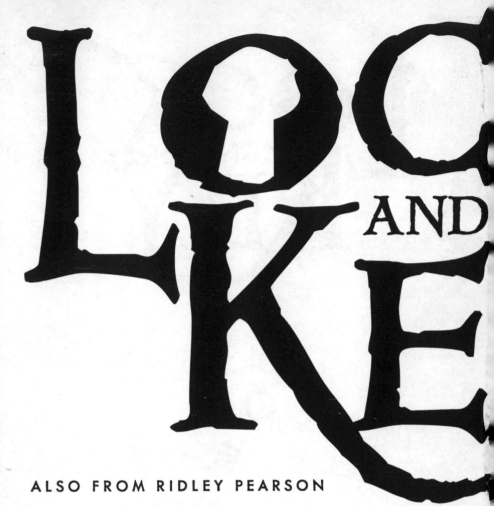

LOCK AND KEY

THE DOWNWARD SPIRAL

BY

RIDLEY
PEARSON

HARPER
An Imprint of HarperCollinsPublishers

Library of Congress Control Number: 2017932860
ISBN 978-0-06-239904-5

Typography by Joe Merkel
17 18 19 20 21   PC/LSCH   10 9 8 7 6 5 4 3 2 1
❖
First Edition

In Memory of Timothy M. Wormser

CHAPTER 1

Awakened by the sound of an outboard motor coughing to a start, I threw my legs out from under the down comforter, toes searching for the fuzzy lining of my slippers. As I stood and headed for the partially frosted window, I pulled a throw off the corner chair, accidentally dumping one of my Christmas presents, a novel, onto the plank flooring. Wrapping my shoulders, and reaching for the pair of binoculars that I'd been given four years earlier on my eighth birthday, I trained the glasses onto the churning waters of Nantucket Sound.

The waves collided, thrown into a gray-green

chop topped with white foam like a latte. The condition had something to do with currents and tides and a lot to do with wind direction and speed. Among the swells moved a flat-bottomed white fiberglass skiff called a Boston Whaler. The whaler threw foam and spray to either side as it cut its way atop the rough waters. I recognized its single occupant, the boy driving, as my brother, James. He wore a blue knit cap over his brown hair, a yellow foul weather suit, and over it, a bright orange life vest. He worked the wheel with his left hand and the throttle with his right. Oddly enough, the binoculars didn't reveal the falling snow. Only as I looked with my naked eye could I see it as a fine white confetti blanketing the seascape.

The sky held an elaborate mix of colors: aqua, gray, pink, and purple. A painter's sky. Our mother had been a painter, a good painter. A fine artist, she was called. She'd hung shows in banks and the library and sold well at the Provincetown summer craft fair, where I remembered her in a straw hat, bright lipstick, and sunglasses. We all smelled like suntan lotion in summers, and hamburgers, and fresh-cut grass. Ice cream doesn't smell or we would have smelled like that as well. I didn't remember my mother clearly, but it's all that's left of her: memories. Father, too. Life stops. Life goes on. As a twelve-year-old I found it hard to wrap my mind around it all. James wasn't doing much better at fourteen. (He looked and acted older—sixteen; seventeen if he wore a necktie—but inside I wasn't sure if he had an identifiable age.) He'd changed in the last few months, during our first semester at Baskerville Academy, a boarding school in north-eastern Connecticut. I suppose I had, too, but it takes others to see change in yourself, and I had few others around anymore. There was Lois, who'd been Father's secretary, then our nanny, and who now was our guardian. Ralph had been Father's driver, and maybe his closest friend. He felt like our uncle. It was odd to spend Christmas break with your family's house staff, in your family's Cape Cod compound that had been in the Moriarty family for three generations.

Tragedy had brought us together; tragedy had torn us apart. The four of us existed in a kind of limbo, feeling halfway between blood relatives and unwanted second cousins. Thankfully, neither Lois nor Ralph had tried to play the father or mother card. Nonetheless, there was no getting around the awkwardness that these two adults were now employed by my brother and me.

The skiff survived the chop to reach a sailboat that had arrived quickly from around the point that formed Lewis Bay to the west. Its white sails suddenly made to luff; I watched them flapping and knew the deafening sound of it. I watched shivering as James threw a bow line and was pulled to. A stern line pulled him parallel. He climbed aboard.

The binoculars lacked enough power to reveal any faces. It was more like watching a stage play from the back row. I took away the general gist of the story: two adults—men, by their size—met James and led him into the cabin belowdecks, while the crew dropped a pair of bumpers between the whaler and the sailboat. There was someone in foul weather gear at the large wheel at the back of the cockpit. There was a sense of urgency on the part of all, even seen from this distance.

James came back out of the cabin exactly five minutes later—I timed it. The same two men accompanied him back to the rail, shook hands with him, and saw him safely over the side. As the outboard engine started, it burped purple fumes. Lines were cast off and the skiff headed back toward shore. I confess to feeling something like relief. The ocean had no respect for humankind. I wanted James, the last of my living blood relatives, home safely.

When I saw him later, I didn't mention my having witnessed the rendezvous. I waited for him to say something, and when he didn't I resented the kept secret. The time of day alone told me it had been prearranged and was clearly important; James was no early riser. His silence not only hurt, but scared me a little.

Father's untimely death, a scant six weeks behind us, had been surrounded by a great many unusual and sometimes dangerous events. My brother and I had been at the center of those events. I needed no reminder of the tragedy, or the shroud of suspicion covering our loss. James and I had sworn an allegiance to determine what exactly had happened to Father, and by whose hand.

That same Friday night, we headed back to our Boston home, Ralph at the wheel, Lois in the passenger seat where my father should have been. Winter break was over. School would be starting up on Monday. The four of us made the ride as disconnected as strangers. I wondered if everyone else was thinking of Father as I was. Riding in the backseat with James, I repeatedly made eye contact, hoping he might tell me all about his dawn boat ride to the mysterious sailboat.

He never did.

CHAPTER 2

AFTER FOUR HOURS OF HEAVY TRAFFIC IN LIGHT snow, and a meal of Cluck-and-Crow sandwiches and soda, Ralph delivered James and me to the front door of our Boston home in the Beacon Hill neighborhood. Ralph jumped out and opened the car doors for us—like the chauffeur he was—led us up the snow-covered stone steps, unlocked the royal blue front door with its gleaming brass horse head knocker, leaned in, and switched on the lights.

Ralph's body type might have been responsible for the term "barrel-chested." Calling him sturdy would be an insult. Calling him young would be incorrect, but calling him old would get you clouted. Calling his heritage anything but Irish would drive blood into his face.

The way he handled himself, I'd often wondered if Ralph hadn't been hired partly as Father's bodyguard. He had sneaky eyes that saw everywhere at once. When I started looking for it, I could see he always put himself between us and the street, or us and strangers. Looking back, I realized he'd done the same for Father. If Ralph had been part bodyguard it helped explain why he'd taken Father's loss so hard. Father had died falling off a ladder while winding a clock in our vestibule—a task typically handled by Ralph. He probably felt guilty about that.

Or, maybe like James and me, Ralph didn't believe Father had been up the ladder in the first place.

Thanks to James's roommate at school, a boy named Sherlock Holmes, my brother and I now had our own opinions of what had and hadn't happened that tragic night. We no longer believed it an "accident." We had shared our theory with exactly nobody, but had pledged to investigate it, the three of us, to its rightful conclusion. Ralph should have been in the house that night with Father, but had been called away by a friend. Lois had been up in her room at the time. If by some strange reality warp we found out that either Ralph or Lois had been involved with Father's final hours, James and I would see that person in jail for it. Or worse.

I entered my room feeling heavyhearted. Being home made me long for Father. I didn't want to put away clothes. I didn't want to pile my laundry. I wanted to dive into bed, snuggle with my plush pets—Ellie (an elephant) and Cucumber (a Rottweiler)—pull the covers over my head, and have a meaningful cry.

But first things first. I unzipped and stepped out of my blue wool dress, flushed with annoyance once again that Lois had required James and me to "dress proper for the ride back to the city." This, I supposed, was to counterbalance that she'd allowed us to ride "casual" from Boston to the Cape—jeans and winter sweaters. The dress wool being scratchy, I'd worn a full-length slip beneath. I kept it on because the room was cold. Ralph had turned up the heat, but it would take most of the night for the steam radiators to improve things. I moved quickly, my feet chilly on the wood floor, my arms gooseflesh.

I avoided the wardrobe door's full-length mirror. I was a bit "underdeveloped"—a term I abhorred; as if my chest and hips had anything to do with my development!—more tomboy than princess, more freckle-faced than any girl would want. Nice eyes—a grayish green—good teeth, astonishingly red lips given the lack of cosmetics, the best haircut Boston could buy—which was saying something— and just the hint of an underlying intelligence that I was learning to manipulate given the situation. But unlike my friends at school, I wasn't one to linger in front of a mirror. I was a realist. When things changed, I'd deal with it.

A wardrobe is a piece of tall furniture that serves as a closet and, sometimes, a closet-and-clothes-dresser all in one. The house was old, as in two hundred years old. They hadn't built closets back then; they constructed brick houses with rectangular rooms. Bathrooms were shared by all, typically at one end of a hallway or another. Wardrobes and trunks had held clothing, linens, and blankets. Our house had long since been remodeled so that James and I each had our own bedrooms with our own bathrooms. Dormers had been punched out of the roof line and windows added out to a fire escape. But no closets. My wardrobe had been built in the time of Thomas Jefferson. Its cedar-wood smell reminded me of bunny rabbits and guinea pigs in elementary school classroom cages. My brother had hung an automotive air freshener in his wardrobe: Autumn Leaves.

I pulled open the door with the mirror.

As I tried to scream, a hand slapped over my mouth. The intruder, who'd been but a shadowy shape inside the wardrobe, turned me and stood behind me, arching me backward, his cheek pressed to my ear.

"Not a peep, Mo." A British accent. My family nickname. The scent of orange marmalade blending with a more complex, darker smell of milk tea. Oily hair smearing my freckles. Freakishly long fingers with equally long nails, clean and filed.

I nodded. We both relaxed.

"Sherlock." I gasped. "You scared me to death! What . . . are . . . you . . . doing here?"

He spun me around. We stood terribly close. I quickly crossed my arms. Embarrassed. Reaching past him I tugged a robe from a hanger and slipped it on, tying it tightly.

"What are you doing in my wardrobe?"

"Armoire."

"Shut up!"

"If I shut up, how can I answer?"

Sherlock and I had a relationship—small *r*. I'd only met him in September, on my first day at Baskerville Academy. It felt more like a year or two ago. A brilliant boy with far too high an opinion of himself and limited social skills, he could dress nicely when he wanted to, but apparently he rarely wanted to. He was a bit of a string bean and more than a bit of a conceited brainiac. Anxious to the point of jittery, he was not one to suffer fools gladly. His permanently rosy cheeks, high cheekbones, and royal blue eyes cut through all that. Maybe he'd be handsome someday, but he had his work cut out for him.

"Explain yourself, or I'll scream."

"No, you won't. It's me. I'm not some Peeping Tom, you know? Think, Moria. Why would I be here? Why would I have hidden outside your door until Ralph opened it and sneaked up here without anyone seeing me, if it wasn't something important?"

"You did not."

"Did too."

"Just now?" I asked.

"When else did Ralph open the door?" Sherlock answered.

"You clever, clever boy." It just kind of slipped out.

"We established that a long time ago." He smiled a thin but toothy grin that signaled his own sense of self-importance. "You will recall the last time you, James, and I were here together we discovered the words branded into the back of your father's desk drawer," he said. "I've figured it out, Mo. At least I think I have." What was this? I wondered. A moment of modesty, even insecurity? Maybe being all alone over Christmas break had caused him to rethink the importance of friendships.

What he was talking about was this: before my brother and I were sent off to Baskerville Academy, Father had left me—and only me—specific instructions in the event of his disappearance or any difficulty in communicating with him. I should have taken his precaution as a hint, a warning that he was worried, but at the time I thought he was just being his overly protective fatherly self. Anyway, he'd hidden a key for me in his private study, his office, that had opened a desk drawer revealing little more than some words burned into the back of the drawer.

whenallthat'sleftisright

The words had puzzled the three of us. We'd worked hard to figure it out, but had ended up stumped by it.

Or at least until now.

Heart pounding, I searched his eyes for any hint he might share whatever he'd learned. Sherlock had a way of teasing that was rude and unpleasant.

"So?" I said, giving him exactly what he wanted. He would draw this out until I begged.

The thud of heavy feet on the stairs captured our attention.

"Hide!" I said, pushing him back into the wardrobe and leaving him in there long after the threat had passed.

CHAPTER 3

IF I STOOD IN MY BATHROOM AND SHOUTED toward the air vent, James could hear me.

"In here now!" I called.

James entered, looking perturbed. I closed my door, revealing Sherlock standing behind it. James spooked, speaking a bad word.

It was awkward for the two roommates, who had spent the first semester working out that they needed each other as much as they disliked the other. They shook hands as if concerned about the sharing of an infectious disease.

"How goes?" James asked.

"It was an unfortunate holiday," Sherlock answered in his British marble mouth. "I was saddled with being the guest of the Geissingers for the duration, an arrangement clearly uncomfortable for both sides. Their Lucy took quite the shine to me, I'm afraid."

"Goose Geissinger, Mr. Maestro, conductor of the Cow Chorale, has a daughter?"

"A dog," Sherlock said. "Lucy is a black Labrador, energetic and with a quick tongue. Hounded me, quite literally, day and night. The Hound of Baskerville. Made a point of jumping onto my bed when I was otherwise fast asleep. I don't think I've slept for three weeks."

"Yeah, well, you look it." James eyed us both. "I didn't hear the doorbell, did I?" James took a quick look at my window that led out to the fire escape, no doubt suspecting I'd had a willing hand in letting Sherlock in. But the window was locked.

Sherlock needed to work on his tone of voice, which tended toward condescending. "No, not the window. The front door, while all of you were coming inside."

"Impossible."

Sherlock shrugged, uncaring what James thought. I thought their mutual contempt came from their being so alike. Like Sherlock, brother

James was a clever one, able to see not just what was in front of him, but what was missing.

"You two contracted my services to help investigate your father's accident. Need I remind you?"

"Believe me, that was Mo's doing," James tried to clarify. "I just went along with it."

"Be that as it may," Sherlock said, "are the two of you interested in the solution to the riddle branded into your father's locked drawer?"

"Of course we are!" I said, spitting a little by accident.

James returned Sherlock's early shrug of indifference. Tit for tat.

"There were Boy Scouts at the school over the holiday."

"Yippee," James said, disgusted. Bored.

"They set up caravans in the forest between the old mansion and the hockey rink," Sherlock said. He explained that the term "caravan" applied to what James and I called trailers, but with awnings and tents attached.

"Father supported the Boy Scouts when he served on the Baskerville board of trustees," I said, ever the dutiful daughter. "When empty, the school grounds amount to hundreds of acres of beautiful woods with no one taking advantage of them."

"It wasn't the caravan arrangement," Sherlock

said, "it was the marching."

"Marching?" James questioned.

"They marched to a chant recited by all. Led by the troop leader. A call and response. I quote: 'You have to go home with your left, your right!'"

"Fascinating," James mocked.

"It instructs them when to place their right foot forward, their left, et cetera. It's a rhythm, a cadence that keeps them marching in step."

I covered my mouth so that Sherlock wouldn't see me smiling at his expense. He sounded like a total fool.

"You lost me," James complained.

"It was the reference to left and right, just like your father's desk drawer. And I quote: 'when all that's left is right.' You see?"

"Not at all," said James.

"Marching orders. Instructions," Sherlock said, his lips twisting into a smirk. "It's not a riddle. He branded into the drawer how to use the key. All the way left, then to the right. At least, that's what I think he's telling us."

James stepped forward, and though Sherlock shied, took his roommate's cheeks between his palms, squishing his face. "You . . . are . . . brilliant!"

"Sandwiches are served!" came Ralph's ragged

voice from the first floor.

We three exchanged looks of panic.

James spoke to me, then to Sherlock. "We'll put him in Father's office. You'll wait for us. You'll do nothing until we're there. Agreed?"

"But of course."

"Brilliant!" James repeated, slapping Sherlock for the second time, this time a little too forcefully.

CHAPTER 4

W<small>ITH</small> S<small>HERLOCK</small> <small>TUCKED</small> <small>AWAY</small> <small>IN</small> F<small>ATHER'S</small> office, James and I joined Ralph and Lois around the dining room table. The room itself was extraordinary, festooned with plaster bunting crown moldings, white pilasters, and a matching chair rail. The room's centerpiece, a polished mahogany table from an 1810 Southern pecan plantation, had been in our family since the Civil War. It was the size of a tennis court. Lois had placed James and me on opposite ends, with her and Ralph squarely in the middle of opposite sides.

I needed an intercom to speak to James in my

normal voice. "How's the weather down there?" I called to my brother.

"Pity we can't be in the same zip code," he shouted back.

"Very funny, children," Lois half scolded. "As I pointed out in the compound," she added, referring to the family property on Cape Cod where we'd spent Christmas, "you two will have to grow accustomed to your new roles as head of the Moriarty household, like it or not."

"Not," I said quickly.

"There will be charitable events, public functions. The family plays an important role in this city. You two must fulfill certain civic duties."

"Excuse me for a moment," I said in a silly, haughty voice as I stood. "I shan't be long. A quick visit to the loo, if I may?"

James applauded dully.

I made a quick stop in the downstairs bathroom, but only as an excuse to check on Sherlock, as Father's study was the door at the end of the short hall.

I spent too much time whispering that we'd be finished as soon as possible. With the door partway open, I heard footsteps and turned to see Lois approaching.

Sherlock ducked behind the partially open door.

"Moria, dear? What on earth . . ."

She caught up to me, only the thickness of the door between her and Sherlock. Maybe she smelled Sherlock, who was prone to using cologne to mask his lack of a shower. Maybe she sensed my apprehension.

"Aha!" she said, noticing the framed color photograph-on-canvas surrounded by the study's built-in bookshelves.

It was one of the few family portraits. In it, Father held James, while Mother cradled me as a newborn. Of course I had no memory of the moment, but I'd seen it my whole life and I felt as if I could remember. Taken by a professional, it showed the four of us posed in the green backyard of the Cape Cod house, frothy waves breaking in the distance. Father wore a white cable tennis sweater. Mother, a tennis dress and cardigan. They smiled widely, their skin young and flawless, eyes sparkling.

I played the sympathy card, forcing my eyes to mist over.

"Now, now, we mustn't dwell on those things out of our control, but be grateful for all we have."

"I'm not dwelling. I'm savoring. I'm allowed that, aren't I, Lois?"

"You're allowed that, indeed." She laid a warm

hand on my shoulder, looking at the photo herself. "And I'm an old witch for interrupting. Join us at the table when you can."

"I'll be right there." I felt cheap for taking advantage of her like that. I didn't mind bending rules or altering the truth in my favor when it served a higher purpose, but this struck me as something selfish: a secret I was hiding. An act of betrayal. I had long since set betrayal as off-limits.

So why was I now changing the rules?

CHAPTER 5

James deposited his plate into the dishwasher and was, as always, the first out of the kitchen. I stayed behind, wiping the countertops while Lois washed the remaining dishes. It didn't take long.

I said a polite good night and headed for the stairs. Once into the vestibule, I stole to my right down the narrow hallway that led past the washroom, the library's pocket door, and into Father's office.

James held a finger to his lips and carefully shut the door behind me. He locked it.

I signaled James and Sherlock to stay put as I kneeled in front of the cold fireplace and dug into the ash at the back. I latched onto and withdrew the small key hidden there, the secret Father had shared with me.

His large, antique desk held a multi-line telephone, a Swedish glass paperweight, and a framed photo of James and me, with a green leather desk pad set before the cracked leather office chair.

Sherlock turned, inserting the key into the upper right drawer as a performance. He rotated it counterclockwise while whispering, "All that's left . . ." It rotated fully around once, twice, three times, and stopped. We all three heard the faintest of clicks. No louder than the ticking of a clock.

"No way . . ." James said, almost a moan of regret. For him, everything with Sherlock was competition.

"Is right . . ." Sherlock turned the key to the right.

With a pronounced click, the desk pad popped open on a hinge, revealing a hidden space beneath. We all made a sucking sound of surprise.

"Why'd he tell you and not me?" James complained.

The three of us just stared at the secret hiding place.

Sherlock, whose vast intellect seemed to have missed the chapter on human emotions, launched into an explanation of the mechanics. "The spring-loaded trigger was initiated by the revolution of the key."

James told him to shut up.

I answered James, as careful with my words as I was when trying to pull burrs from London or Bath, our dogs. "I don't think it was trust, or anything like that. You were always the important one to him. Maybe he just wanted me to feel like I had a role in our family."

"I'm not buying that," James said.

"He kind of warned me he might disappear."

"He what?"

"Yeah. He gave me a timetable. I wasn't to use the key unless we hadn't heard from him."

"This is not happening." James had gone the color of the fireplace ash.

Sherlock made the mistake of offering his interpretation. Never wise when it involves someone else's family drama. "We can assume your exclusion, James, had something to do with a boy's proclivity for curiosity. Spontaneity. He didn't want you opening the drawer in the spirit of inquiry. He obviously trusted Moria to simply obey his wishes."

"Give it a rest," James said.

But Sherlock had no off switch. "Think about it. You, Moria, would have discovered the clue burned into the drawer and would have sought your brother's advice."

"I would have, James!"

"Never mind," Sherlock added, "that the two of you would never have arrived at the proper solution to the clue without me."

"He says in all modesty," quipped James.

"Am I wrong?" asked Sherlock. He never was. Never. And we all knew it.

"Arrogant, insulting, and annoying," returned James, "but rarely wrong. And for the record, I agree with you. Father would have expected Mo to include me."

Both boys looked at me for my agreement. I answered by pulling up on the partially open desk pad.

Inside lay a manila envelope.

"Oh, my," I gasped.

Next to the envelope was the unexpected. Lying in the drawer, halfway wrapped in an oily rag, was a gun.

CHAPTER 6

JAMES REACHED FOR THE WEAPON, A LONG-barrel revolver, what was often called a six-shooter in the cowboy Westerns.

"Uh uh uh!" Sherlock said quickly, stopping James dead to rights. "Fingerprints, dear boy!"

"Do not call me that!"

"Might I suggest you avoid the rag as well?" Sherlock produced a pen from his pocket. "Insert it into the barrel ever so carefully."

James adroitly picked up the wrapped gun. He set it down on the desktop as if it were warm to the touch. We stared.

"Father?" James said.

"We don't know," said Sherlock, "hence the precaution. The gun may hold your father's prints, no prints, or the prints of a yet-to-be-disclosed third party." James wasn't impressed by the explanation. Sherlock continued. "The envelope could contain something as benign as take-away menus, or a letter of explanation on how to use the revolver to one's political or financial advantage. Perhaps a photo or a news clipping. It could be a ransom or a threat."

"Oh my word! I never would have thought of that!" I said.

"Nor would you have picked up the gun first," said Sherlock. "The feminine response would more likely be to read the contents of the envelope rather than handle the weapon. Perhaps your father's expectation, and the reason he left the key to you and not James."

"That's—" I was interrupted.

"Entirely possible," James whispered distastefully. "He's right, Mo. I would have reached for the gun first."

"Might I suggest," Sherlock said, "that you, Moria, read whatever's contained in that envelope before we do anything else?"

I picked up the envelope.

Beneath it, burned into the wood, was written:

For the love of money is a root of all sorts of evil, and some by longing for it have wandered away from the faith and pierced themselves with many griefs.
Nevermore

"Interesting," Sherlock said. Pointing out another branding along the right edge of the compartment, he said, "There's another here, as well." The burned lines created five rectangles stacked vertically, like a capital *H* with two additional middle bars.

"'Nevermore,'" James said. "Meaning what? He's not going to let money ruin things? Or is it simply never again? No longer? Fed up? Sick and tired?"

I sat down in a chair by the unlit fireplace and withdrew a single sheet from the envelope. It contained symbols. Some looked familiar. Most did not.

Sherlock looked over my shoulder.

"What do you think?" I asked him.

"It's Greek to me."

"Me too."

"No. I mean it's Greek. Some of the letters are Greek. Though all run together so that it feels more like a cipher. May I?" he asked. I handed it to him.

The front doorbell chimed.

The three of us froze. Sherlock folded the sheet and tucked it into his back pocket.

"Not . . . good," said James.

"Here's what we do," I said, knowing that Lois would be making the trip from her second-floor bedroom behind the kitchen. The bell rang again. It would take Lois a minute or so. "Sherlock, you put everything back as it was. You'll stay here, in this room—all night, if necessary. You don't leave until we come for you. James, you get the front door. I'll head upstairs and get ready for bed, as that's what Lois would be expecting me to do."

The boys looked as if they were about to argue with me.

"Now!" I said, unlocking and opening the office door.

To my delight, James followed. I hurried up the front staircase as silent as a ghost and glanced back to see James looking up at me. Waiting for me. We connected, brother to sister, conspirator to conspirator. I felt positively wonderful. James nodded at me proudly, and turned toward the front door.

I fumbled with my clothes, racing to start a bath.

CHAPTER 7

JAMES HAD BECOME THE CAUTIOUS SORT EVER
since his initiation into a secret society called the
Scowerers that I wasn't supposed to know about.
(Credit Sherlock.) He'd also become more distant
toward me, which broke my heart.

With our having returned home only hours
ago, he reasoned, whoever was at the front door
must have known our schedule. Already past nine,
it was too late for a random caller. That drastically
limited who might be ringing our bell at this hour.

Father had been a cautious man as well. A state
of mind that had evolved into outright paranoia

toward the end. He'd upgraded our home security to include at least two video cameras—that I knew of—covering the front and back doors. The windows were alarmed. Movement-sensing floodlights had been mounted high up near the roof gutters.

A small video screen inside the door revealed two men in topcoats. James used the intercom to ask they take a step back and show their faces. Mr. Lowry, Father's lawyer, and Dr. Crudgeon, headmaster of Baskerville Academy. Venerable company, indeed.

"Sorry!" James said, speaking through the intercom. Lowry and Crudgeon had been behind James's initiation into the Scowerers, the secret society that had links to generations of Moriartys and also to Baskerville Academy. Now officially a member of the group, James was being "groomed" to take over leadership of the Scowerers, an entity he still knew little about. These two men were his tutors, his advisors, his guides. The idea of following in Father's footsteps, of running a secret group of men and women, charged James with purpose, provided him a newfound sense of self-importance, and influenced his every decision. Since his initiation (something Sherlock had secretly witnessed) James had grown colder to me and Sherlock. He'd formed a select group of friends at school and pulled them around himself in a way that reminded me of Malfoy. But unlike Malfoy, James was no coward. He was no one to mess with; as his sister, I knew that only too well. He could be cunning, creative, and cruel. He considered himself a prince in line for the throne. The arrival of Lowry and Crudgeon told him: a) either he or our home was being watched, for the Scowerers knew we'd returned, b) something important was happening, or else why would they visit the house so late at night, and c) he, James, was central to whatever was going on. This last bit gave him a keen sense of importance.

Pulled between the excitement of our discovery only minutes before in Father's study, and the unexpected arrival of these two, James felt unsure of his footing. He felt compelled to keep Sherlock's presence secret. At the same time, he was part of the secret society and sworn to loyalty.

He unlocked the door's double locks and admitted the two men into the vestibule. They stomped snow off their shoes and pulled off their overcoats without invitation.

"Please . . . come in, why don't you?" James said, to put the two men in their places and remind them whose home this was.

"Yes. Sorry. Kind of you." Dr. Crudgeon's wide shoulders and stout frame made removal of the overcoat something of a struggle. Lowry helped the man out of it then shook some of the melting snow from it before finding a hook.

Crudgeon patted down his gray-tipped hair where the overcoat's collar had ruffled it. He cleared his throat and checked the small mirror hanging on the wall. In its reflection he saw the stony face of Mr. Conrad Lowry, Esq. looking over his shoulder. The cold had nipped the tip of Lowry's long nose a brilliant red. The lawyer's bushy eyebrows were matched in peculiarity only by the dark tufts of hair escaping his ear canals. He looked something like a human woodpecker, at once both menacing and intelligent.

"Snow flurry," Lowry said overly loudly.

"Ah! Good evening, gentlemen!" Lois called as she came from the kitchen. "I see you're in good hands!" She caught up to James and placed her hand on his shoulder.

"Perfectly!" said Crudgeon, eyeing James. "A fine host."

Ralph said hello as he slipped behind Lois, a mug of something steaming hot in hand, and climbed the staircase. Lois greeted both guests by mentioning the snowstorm. Idle chitchat gave way to a moment's silence.

"Well, I'll leave you then," Lois said, getting the

message she wasn't wanted. She retreated toward the back of the house.

"Good to see you, James!" Lowry clapped James on the back. "How was the Cape? I hope you'll tell us all about it!"

The three moved through the foyer and into the library. Like Father's office, the library walls held floor-to-ceiling bookshelves with not a sliver of empty space for an additional volume. The drapes were a rich burgundy velvet, the hand-knotted rugs Afghan. An antique world globe rested alongside a brass lamp with a green glass shade. The library was among my favorite rooms. James was indifferent to it, preferring Father's office for its intimacy and the power it represented.

James slid the pocket doors shut and ensured the other door leading to the hallway outside Father's office was pulled snug as well. Their conversation, he knew, would not be meant for Sherlock's ears.

The three sat down. Crudgeon glanced at his wristwatch.

"Fancy seeing you two so soon. What's going on?" James asked softly.

"Your sister?"

"Upstairs taking a bath, knowing her. Why?"

"Just crossing the t's and dotting the i's."

Crudgeon cleared his throat. "You will remember we mentioned we might have an assignment for you."

"Out on the boat this morning. Yeah, of course! Not an easy thing to forget," James said.

"Events have moved more quickly than we anticipated," Lowry said.

"We barely just got home," James protested. "It's not as if I've had time to go looking for Father's journal. We just finished dinner!"

"No, no! We understand. It is something else entirely," Crudgeon said.

"The city councilman. The at-large guy. No connection to a particular district."

"You were paying attention. Very good," said Lowry.

"That's it exactly," said Crudgeon.

"He's a hassle to us," James said.

"He's become an annoyance to our little society," said Headmaster Crudgeon.

From what James knew about the Scowerers, the group was anything but little. But he kept his mouth shut.

"So let us begin there," Lowry said, sounding lawyerly. He glanced at Crudgeon, who spoke next.

"Boarding students return to campus Sunday night. We talked on the boat, among other things, about your transition into a leadership role, that the Scowerers have pledged fidelity to you and your family. You may find it odd that men and women far older than you will follow orders from a boy your age, but I assure you they will. Especially if you prove yourself worthy of such fidelity."

"I understand," James said. "And I'm eager to prove myself, as I said."

"Good!" Lowry said. "Because there's a job that needs doing. It provides you just such an opportunity."

James bit his lip to keep from speaking, excitement getting the better of him.

Crudgeon cleared his throat again. He swallowed. It was gross. "I take it you are familiar with the sophomore Alexandria Carlisle?"

"Lexie the Loser? Yeah, sure. I know her. Why?"

"We want you to befriend her." Lowry's eyes narrowed.

"Wait! What?"

"We need you to gain entrance to the Carlisles' home north of Boston, in Nahant." Lowry allowed this to sink in. "We told you about her father, retired Rear Admiral Copperfield 'Coop' Carlisle, who keeps an appointment book in his study. The contents of that appointment book are not online in any manner. We need you to photograph the upcoming four weeks of his schedule. You must not be caught or give away your intentions. Can you do that for us, James?"

"Befriend her? Meaning?" James processed the rest of the message. "You want me to spy?" The idea of spying thrilled him. The thought of trying to make friends with Lexie Carlisle made him sick to the stomach. Never mind she was kind of pretty, he thought. She was a girl, a loner, and a nobody.

"You will hint at wanting to visit her home."

"I will what, Headmaster? Are you kidding?"

"Alexandria takes breaks to Nahant every other week," Crudgeon said. "You must get yourself invited to join her."

"But that means we'd be . . . serious! That's like boyfriend/girlfriend stuff! That's not going to happen. Me and Lexie? You expect me to make Lexie the Loser my girlfriend?"

"We expect you to carry out the assignment. Don't complicate things," said Lowry. "This is not a request, James. Time is of the essence."

"But you mustn't rush things," Crudgeon added sharply. "Not with a shy girl like Miss Carlisle. You can't afford to scare her."

"Shy? Lexie is friendless."

"Not any longer, she isn't," the headmaster said, his lips curling. "Do we understand each other?"

"How's that not supposed to not look staged? This is me! And her? Are you kidding?" James said. "She'll never fall for it."

"Girls rarely give boys second chances, James. If you should fail—and we trust you won't—you'll force our little group to adopt a more aggressive policy."

"In other words," James said, "I handle it perfectly or I ruin everything."

"Something like that," Headmaster Crudgeon said.

"Exactly that," said Lowry. "Others have already failed to obtain the information. We need this, James."

"Others?" James asked. A heaviness hung between them, tightening James's throat. "Why are you both looking at me like that?"

"This leads to something of a more personal nature, the second point that needs discussion, James," said Lowry, checking his watch for a second time. "Tommy, would you mind checking if Lois could bring us some ice water?"

"I can!" said James. But Lowry grabbed him by the wrist.

"No, that's all right," said Lowry.

"Back in a jiffy," said Crudgeon. "Catch him up on where we stand." He slipped out the pocket doors and slid them shut. Lowry loosed his grip.

James felt a bit turned around. The two men seemed to have rehearsed some of this, and James found himself lacking the script. "What's going on?" James asked.

Lowry spoke softly. "There's the very real possibility you or your sister may be targeted by an opposition organization."

"I don't understand."

"Competitors to the Scowerers in Europe."

"You told me we have investments there."

"Indeed."

"Competition's a good thing, right?" James said.

"Can be. Not always."

"Go on."

"News of your father's tragedy will have spread quickly in certain circles. Investment groups like ours. There will be an effort to fill a perceived power void, especially in distant territories where our immediate control is a bit out of reach."

"Who are they?" James asked.

"They call themselves the Meirleach. Literal translation from the Gaelic is 'thief.' They are an Irish group, formed well over three hundred years ago. Well organized, well funded, ruthless, and powerful." Lowry pulled out a handkerchief and mopped his brow. It was not warm in the house. Not at all warm.

"Investment groups?" James said.

"Your father was engaged over the past three years or more," said the headmaster, "negotiating with the Meirleach over our Eastern Europe . . . investments."

"Our turf. Our territory," James said.

"Our investments," Lowry repeated. The doors slid open. James caught something in Lowry's eyes as he looked behind James at Crudgeon, who entered carrying a tray with three glasses of water. By the time James spun around there was nothing to see but a smile on the headmaster's unwilling face.

"Our choice of words is so important," Lowry said, reminding James he was a lawyer first and foremost. "Headmaster Crudgeon, why don't you explain the situation at school?"

They all took a glass and a few sips.

"Of course! Our little group has placed a security detail on this house until Sunday. When you arrive to Baskerville you may see the occasional adult keeping an eye on you. Don't draw attention to it, and play dumb if anyone asks. You don't know who they are or what they're doing on campus. I will announce that there are some inspectors and engineers having a look at the place. That will be all the students are told."

"For my security or to make sure you know what I'm up to?"

"Are you up to something we should know about, James?" Lowry said. "Are you in need of a babysitter?"

James wondered if these men somehow knew about the efforts to find out who had killed Father. If they felt threatened by the effort. If they were lying to him about the purpose behind the surveillance.

James asked, "What are these Meirleach after?"

"James, these are ugly people who would not think twice about using you or Moria to pressure us. It's as simple as that. You don't want that. We don't want that. Your father wouldn't want that."

"Don't speak for my father, please. You have no right. No one has any right." James saw through his own anger to a flicker of truth, of realization: Lowry was deeply concerned about the Meirleach. He filed it away. "So they're criminals," James said. "Irish thieves. Why would they bother kidnapping me? What is it they want? What leverage are they trying to gain?"

"Your abduction would be used to force us to surrender certain investments," Lowry said.

"The European turf you were talking about," James said.

Crudgeon sucked air.

Lowry reminded James to consider his vocabulary. "We live in an age when you never know if you're being recorded, or if someone's listening. We must take every precaution."

James apologized. "What you're saying makes sense. It's just a lot to take in."

"Of course it is," said Crudgeon. James couldn't get over Lowry having called the man "Tommy." Crudgeon didn't have an informal bone in his body as far as James could tell.

"Moria's going to spot these guys watching us. Have you thought of that? Moria notices everyone, everywhere. She's freaky that way."

"If she says anything, just remind her of my explanation at assembly. Play dumb, is my advice." Crudgeon returned his partially drunk glass to the tray.

"Mo knows I'm not dumb."

"We all have our moments," said Crudgeon, a wry smile playing across his face.

Lowry drained his glass, the ice clinking. James wondered if his contained something stronger.

"What's that sound?" James asked. "You hear that? Is that running water?"

A moment later there was the clap of a nearby door shutting—Father's office!—and thunderous footsteps up the stairs. Too light for Ralph. Too fast for Lois.

CHAPTER 8

I AWOKE TO SEE SHERLOCK TOWERING OVER ME as he drove his hands below my rib cage in an effort to expel water. Though I was covered in a towel, the location of someone's hands—especially a boy's hands—in that particular area of my body caused me to sit up sharply. Sitting up sharply caused me to vomit. All over Sherlock.

He smiled.

"That'a girl!" he said. I coughed, threw up some more water, and felt him banging on my back. He seemed to be enjoying this.

"I heard water coming down the wall. It came

under the bookcase. I just knew . . ." he said. Lois arrived, out of breath and red in the face. "You?" she shouted, presumably at Sherlock. "Moria?"

"She was passed out . . . in the tub."

"And you—?"

"Yes," Sherlock answered. "I scooped her out, but with my eyes closed, I assure you. And I put a towel over her before opening them! I am not a cretin!"

"Oh, good golly," Lois said, trying not to cuss. "She could'a drowned! You . . . saved . . . her." Then her face bunched. "What are you doing here, young man?"

"Saving her?" Sherlock said, sounding thoroughly guilty.

I coughed horribly, this time intentionally, trying to return the favor by saving Sherlock from Lois's interrogation. Lois pulled Sherlock away, telling him she'd "take it from here," and in the process knocked the hot chocolate off the sink and onto the floor, breaking the mug and sending pottery shards everywhere.

As if that weren't enough, our dog Bath charged into the bathroom, knocking down Sherlock as Lois had nearly tripped over me trying to catch the falling mug. Bath began licking the floor. Sherlock began mopping my vomit off his shirt. I began coughing, again. And Lois began crying.

James entered in a huff, testing the *Guinness Book of World Records* limit for how many people could fit into a bathroom.

Things got crazier before they improved, but it wasn't long before James was sitting next to me on my bed. I was wearing a nightgown I didn't even know I owned. His hand was touching my neck, his thumb stroking my cheek.

I could see he'd been crying. I loved him for it.

Brothers can be tricky.

I was exhausted. All I wanted was sleep and I said so. James gave me a long, ardent hug and I returned it. He whispered something I wouldn't ever forget.

"Glad you're OK, Mo."

He brought a tear to my eye, an added ache to my chest. I kissed him lightly on the cheek, and chuckled to myself as I saw him rub it off as he moved into the hallway.

CHAPTER 9

"Come on, Mo! You've got to see this!"
James dragged me by the wrist and out of bed.

"I'm sleeping! I almost died!"

"Shut up! You're fine! Here." He handed me my warmest robe.

My brother led me down the hall a short distance to his room. I was still coming awake, still upset he'd dragged me off with him.

"Sherlock sleeping on your floor?" I said, upon our arrival. Lock was sleeping soundly though not snoring, his long frame awkward beneath a pair of blankets, his stocking feet sticking out off the air mattress.

"Not him! Who cares about him? Bath! Look at Bath."

Our family dog was sprawled on the bare floor, legs out straight, his ear cocked funny on his head as if he'd been listening intently before falling asleep.

"The hot chocolate!" I gasped. "He's sick! We've got to get him to—"

"Wrong!" James pronounced. "It takes an ounce of chocolate per pound of dog. I looked it up. He would have to have eaten *four pounds* of chocolate to make him seriously sick. It's not the hot chocolate. I think he likes me all of a sudden."

"Well, that's bizarre," I said.

"Right?"

"Probably Sherlock, not you," I said, trying to come up with a reason Bath would finally—after five years—voluntarily sleep in my brother's room. He would scratch, cry, and bark to get out of sleeping with James.

"Can't be," James said. As one resistant to anything having to do with Sherlock Holmes, James clearly refused even the notion that Sherlock might be responsible for accomplishing something James never had.

"Maybe Lock smells funny or something like that," I suggested.

"He smells awful. And his feet. Oh, man, his feet!"

"So maybe Bath likes that."

"No," James said, "I don't think so."

"So now you're the Dog Whisperer? James Moriarty, master canine trainer?"

"Just because you're good with horses doesn't make you an expert, you know?" He said this defensively, though it made no sense to me. I let it go, not wanting to argue with my brother at 1:00 a.m.

"You haven't done your due diligence," James said.

"Ew! That's disgusting."

"It's a business thing, Mo, not a bathroom thing."

"Well, it sounds dirty."

"It means your research, your homework, your fact-finding. Thoroughness."

"Dog. Asleep. On floor," I said, sarcastic to the bone. "Dog who hates my brother."

"Does not!"

"Dog who has never slept in my brother's room.

How's that for thorough?"

"Not enough," he said.

"I nearly drowned tonight, Jamie. I'm tired. Embarrassed. I have a wicked headache. And I'm basically totally confused by a million things, starting with the gun in Father's desk. Pardon me if I don't care about Bath sleeping on your floor!"

Sherlock snorted, stirred, and returned to his heavy breathing.

"Keep your voice down!" James said. "Go ahead, try to wake him."

"But he looks so peaceful."

"Not jerk-face. Bath, you idiot!"

"Oh, shut up!"

"Try to wake up Bath. You can't!"

That proved enough of a tease to cause me to try. He was right. Shake him. Pat him. Pull him by the collar a couple inches. Bath was spark out.

"Well," I said, "that's not right. At least he's breathing! No wonder he's in here. He couldn't leave if he wanted to! Should we get Lois? Call the vet? Now you're freaking me out!"

"No!" said James. "Not yet, at least."

"Chocolate," said Sherlock, jolting James and me. I was sure he was talking in his sleep. "Hot chocolate. Lois. The dog." Sherlock held the blankets as he sat up. The air mattress shifted and he nearly lost his balance. "Lois bumped the mug when she was trying to get me off you," he said to me. "Not that I was on you. I was over you. I—"

"We get the point!" James said. "So?"

"Lois bumps the mug. Mug shatters. Dog licks up the hot chocolate. Dog falls asleep minutes later, right where he now lays."

Somewhere far in the distance a siren wailed. From the other side of James's bed, the radiator clanked as it did throughout the winter months. I could hear James and Bath breathing. Either Sherlock farted or the air mattress squeaked. The silence was broken.

"Where'd you get the hot chocolate?" James asked me hoarsely, his voice scratchy and dry.

"Ralph brought it. Left it outside the door. Knocked to tell me it was there. He does that all the time in the winter."

"Ralph." James could barely be heard.

"But Lois would have made it, right?" I was speaking rhetorically. Ralph couldn't boil a pot of water without directions.

"Lois," James said. "And Crudgeon left the library at one point to get us all water."

"We have a saboteur in our ranks," said Sherlock.

I looked to my brother. "You're saying one of

those three was trying to kill me?" I felt a kind of cold the robe couldn't help.

"There must be another explanation." James gasped.

CHAPTER 10

"Stalker alert," I warned Lois. The day after my "unfortunate incident," as I shall forever call it, we were passing a tea store, one of Father's favorites, when I happened to turn my head and happened to see the two men in the reflection off the glass. I meant it as a joke. Seeing Lois's reaction—stiffening shoulders, a catch to her stride, a straightening of the spine—I felt bad. "Just kidding."

"Don't do that!" Lois said.

I didn't want to be with Lois—one of the three people we suspected of having tried to hurt me.

I wanted to be with James and Sherlock and my friends at Baskerville. But James had driven off with Ralph a few hours earlier, and Sherlock had been required to take a bus rented by the school that departed Boston in another hour or two.

I was stuck, though determined not to be.

"Well, I mean, there are two men back there. And they happen to have been somewhere in sight for the past three stores, but I doubt they're stalkers. Oh, and I saw them in the parking lot, too."

Lois did not look back, which surprised me. Who doesn't turn around when someone warns them they're being watched?

"Washroom," she said. It wasn't a request. We turned down a short hallway. At the door to Women's, Lois and I shot a backward glance. One of the two men had followed, heading to Men's. The other stood by the shoe store at the end of the hall.

This was the same Lois in consideration as one of three people who might have tried to drug me unconscious so I would drown in my bath. A Lois I had known basically my whole life. A Lois I loved like a mother.

"Caprese," I said, which was as close as I got to cursing. "Hamlet!" was another (never hurts to quote Shakespeare). And "Oh, ship to shore!" came in handy as well.

Lois was accustomed to my shorthand potty mouth. "Inside."

Standing by the sinks, surrounded by pale green tiles and a smell that defied description, Lois questioned me about when I'd first seen the two men, how I'd noticed them.

"I'm an observant, sometimes brilliant, young woman. You have to ask?"

For a moment, she thought I was serious. Then she smiled crookedly (Lois avoided showing her teeth when she smiled). She did something unexpected then: she put her phone into her purse. The move caught me off guard. Lois didn't like anything that operated with an on/off button, especially the phone that first Father and now Ralph required her to carry. What troubled me was why she'd had it in hand in the first place. Had it been dialed to 911, awaiting her thumb to put the call through? Had the men scared her that much?

Or had she allowed someone to listen in on my discussion with her?

"What's going on?" I asked her.

"Just taking precautions."

"Did Father have enemies?"

"What a strange thing to ask." Lois looked at me askance.

"That's not an answer."

"This is not the place. It smells like yesterday's breakfast in here."

Whatever that meant.

She inspected herself in the mirror, tucking a strand of hair behind her ear. She brushed her front, smoothing out the fabric of her navy blue dress. Then she addressed me as an afterthought, regarding me in the mirror. "Any person, man or woman, who is as successful and intelligent as your father is bound to separate himself from certain groups and find himself aligned with others, Moria. The term is 'competition,' not 'enemy.'"

"Why would the competition be interested in me?"

"Or me," Lois said. She and Ralph were experts at making themselves invisible. They could be in the same room with me and I wouldn't notice them unless they wanted me to. I'd made the mistake of not thinking about Lois as the target.

"Because you know more than any of us about Father's businesses," I exclaimed. "Oh, Lois, I'm so sorry! I hadn't considered that!"

"Don't trouble yourself with such nonsense. And it's just that: nonsense! I'm sure we're wrong about these two. Only one way to find out." She led me out the door, down the hall, and back into the mall. We passed the man who stood waiting.

Tall-ish, dark-ish, nondescript-ish. Moroccan or Egyptian. Swarthy, in a handsome, intriguing way. He didn't give us a second look, much to my disappointment. We passed several more stores. Lois impressed me with the clever methods she used to steal a look behind us: a mirror on a kiosk cart; pointing up to store signs and pivoting as if lost; dropping a Hello Kitty notepad intentionally and glancing back as she retrieved it. The methods not only struck me as shrewd, but practiced.

"We're clear," she told me. Not "good," or "OK," or "alone," but "clear." They said that kind of thing in cop movies, not real life.

I mentally replaced the word "practiced" with "trained." Lois was comfortable, I realized, not uptight the way I was. She was calm and collected, the experience not entirely unfamiliar. She'd been trained.

Either the air-conditioning had switched on, or thinking of Lois had given me a chill, but gooseflesh ran up my arms and tingled at the base of my neck and I squirmed.

"Didn't you hear me?" she asked. "We're all right. We're fine."

But all I heard was, "We're clear."

A mall security woman passed us on a Segway.

Three girls in extremely short shorts and bare midriffs paraded past, leading a group of six guys by about ten feet. In January, no less. I couldn't tell if the two groups knew each other, but I thought they probably did. The same groups had existed in the hallways of my middle school, before I'd started at Baskerville Academy.

"I'm actually looking forward to getting back to school," I said to Lois. "I can't believe I'm saying that, but there you have it."

"If you're trying to convince me otherwise, know this: we all think it a good idea to keep you home an extra day or two."

"It's not being with you, Lois!" I lied. In fact I was terrified to be in the house alone with her and Ralph. "It's just the last thing I want is more special treatment. James and I already take a lot of grief for our ancestors starting Baskerville. That's bad enough. What am I supposed to tell them? I almost drowned taking a bath, but my brother's roommate saved me and my governess decided I should take a couple days off."

"That would be a pretty dress for you," Lois said, apparently forgetting we wore uniforms at Baskerville.

I jumped back suddenly, wishing I hadn't. My

reaction wasn't because of the outrageously ugly dress. It was because I was a quick learner, me being me.

I caught a figure in the reflection off the glass.

Not either of the stalkers. This time it was Sherlock staring back at me.

CHAPTER 11

Given my newfound respect for Lois's powers of observation, my options were limited. Because
of the men we'd seen following us—though they
were currently nowhere in sight—she wasn't about
to leave me alone.

We stopped in the food court. She, for a cin-
namon bun. I, for a peach gelato. While I was
conspiring on how to break free in order to meet
secretly with Sherlock, a guy in a green apron,
pushing a rolling trash pail, cleared a few things
off our table.

He knocked some litter into my lap. I was about

to complain when I saw it wasn't litter at all.

Moria

Written in pen across the folded piece of paper.

By the time I looked up, I saw only Sherlock's back and a green apron string.

"Everything all right, sweetie?" Lois asked. My reaction to the trash in my lap had been excessive.

"Fine, thanks." I thought it strange and somehow predictable that neither Lois nor I had looked to see who was cleaning our table. I condemned myself for not even thinking of this act as being performed by a fellow human being. Worse: Sherlock had known we wouldn't look up at him, and that disturbed me most of all.

I unfolded the note in my lap, where I also held my phone. Lois knew I could spend hours looking down at my phone, oblivious to everything around me.

On the sheet of paper he'd drawn a bunch of boxes in ballpoint pen. Not boxes, I realized, a diagram. Not a diagram, a floor plan with a half-dozen question marks on some of the lines.

Not just a floor plan. It was the ground floor of our house.

Sherlock was asking me for measurements.

CHAPTER 12

Late Sunday, students began returning to Baskerville from break. Sherlock didn't pay much attention. Asocial by choice, he kept to the library, skipping dinner.

The DuPont Library, a concrete abomination that had no business on a campus of Colonial brick buildings, occupied ground to the west of the dining hall with an apron of brick terrace out front. The bricks held names of alumni and donors. Sherlock, who'd become absorbed in a good mystery, was the last student to leave. Mrs. Hornknocker, a grandmother to all with silver cotton-candy hair and a loose and flabby neck, wished Sherlock good night and locked the doors behind him.

As usual Sherlock was in two places at once. His feet were moving, but his mind was on the plot of the book clasped in the vise of his arms against his ribs.

As Mrs. Hornknocker switched off the building's interior lights, an unintended darkness overtook the terrace.

Sherlock spoke loudly into the empty courtyard. "You'd be fools to try it! She's not blind, you know."

Two figures hunched in shadow on the side of the building looked at each other in the gloom, wondering if Sherlock could possibly have seen them.

"Whatever hazing you may have in mind, I'd rather take a rain check." He sighed heavily as he heard them rush toward him from behind. He and James had been warned in the fall session to expect some hijinks from upperclassmen. They had never come, which had been fine with both boys. "This stuff is so childish!" Sherlock hollered.

He was scooped up off his feet, his two attackers seizing him beneath his arms. Things became a little more aggressive and confusing when a foul athletic sock was stuffed into his mouth and a section of tape slapped across his lips.

"Buferfuff . . . nunshish," he muttered, not liking this at all.

The mystery book fell to the terrace.

He was struck on the head. His legs sagged.

Sherlock woke up in one of the six music rehearsal studios beneath Hard Auditorium, an exceptionally small, closet-sized space.

"Nufflegger . . . hmff." The sock was still down his throat.

The boys let loose on him, delivering a pounding. If this was hazing, it was not what he'd expected.

His punishers wore balaclava ski masks, though that hardly deterred Sherlock, so honed were his skills of observation. Even with one working eye (the other swollen shut), a broken nose (bleeding), and a sprained wrist, Sherlock took note of the two pairs of worn running shoes and one pair of socks marked NFL.

When the thicker of the two boys said, "You don't wanna go busting into people's houses without asking."

"Hummercunch . . . affterally."

"You put your beak where it doesn't belong and we'll spread you around the forest to where your hand won't know where your foot's at."

"Meffer-flef," groaned Sherlock.

The taller boy had to be a varsity soccer player the way he delivered the final kick to Sherlock's chest. Something cracked loudly.

It surprised the two punishers and quickly put an end to the event.

As they left, the boys shut off the room light and switched on the sign that was mounted outside each of the rehearsal rooms.

QUIET PLEASE
REHEARSAL IN PROGRESS

Sherlock knew that sign well. Through all his pain and soreness he managed to find amusement. It hurt too much to laugh, but he was thinking that if that was the rehearsal, he didn't want to be part of the performance.

CHAPTER 13

I ARRIVED AT BASKERVILLE ACADEMY MID-Monday morning, having talked Lois into cutting my two-day imprisonment down to one. I was later than all but a few students whose flights had been delayed by winter storms.

My brother skillfully avoided me throughout that afternoon and evening. His avoidance told me something had to be wrong. Very wrong. He'd left for school an ally and companion, my nurse and protector. Suddenly, I didn't exist.

Something was up, and I knew it.

I was not to be deterred. I finally cornered him

by using the element of surprise, taking advantage of the one place where only a sister would dare. It required impeccable timing and thorough scouting, but James and I had grown up playing endless hide-and-seek. Cops and robbers. Spy versus spy. An expert at covert surveillance, contortion, subterfuge, and diversion, I was well positioned to literally catch him with his pants down.

I slipped into the only washroom on Bricks Lower 3. The boys' washroom. I pressed my back to the door to prevent anyone entering, while trapping the only boy, my only brother, inside.

"You've been avoiding me!"

James was scrubbing his soapy hands together under the faucet. He tried and succeeded to keep from looking surprised.

Impressive, I thought.

He spoke in a calm but deliberate tone. "If Can't-Tell catches you, you'll be expelled."

"Mr. Cantell's the assistant wrestling coach. He won't be around for hours. Why are you avoiding me, Jamie?"

"I'm not. Who said I was?"

"Bull roar!"

"There was a mix-up. It may have started with me. Probably did, but I'm handling it."

"Where is Lock? Why haven't I seen him?"

"That's the mess-up," James said. I could tell he felt ashamed.

"Jamie?"

"I'm going to handle it."

"Handle what?" I felt butterflies, and not the good variety.

"I would check the infirmary."

"Jamie?"

"Stop saying my name like that. You're not Father."

"What's going on?" I asked.

"I might have mentioned to a couple guys what went down at the house, that your boyfriend was involved."

"He's not my boyfriend."

"I think one of them checked with Natalie," James said. "And I guess you'd been texting with Natalie, and maybe she'd been texting with Ruby Berliner. Anyway, Ruby told this guy that Sherlock broke into our house."

"What?" Natalie Sekulow, one of my two roommates, had an unspoken crush on Sherlock. It was my own fault for talking about him so much. By the time the fall session had ended, I'd sold Natalie on all of Lock's good qualities. That she might gossip about him was no great surprise. Ruby, on the other hand, I'd have expected better of. An artist and thinker who hated tests but loved old TV shows, Ruby didn't strike me as a girl to get catty.

"That he hid in your room while you were undressing."

"What?!!" I felt livid. And embarrassed. "He saved me!"

"I know that! That's not the point! It got all messed up. And anyway, I'm going to handle it! How many times do I have to tell you?"

"The infirmary? Oh my gosh! Sherlock's in the infirmary?"

"Give it a rest, Mo! It's done. We can't undo it. I can't undo it! I'm new to this stuff."

James caught himself. I wasn't supposed to have heard that. I pretended I hadn't, but it hung between us, causing a cavernous pause.

A boy pushed on the door. I stuck my head out into the hallway and told him to go away. I was not polite. Speechless, perhaps even frightened, the boy hurried off. I felt surprisingly powerful at that moment. Abnormally good.

"Lock's on our side," I reminded James.

"I know that."

"What side are you on?"

He stuck his hands into the wind machine hand dryer. It roared. He looked over at me cruelly.

"He's not my boyfriend," I said. "That's just plain wrong."

"That's another conversation."

"The infirmary??"

"Wait," my brother said. "Wait until you calm down before you see him. And when you do see him, make sure he forgets who did that to him."

"I will not!"

"You will, too!"

I loved my brother dearly even when he gave way to his short temper and grew heated like this. I knew the brilliance with which he approached practical jokes and "operations," as we'd called them in our childhood years when pretending to be spies or criminals. Jamie had always delighted in playing the criminal—always the thief, never the detective—and I in the opposite role.

Hearing such a forceful tone from him now made me wonder if our games had shaped us, if we were bound to the things of the past the way trees along the coast lean forever away from the sea.

If, by our own decisions, we become unchangeable.

CHAPTER 14

THE SCHOOL INFIRMARY HAD THE LOOK OF A movie where you're supposed to be in heaven. It was in a converted part of the top floor of the humanities building, which had once been the original library, with tall, arched-top windows admitting an abundance of natural light, white walls, and metal-framed beds with white linens. The school nurse, a matron of Germanic proportions and pleasant demeanor, wore a white apron over office clothes. She had big teeth and a broad smile.

There were already two cases of flu, both girls in a closed room designated for the contagious, and then Sherlock in the third bed of six that shared a kind of dormitory.

"Hey, you," I said, trying not to cringe. I pulled out a chair, but he tapped the bed, and I willingly sat down at his side. "Oh, man," I let slip out.

"Ran into a door," he muttered through cracked lips. His nose was covered in white tape and a bent piece of metal.

I felt myself choke up. James had had nothing to worry about. Sherlock Holmes was no tattletale. I could have kissed him. I actually thought about it, which was something so new to me I probably blushed. I grabbed some tissue and blew my nose.

"That bad?" he said, fighting to not smile.

"Yep," I said. "Maybe worse."

He winced as he lost the battle.

"Some door," I said.

"The mother of all doors."

Some tears spurted out. I hated myself. I caught them with the tissue.

"Not that bad," he said.

I had to use the tissue yet again.

"I got your diagram."

"Mmmm."

"Tricky of you to deliver it like that."

"You know me," Sherlock said.

"Got the measurements for you."

"Mmmm."

"A hundred and forty-four square feet."

"Missing," he forced himself to say.

"Yes."

He had trouble speaking, but there was no stopping him. "The bath water. Other side of the bookshelf. A meter or so of bookshelf."

"Where it was damp? Four feet. I measured, remember?"

"The code," he said, his one good eye blinking slowly. Expressive. Deep. Richly blue.

I probably blushed again.

He was nodding off. I was watching him fall asleep and there was something so intimate and peaceful about it. I wanted to pat him or stroke his cheek, but he looked so banged up I didn't dare touch him.

"The code," he mumbled again.

I wondered if he was already dreaming.

CHAPTER 15

At 2:00 a.m., James slipped out of bed, into his slippers, and sneaked quietly down the Bricks Lower 3 hallway. Lower 2 adjoined Lower 3 in a staircase area with an exit to the outside and a janitor closet tucked under the rising staircase.

Father had shown James the closet and its removable floor panel back in October. He'd told his son stories of his discovery of the utility tunnel years before when he'd been a student at Baskerville. It was a father-and-son secret that James held dearly.

It was a gloomy and claustrophobic area filled

with pipes and wires and a low ceiling that prevented standing. But it was private and secret, and therefore to James and boys his age more like a fort than anything else. He used it as a meeting place.

Its limited space was crucial to James's plan. He'd asked two boys to meet him.

Quietly lifting the steel floor plate, James spotted Ryan Eisenower's buzz-cut hair atop the boy's oversized head. James climbed down into the cramped space and joined him.

"Where's Bret?" James asked.

"Haven't seen him. Didn't know he was coming."

"Do you know what this is about?" James asked.

"Probably. I think so."

"You either do or you don't. So let me ask you again: Do you know what this is about?" James understood the importance of expressing superiority. A certain tone of voice and eye contact could establish a confidence that others would not challenge. Size didn't seem to matter. Likewise, physical strength, for Eisenower was twice James's physique. It was one's sense of purpose that made one person more of a leader than the next.

"I'm pretty sure I know what this is about."

"Good," James said. "Then say that the first time I ask."

"Who put you in charge?" Eisenower growled.

"I did. You complaining? It sounds like you're complaining."

"No."

"We're good?"

"Yes."

"Good." James settled, brushing concrete dust off his hands. Though twice his size, Ryan Eisenower was maybe half his bandwidth. James felt a sense of the primitive rising from within him. Maybe it was the heat of the tunnel that resulted from the overhead pipes. Maybe it went back a million years to fire-lit caves. Competition. Survival. Domination. The same forces that fielded varsity teams, that gave way to tug-of-war contests in the spring. Boys weren't boys, they were cavemen in Vineyard Vines and Under Armour.

James knew this. Crouching, he shuffled forward and slugged Eisenower in the stomach without warning. He swung his elbow out like a wing and cuffed Eisenower on the ear. Kneed him in the chest. Prepared to elbow him in the back. But Eisenower grabbed and pulled James by the legs, tackling him onto the concrete floor. James, the

wind knocked out of him, managed to kick Eisenower in the chest, which stood the boy straight
up. Eisenower's head banged into a pipe. The boy
blinked, seeing stars.

James took measure of the low-hanging pipes
as he drove his shoulder into his opponent, knocking Eisenower over. He took the kid by the shirt
while straddling him.

"Don't you ever do me any favors without
checking with me! You got that?"

Eisenower's face bunched, part anger, part
shame. "We were just helping you out. Sheesh!
Some kind of thanks!"

"You messed things up. You got it all wrong.
Sherlock saved my sister, you idiot! He deserved a
medal, not a beating!"

"What?" It was Bret Thorndyke, just coming
down the short ladder-like concrete steps into the
tunnel.

"You two went to town on the wrong guy at the
wrong time!" James said, spinning to face Thorndyke. Not nearly as big and powerful as Eisenower,
Thorndyke was nonetheless an upperclassman,
older than James, and therefore more frightening.
He was also an athlete, agile and daring. Thorndyke
presented James with a different kind of opponent.
His childish look—in NY Knicks pajama bottoms

and a Baskerville Athletic Department T-shirt—belied the threat within.

James knocked him down quickly and leaped to straddle Thorndyke while pinning the boy's arms. Thorndyke bucked to get James off. James reached for his throat.

"Are you listening?" James asked, marveling at the sense of control having his hand on the boy's throat afforded him. He felt intoxicated.

Thorndyke worked hard to nod in response. James lessened his grip.

"I know it was your idea, Bret." James glanced back to see Eisenower getting up, but the fight was gone from the boy's eyes. This in stark contrast to the one beneath him. "I know you like that kind of thing. This kind of thing." He squeezed the boy's throat tighter. "You love it, don't you? But you and Boy Blunder got it all wrong." James relaxed his grip, seeing the redness and swelling of the boy's face. James didn't remember tightening his grip like that. "Never again. Do we under—"

Thorndyke heaved up and threw James off. James twisted his leg in the process. He rolled, but Thorndyke throttled him with a series of blows. James would have been beaten unconscious if Eisenower hadn't pulled Thorndyke off and held the boy.

"You listen to me," Thorndyke growled at James, struggling to break free of Eisenower. "You try something like this again and I'll finish you."

James recovered nicely. "No, Bret, you won't. You hurt me and you will pay in ways that I won't be able to stop. If either of you don't want to work with me—for me—I could care less. So be it. Good riddance."

"I didn't say that," Thorndyke said.

James said, "You beat the snot out of *Sherlost*, and while he may have deserved it for being the dork that he is, he didn't for anything he'd done, which is why you will never do me a favor without me asking for that favor. We're mates, the three of us, and there are more of us, many more, than you know about. There will be more, soon. What I'm doing here is for real. It'll continue after we graduate. I can do it with or without you, believe me. You might want to remember that. It may not make much sense right now, but it will soon enough. Change is coming. You want to be part of it, you need to pay attention. Strict attention." James was up and inches from Thorndyke's face. James nodded to Eisenower, who loosened his grip on Thorndyke, who brushed himself off. All three boys were white with cement powder, red-faced with rage.

The fiery look in Thorndyke's eyes said he wanted to go at it again. But something about James—the same unnameable something James had possessed his whole life—stopped Thorndyke.

The older boy stepped aside, allowing James to squeeze past.

"Thank you," James uttered, once at the bottom of the ladder. "What you did shows loyalty, and I appreciate it more than you know. But we need to work as a team."

He climbed out of the hole, expecting some kind of rebuttal from Thorndyke, for he was the type to want the last word.

But neither boy dared to speak.

CHAPTER 16

THE BASKERVILLE COMMON ROOM, THE LARGE
lobby area of couches, comfortable chairs, and
game tables, was shut off from the dining hall by
a pair of massive double doors. It served as a holding area and gathering place for all students prior
to meals, as student waiters prepared the hall.
Teams of like-minded students tended to cluster
in circles, their backs to others. Girls huddled by
themselves. Boys huddled by themselves. Jocks
huddled. Nerds huddled. A few foursomes played
bridge. Rabid hunger, social anxiety, potential
and failed romance all made for a mixture of loud

voices, and generalized cruelty.

James spotted Thorndyke and Eisenower approaching. Maverick Maletta trailed them by half a step.

"We have some unfinished business," Thorndyke said. Eisenower nodded.

"Did you not pay attention in Cummings's class when he lectured about cliché? That's pathetically unoriginal, Bret." James stood up, nose-to-nose with the boy.

"Outside," Thorndyke said. "After lunch. The Dumpsters."

"And again. Are you binge-watching *The Sopranos* or something?"

Some strays, sad-looking students who could never find a circle with enough social gravity to bind them, turned to observe the confrontation. James, whose sense of personal space and his surroundings had heightened since the warning from Crudgeon and Lowry, lowered his voice.

"Do you sleep through World Religions?" James asked. "Or are you familiar with the quote 'For now we see through a glass, darkly; but then face to face: now I know in part; but then shall I know even as also I am known'?"

"You've lost it."

"No, actually. Quite the opposite. You and

I are face to face, but I happen to see through a glass, darkly, and I happen to enjoy it. Savor it. You messed up, and for that I gave you and Ryan here a little tune-up as a reminder to stay in line. You want to meet out at the Dumpsters, fine. But I'm going to leave you there, facedown on the asphalt. And if by chance I don't, if I should take a lucky punch from you and go down myself—and I don't rule out that possibility—then you had better not sleep at night, you had better bring a baseball bat into the shower with you. Because I like where this is going, Bret. I get off on it. And I finish what I start, and I start only those things that are winnable. You start this up again, you will not like how it ends. I'm committed to seeing this through, Bret. How about you?"

If James leaned any closer they'd be touching noses, or leaving butterflies on each other's cheeks. His dry windpipe made his words ghostly and ominous.

Then, as if a switch had been thrown, James became an entirely different person. His eyes brightened, his snarling lips swept upward into a smile. Even his voice mellowed and sweetened.

"Alexandria!" he called out to a girl just passing. Her shoulder-length colorless hair needed attention, her hunched posture correcting. Her skin could have benefited from a reliable acne cream, but that was not an uncommon problem at Baskerville. Hidden within the ruins of neglect was a pair of interesting green eyes and a face that might someday mature into being "almost pretty."

"Lexie the Loser?" Thorndyke murmured.

James took the boy by the neck of his shirt and twisted it to where he choked him. He hissed into Thorndyke's ear. "You say that again and you won't have teeth." With his other hand, James grabbed Lexie by the upper arm, and quickly let go so he didn't seem too aggressive. "Hang on," he called to her as he pushed Thorndyke back.

"James?" she said. Timid. Cautious, but not afraid. Curious, but not convinced. A deep voice, like she was speaking into a well.

"You like sailing, don't you?" James said.

"I do. Yes. Very much."

"You sitting with anyone at lunch?"

"Me? With nine others, like everyone else."

"Can I join?" James asked.

"It's mostly girls I sit with, James. In fact, it's all girls."

"Neutral territory? Randolf's table?" Though seating wasn't assigned, each table at lunch and dinner included a single teacher who kept order and tried to instigate conversation. Randolf was a math teacher and liked by all.

"What's this about?" Lexie asked.

"I just . . . want to sit with you, I guess." The lying came far too easily.

"It's a dare, isn't it? I'd rather know up front, James. I don't know you well, but I don't think of you as cruel. If you need me to play along for you to win the dare, if it's nothing too demanding, I'm happy to do it."

"It's not a dare."

"James? Please. Tell me, and we can get this over with."

"Is that really your opinion of yourself?" he asked.

"Should I be immune? 'Lexie the Loser.' That's rough when you're on the wrong end of it. And inaccurate, I might add. What have I ever lost at, that you know of, James? That others know about? No one at this school knows me that well. Sure, they judge me by my looks, I suppose. The fact that I'm quiet. I'm sure you do, too. And I won't say I don't care, because I do. Believe me, I care. But a loser? Never."

"I don't call you that. That's high school stuff. It's for idiots who can't think for themselves."

"Cummings's table?" Lexie proposed. An English teacher. The conversation might be a little intense, James thought.

"Ms. Morgan's," James suggested. The art teacher. Neutral turf.

"Done. Whoever gets there first saves a seat for the other," she said. "If you burn me, James Moriarty, if you leave me standing and unable to find a seat, or waiting for you to take one I'm saving, I will never, ever, forgive you. Understood?"

Lexie had pluck. Backbone. Mettle. Who knew? James thought. "Our fathers were friends, weren't they?" he asked.

"I think. Maybe. Business acquaintances at least," she said, being more specific. "My father's on the city council and I think yours knew him through his work. I was so sorry to hear about your father, James."

"Well, at least we have that in common," he said, trying to make light of it. But she wasn't amused. "Whoever's there first," he repeated. "No tricks."

"Hmm," she said, "I wonder." She headed off, her incredulity trailing her like the train of a gown.

CHAPTER 17

"I'T'S NOT THAT I'M COMPLAINING." LEXIE SAID in her pleasantly deep voice. "But I'm still curious as to why you would sit with me, James."

"I heard you're a sailor. So am I. When you said you never lose, did you mean—?"

"I meant I never lose, James. I made the Headmaster's Society last session. A four-point-one—the only student in our class to make it. Suddenly, I'm 'Lexie the Loser.' Sticks and stones, right? And yes, that includes sailing."

James set down his milk. Wiped his lips with his napkin. Lifted his fork to attack the pork. Thought better of it and placed the fork gently onto the side of the plate. "I promise, it isn't a dare," he said.

"Well, then it's something you aren't explaining."

She was as perceptive as she was smart, he thought.

"Why can't I just like you?" he asked.

"You can, but you don't, because you don't know me."

"Then help me get to know you."

"Why should I?"

"Because I'm interested," James said.

"No, you're not. We've never said two words to each other. You want to talk about losers? The guys you hang around with are losers. You don't fit in with them, James. What's that about, anyway?"

"Ouch," James said.

"Yeah. Sorry about that," Lexie said. "I tend to lack a few filters." She smiled sweetly and James saw an authenticity he liked.

"Sailing," he said.

She giggled at his changing the subject. "Yes. Real fun."

"You don't lose."

"Not lately."

"How long is lately?"

"Five years. Club cup for five years. We race 470s. They're a—"

"Trapeze dinghy. Two-handed. Summer Olympics."

Another of her smiles. Not the same as the first. Wry. A bit flirty.

He returned to eating. If he took his time, all the food for seconds would be gone. "You've never had a crew like me."

"Is that so?"

"Won't know until you find out."

"Then I'll never know, will I?"

"Ouch again," James said.

"Is there an invitation in there somewhere that I missed?" she said.

"Our boats are on the Cape. Put up for the winter."

"Mine is in Nahant, and ready to sail."

"Winter sailing."

"Yes."

"Hmm."

"Does the idea scare you?" she asked.

"Hypothermia. Death. Isn't it supposed to?"

The second smile again, the one felt at the back of his neck. They laughed together.

"Being scared of something," James said,

looking directly at her, "doesn't mean it isn't worth a try."

"Danny Double Entendre," she said. "Am I supposed to melt into a puddle of Jell-O and start batting my eyelashes?"

"Are you?"

"Not going to happen," she said.

"Good," said James.

"If I'm supposed to invite you, you shouldn't hold your breath."

"Best crew you've ever sailed with," said James. "You won't know until you try."

"You and the lines. Is that the only one you know? You're lying to me about something, James. I won't allow you to hurt me."

"Why, because you like me?"

"Not even the least little bit," she said with a smile.

They ate in silence. Serving plates passed. James loaded his plate repeatedly. They stole looks at each other. She smiled more than once.

CHAPTER 18

I SAW THE FOLDED POST-IT NOTE STUCK TO THE wood panel of my dining hall chair. Before I sat down, as I swiped my skirt beneath me, I snagged it.

Computer center, ASAP.

I wadded the note into a ball and let it fall to the floor beneath the table.

There was something wonderfully exciting about receiving a secret note, especially from a boy, a particular boy whose handwriting was familiar to me. A boy clever enough to know what chair I would choose.

For a moment, I didn't believe I could possibly be so predictable. I couldn't possibly sit in the same chair at every meal! Was I that much a creature of habit? It was true that I liked looking out the bay window to the view of the forest to the west. It was also true that I often—perhaps more than often—claimed the chair to the left of Mrs. Habersham, teacher of Western Civilization and assistant soccer coach. I liked Mrs. Habersham, considered her a good teacher and someone I looked up to. But could I afford such predictability? Weren't people considered boring when they did the same thing over and over?

I snagged the mashed potatoes. I might allow the roast pork to slip past, the soggy green beans. But butter-infused, creamy mashed potatoes? Never.

I ate hungrily, eager to excuse myself. After wolfing down the potatoes I received permission to go to the washroom and headed in that direction. The same direction as the staircase leading down to the computer center.

Sherlock had never explained his possessing a master key to the school's locked doors. If he didn't want to tell me, I wasn't going to ask a second time. With the rumble of voices and dishes clanking overhead, Sherlock admitted us into the off-limits computer center. This wasn't the computer lab, where programming and technology was taught. The computer center was the brains of the administration—the school's network routers, administrative backup, academics, admissions, alumni. The way Sherlock described it, the room had massive storage capacity and something he called "redundancy," which I took to be backup of the backup.

As far as Sherlock and I knew, no one came down to the center unless there was a glitch. We were likely safe until lunch ended and classes resumed in another forty-five minutes.

I didn't consider myself a rule breaker. Father had raised James and me to comport ourselves admirably. Yet here I was, breaking and entering. Growing up wasn't so great after all.

"Why am I here? What's going on?" I asked, feeling horribly guilty about our trespassing.

"Making progress," Sherlock answered, adjusting his sling so that he could type with two hands.

"Please. No games. I'm not in the mood." I offered to do the typing, but this was Sherlock.

"Did you attend chapel last night?" he asked rhetorically. "No, you didn't. I was looking for you. If you had, you might have shouted in the middle of the scripture reading at the start of the service."

"You attend chapel?"

"International students are required to attend all religious services."

"No way!"

"I promise you, it's true. I actually find it relaxing, and the music's wonderful, but may I continue?"

I nodded, feeling something different about Sherlock Holmes. Once again, something mysterious.

"The scripture was from First Timothy. It was about bringing nothing into this world and carrying nothing out."

"Sherlock . . . is this really—"

"Important? Yes, of course it is relevant, Moria." We were sitting side by side in front of one of the many terminals in the center. Behind us was a glass wall partitioning off a second section of the center, where rows of racks held dozens of boxes with blinking lights and a dizzying number of colorful cables.

"I happened to have followed along with the scriptural selection, you see?"

"Not at all," I said.

"It was First Timothy six, verse six and seven."

"Fascinating," I snapped sarcastically. All I could think about were the mashed potatoes I was missing.

"Any guesses as to First Timothy six, verse ten?"

"None whatsoever. Did you try any of the pork roast at lunch? I missed the pork."

He arched his left eyebrow at me in a menacing way. That eyebrow of his could communicate more than his spoken words.

"What? I'm still hungry," I said.

"First Timothy six, verse ten: 'For the love of money is the root of all evil—'"

"Stop!" I said. It was just an expression, but Sherlock apparently took it as a direct order. "Go on," I said.

"Which is it, stop or go?"

"That's the saying burned into Father's desk," I reminded myself aloud. "In the drawer with the gun and the page of gibberish."

"You and I," Sherlock said, "suspect your father scanned your family Bible. Our one attempt to prove or disprove that fact was interrupted by Proctor Sidling. That is, until now." He adjusted his sling at the shoulder. I helped him and he didn't stop me.

"What does that have to do with a verse from First Timothy?"

"I'm getting to that," Sherlock said, in a tone of voice I recognized as unintentionally irritable and intolerant. My friend was running out of patience with me. He refreshed the screen and logged on to the system using Mr. Randolf's name and password.

"How can you possibly know his log-in?" I asked.

"He's a math teacher, Moria. An older man. He types incredibly slowly. My third or fourth day of class I stood by his side as he logged on. Observation, dear girl, is the key to undoing all secrets. Don't forget that."

The system admitted him. I could hardly believe his arrogance.

"We don't even know if there is a scan of the Bible," I reminded him, wanting to interject some reality and pop his bubble.

Rather than take it as an insult, he took it as a challenge. So Sherlock of him.

"We have the benefit of two facts, Moria. Hmm? We know, within a day or two, the date the Bible was stolen. Ergo, the dates the Bible might have been scanned. Secondly, it's a large volume, with a good deal of content on every page."

"A big file."

"Exactly! Precisely! Brava!" Sherlock crowed. "An extremely large file."

"So," I said, beginning to understand, "we limit our search to only a few days, and we look for the biggest files created on those dates." I made it a statement not a question, because I could see he was already querying the system to make just such a search.

Seventy-two files had been created during the three-day period in early September when the Bible had been discovered missing. Of those, only three were over ten gigabytes.

Artwork_submission.pdf

14_5_22_5_18_13_15_18_5.tiff

Admit_early914_c&ghl.tiff

All three were further password protected.

"We're cooked," I said.

"Nonsense," said he. "Challenged, but who doesn't love a good mystery? Look at the one with the numbers. You see the three fives? The ones by themselves—you can't count the one that's in fifteen. Isn't it obvious?"

"Not to me it isn't," I said. "I have no idea what you're talking about."

"You must!"

"Not a clue."

"But it is just that: a clue. I might have missed it except for the repetition. But then it just jumps right out at you!"

"Does it?" I said. "The two eighteens or the three fives?"

"For me it was the three fives," he said. "The fifth letter of the alphabet is . . ." He waited.

I counted. "The letter *e*."

"So a word with three *e*'s in it. That's where it started and stopped for me," he bragged.

I was already counting through the alphabet up to eighteen. "*R*! Eighteen is *r*." I pulled a pen from Sherlock's pocket and wrote on my fore-arm: _ *e* _ *e r* _ _ *r e*. "No clue," I said again.

"Two words, maybe? A name?"

He spelled: "N-e-v-e-r-m-o-r-e, dear girl. Nevermore." He clicked on the file.

"Did you really figure that out in your head?"

"I did."

"Wicked!"

"So," said he, turning to me, "what's the password?"

"You're joking."

"You know perfectly well what the password is. Or close to it, anyway."

"Do I?" I said. "Is everything a competition for you?"

"Of course! Where's the fun in it otherwise?"

"I'm a girl," I said, as if that explained it. He looked at me curiously.

"It was only a hunch, mind you," Sherlock said. "I suppose I should have prefaced my invitation as such. But since you and I do these things together, Moria . . . Well, don't we? They're far less fun when done alone. . . . Aren't they?"

"Yes. Far less. Absolutely!" I heard my voice crack and regretted trying to speak.

"Your father, being a smart . . . even brilliant man, left you breadcrumbs to follow, starting with the key in the ashes. Remember, that was intended only for you. He would have left you several paths to follow. No two of us think the same."

"He couldn't have expected I'd find this scan, if that's what it is."

"Oh, that's what it is. 'Nevermore'? Are you kidding?" Sherlock said. "But whatever the paths, there had to be commonality."

"I'm sooooo confused."

"The file is named 'nevermore.' Thus a connection to the hidden space in the desk. The password is . . . ?"

"Just quit it, would you?"

"First Timothy six-ten. The scripture selection."

He typed in Timothy6:10 for the password.

INVALID ENTRY

"*First* Timothy," I said.

Sherlock tried 1Timothy6:10.

INVALID ENTRY

1Timothy610

INVALID ENTRY

"Father liked acronyms," I said. "Try—"

Before I could complete my thought, he typed 1T610.

INVALID ENTRY

1T6:10.

The screen refreshed.

I threw my arms around his neck from behind and kissed him somewhere in his head of hair. He didn't seem to notice.

"It's from 1696," he said breathlessly. "Good Gatsby."

I felt tears push for release and I wasn't sure why. Sherlock began advancing pages. There was an elaborately drawn family tree beginning with Noah and continuing for several pages. Then, a hand-colored illustration depicting a portly man dressed in a brown tunic with a lace collar, Van Dyke beard, and groomed mustache. He was seated. A ship occupied the upper left corner and there was some Latin to the right of his head. All I could make out was "James Ashlyn Wilford." The name was familiar to me, I realized. In his left hand he held a cross on a long necklace. In an otherwise dark painting, sunlight burst from the bottom of the cross, casting a rainbow of faded color onto a heavy book in his lap. To his right a globe of the world sat on a dark table.

"I know him," I said.

"From?"

"I've seen a painting like this. I'm related to

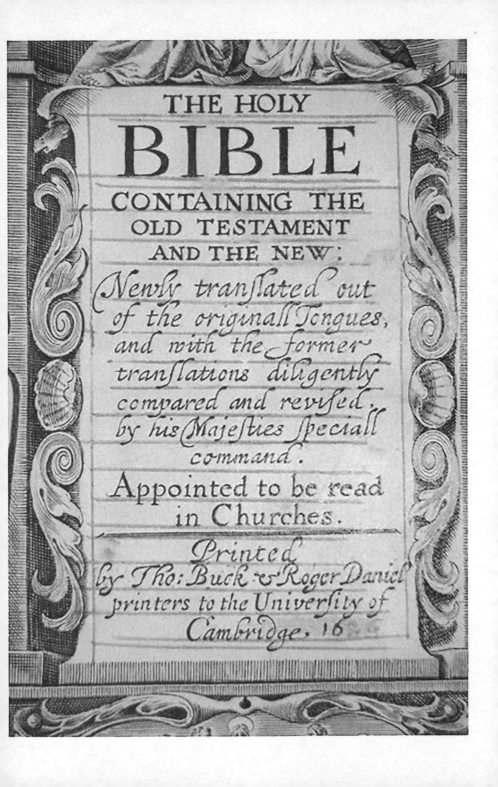

THE HOLY
BIBLE

CONTAINING THE
OLD TESTAMENT
AND THE NEW:

*Newly translated out
of the originall Tongues,
and with the former
translations diligently
compared and revised,
by his Majesties speciall
command.*

Appointed to be read
in Churches.

*Printed
by Tho: Buck & Roger Daniel
printers to the University of
Cambridge. 16*

him. He led one of the first trading expeditions into China. I'm pretty sure that's right. He was nearly killed a bunch of times. One of my great-great-whatever-grandfathers was named after him. My brother, too. He started the trading company. The Moriartys came to run the company by marriage in the mid-1800s. Father explained all this to James and me after Mother . . . left. I don't remember most of it."

The following pages held the Moriarty family tree, with this man's name at the top. He'd made himself into God with all his descendants following. The branches went on for pages. The surname Wilford became Moriarty, confirming what I remembered. Small, elegantly drawn boxes held names written in delicious calligraphy. James and I were on the second to last of the added pages, blank beneath us.

Once into Genesis, certain letters were circled by smudged chalk, pencil, or ink.

"Code," he whispered reverently.

"You can't possibly know that."

"I suspect it's a code of some sort."

"You read too many mysteries."

"You can never read too many of anything."

I laughed. He smiled.

"Codes, if it is coded, have keys to unlock them. The key for this would have to be something quite old. This Bible has been in your family for hundreds of years. Each generation would have had to be able to find the key in order to decipher it. So it's something mathematical. Something easily passed along."

"Look at the light in the painting," I said, pointing out a Godlike beam that shone from the end of the cross and onto the book.

"Never mind how pretty it is," Sherlock snarled. "Can you think of a date, some number that's been passed down to you?"

"The date of the expedition, I suppose. Not that I know it."

"Brilliant!" he barked.

I startled and probably blushed as well.

He turned back to the illustration. There was no date to be found.

"Simple enough to research," he said. "That could easily be it, Moria! Brilliant bit of logic there on your part!"

"Thank you." I don't know why I said it. I bit my lip out of embarrassment.

"I don't think we can fill in the pieces without finding that hidden room in your house."

"*If* we find a hidden room in our house. We don't know if it even exists."

"We did the math, Moria. One hundred forty-four square feet. Numbers don't lie."

CHAPTER 19

Leaving lunch, James had a bout of creep-ing flesh, spiders up your sleeves, shiver-and-gulp. He was being watched, just as Crudgeon and Lowry had told him he would be. He spun and looked carefully all around. No one.

Impossible.

He passed Eisenower on the common room steps. "Follow me," James whispered. "When I slap my side, I want you to catch up and tackle me."

"What the bells?"

"The moment I'm down, take off."

"You're serious?"

"No," James snapped sarcastically. "I'm making conversation. Get a brain, would you?"

He took the path leading toward the chapel. Nearing the little church, as he veered onto the lawn, he gently slapped his leg while never breaking stride.

He heard Ryan coming toward him. Eisenower hit him like a truck.

James went down hard, banged his head off the ground, and felt dazed. He'd had a plan. What had it been?

Eisenower let go of him. But not voluntarily. He'd been pulled off, not an easy feat given Eisenower's solid weight.

"Hey!" he heard Eisenower complain.

James rolled over to get a look.

A thin man in school overalls threw two blows: one to Eisenower's side, and a second into the boy's middle. A red-faced Ryan Eisenower woofed out air, staggered back, fell to his knees, got up, and ran off.

The thin, sinewy intruder pulled James to his feet and over to the east wall of the chapel, out of view of all but the state highway. James reversed their positions at the last second, pushing the man against the chapel's ivy-covered wall. The man could have easily prevented James from doing so. The fact that he allowed it told James everything he needed to know.

"*The tree grows roots and limbs,*" James recited.

"*Of equal reach without and in,*" the man said. A Scowerer.

"You've been assigned to protect me."

No comment.

"You, and how many others?"

No comment.

"Listen, we both know you've sworn some kind of oath to me."

"A blood oath, to be sure."

TMI, James was thinking. Blood? He couldn't see the man's face well under the golf cap, only the shape of a narrow head and pointed jaw of stubbornness.

"Your name?" James asked.

"Espiranzo."

"I need you to tell me something, Espiranzo. You're protecting me from the Meirleach?"

"I'm protecting you from anyone who might try to harm you."

"What is it the Meirleach want? What do they

really want?" James asked.

"We face competition from the Meirleach. It is true. It is not my place to explain this. You must forgive me."

"I will not. I want answers, and I'll have them." Father had used expressions like that with James when disciplining him. James regurgitated them without thinking. To his total surprise Espiranzo replied immediately.

"The loss of your father—God rest his soul—allows our enemies a brief moment of opportunity."

"Enemies."

"Of those we have many."

"But me?" James said. "What can they possibly want from a kid?"

"Your father possessed documents, personal treasure, secrets. History of our society. These materials naturally pass to his successor. You, sir. The firstborn son. It's possible the Meirleach may believe they can use you to arrive at this information."

"You mean torture me or something?" James said. On the boat on the cold Cape Cod morning, James had been told to look for a journal or diary Father might have kept. Lowry had told him it wouldn't be a computer file, but something more permanent and private. He was to search Father's bedroom top to bottom, his office, the basement and attic. James wondered if Lowry's impatience to find the thing had anything to do with the Meirleach.

"I doubt they would risk that kind of treatment."

"Trade me."

"Possibly. But no one is going to harm you. I promise you. The boy should not have been allowed to reach you like that. Report me if you want."

"No! And I appreciate that. I really do. But what about these materials? Would the Directory know how to get them?" The Directory, a group of ten or twelve, ran the Scowerers. James would someday be the head of the Directory.

Espiranzo hesitated, taking time to blow into his cupped hands for warmth. "I know nothing of the Directory."

"The materials, then."

"Like any successful business, our society prizes information. The Meirleach as well. Names. Contacts. Contracts. Alliances. Possessing such information could help advance the cause of the Meirleach, and it would certainly hurt our own."

"What about my sister?"

Espiranzo nodded. "I understand your concern, but it is you who are prized. It is said a record was kept by your family for many generations."

"Our family Bible," James blurted out. The Bible had been stolen at the start of the school year. No wonder Crudgeon had thrown a fit when it went missing. Not Father's journal? James wondered.

"It could be anything. A bank box. It could be hidden somewhere. There would be valuables as well."

"Treasure, you said." James thought of the Cape house, the basement of the Beacon Hill house. He thought of all the trips Father had taken—solo trips lasting weeks. It might be in Hong Kong, where the family fortune had begun.

"Anything is possible," said Espiranzo. "I meant it only in the broadest terms."

"Moria's safe." James made it a statement.

"There is no reason to think otherwise," Espiranzo said. "I knew your father, of course. I had the honor of . . . providing my services for him over the past several years. I've watched you grow up. It is my honor and pleasure to serve you as well."

James twitched with the thought he'd been under surveillance for years without knowing it, without Father saying a thing.

His throat tight, unable to speak, James nodded at the shape of the man before him, wondering, not for the first time, what he'd been born into.

CHAPTER 20

THE FOLLOWING DAY AFTER CLASSES, I WAS TOLD a boy was waiting for me in the Bricks Middle 2 lounge. It was the only place boys were allowed to visit us.

The furniture was dentist-office modern, the decor a result of a dozen eighth-grade girls trying to give personality to a lifeless space. Throw pillows had been added, mostly of Disney characters. A fake plant. A real cactus. Some artwork on the walls that might have been better left in closets. The artistic Ruby Berliner had hung a string of prisms in one of the three windows, which flashed, winked, and occasionally threw rainbows about the room. Mrs. Tiddly, an assistant coach, currently occupied the dorm proctor's chair, duchess of the grand desk, commander of the computer, sultana of the schedule.

The boy turned out to be Sherlock, not my brother, which was fine with me. Lock and I spoke quietly, though not in whispers, as that would result in curiosity and condemnation from the desk.

"July third, 1811," he said. "The first successful expedition into eastern Asia by James Wilford. Two years later he formed the Wilford and Stiles Company, though the sign they hung out read with that earlier date. It's all in Wiki. It also says that Wilford's ancestors were rumored to have been pirates in and around Hong Kong for decades before that. He was slandered in the London papers at the time of his forming the company, but that's all it said."

"You see? You now know more about my family than I do."

"It's nothing to be proud of, your not knowing."

"Shut up," I said.

"I tried to use those numbers as a cipher—"

"You went back into the computer center?"

"Of course! We're conducting an investigation here, Moria! The game's afoot!"

"Whatever that means!" I said.

"It means what it says it means. Game on!"

"It's not a game. It's my father's death."

"I know." He placed his hand sympathetically on my knee. Mrs. Tiddly clucked loudly. The hand came off my knee. "And I aim to help determine the cause of it, as requested. Sadly, the date of the founding of your family company was not the key to the Bible."

"If there is a key to the Bible," I said.

Sherlock raised his hand to fend off the prism light orbiting the room. It was partly my fault, because as I'd entered, upon seeing Sherlock, I'd nervously stirred the prisms. They were still spinning and moving slowly in the light. One fell across a photo of a lioness and her kitten.

Sherlock stood and leaned over me awkwardly, studying the colorful light as it played out onto the photo. He put his tummy in my face, forcing me to scramble to the side of the couch. "Get off me!"

Another clucking sound from Mrs. Tiddly.

One of Sherlock's more annoying personality quirks—and there were many—was his utter silence after questions were asked. He could focus to the point of exclusion of all stimuli around him. At times, admirable. At others, like now, maddening.

He looked back and forth between the crystal in the window and the light on the photo.

"Have you never seen a prism before?" I asked him. "You look like my friend's cat."

He collapsed onto the couch alongside of me with a kind of splash. He broke the rule of no whispering. "I know what it is!" he announced, his conceit apparent. "I know what we're looking for!"

"Shh."

"It was right there, Moria! Right there for the seeing!"

"Well? Are you going to tell me?" I asked in a hush.

"The illustration in the Bible of James Wilford showed him holding a cross. Remember?"

"Of course."

He closed his eyes. I somehow knew he was imagining the painting, so I shut mine as well. We must have looked pathetic to Mrs. Tiddly.

"Sunlight streams in from the right," he said.

"Yes." I could see it now. I was practically in the room with James Ashlyn Wilford.

"It catches the cross and bursts into . . ."

I thought he was trying to see it clearly in his mental image when in fact he was waiting for me to finish the sentence. I peeked out of one eye. His remained closed. I shut mine quickly and said, "colors." Hearing myself say it, I understood immediately. "Rainbows! Rainbows of color!"

When I opened my eyes he was looking at me intensely. "Correct. Rainbows of color. Brilliant color. As in?"

"A prism," I said.

"I'm betting there's a jewel attached to the bottom of the cross we can't see. Where is the rainbow of light aimed? In the painting, where is it aimed?" He seemed agitated again, rushed and in a hurry.

"Onto the book in his lap."

"The Bible in his lap. Yes! You see?"

"Our family Bible."

"Precisely. The painting in the book is a message to all generations for how to decode your family Bible. All that's missing . . ."

"Is the necklace with the cross," I said. "But I've never seen it. If it was going to show up anywhere, wouldn't it have been in the hidden space in Father's desk?"

"I told you before, Moria. We need to find the extra room in your house. The room we can't account for in the measurements."

"We don't know there's any such room, Lock. The extra square feet could just be the chimney or something." I'd been struggling with the idea of Father keeping so many secrets, our family's legacy dating back to James Ashlyn Wilford, my brother being initiated into a strange society. I was resisting instead of allowing the truth. It was unfair to Sherlock and everything he believed in. "The evidence," I said, trying to sound strong. "We need to follow the evidence."

"Just so!" Sherlock said. "First things first: once they open up weekend passes, you need to invite me to visit you in Boston."

CHAPTER 21

Jᴀᴍᴇꜱ ᴡᴀʟᴋᴇᴅ Lᴇxɪᴇ Cᴀʀʟɪꜱʟᴇ ʙᴀᴄᴋ ᴛᴏ ᴛʜᴇ Bricks—the long line of four consecutive brick dormitories attached one to the other like giant railroad cars—after every dinner that week. It was the talk of the third form—the freshman class— as well as my own. I was asked about it, teased about it, and told about it by most of the girls in my dorm. "Lexie, of all girls!" "Do you think it's a dare?" "Has your brother gone deaf and blind?" There was no end to the cruelty of eighth-grade girls.

On Wednesday, he took her on a detour into

the chapel, where the magic of the stained-glass windows, lit by outdoor path lighting, colored the darkened walls.

"Wow," she said. "I've never been here at night. Not in the dark, at least."

"Pretty, isn't it?"

"Stunning."

"Like you," he said, touching her hand. The chapel pews faced inward toward the center aisle, not forward as in most churches. The benches were two-hundred-year-old dark wood with no pillows or padding. Kneeling steps folded down from the railing in front of each one. James played with the step with his foot, opening and closing it nervously. The sound of it echoed throughout.

"You don't think that, and we both know it, James Moriarty. So why do you say it? Why tease me like that?"

"Way to kill the moment."

"There is no moment. That's just it. You're feeding me lines and I don't know why."

"They're not lines. Forget I said anything," James said.

"Don't be like that," Lexie said. "Of course I won't forget. That's the point, James. I won't forget! So if you're being cruel, if this is some kind of game to you, I'm asking you to stop. I've enjoyed your attention. Your company. Our talking. I really have. But it's got to stop or you're going to hurt me horribly."

James placed his hand between her hair and the back of her neck. He gave her a moment to pull away, to object. When she did not, he leaned in ever so slowly and kissed her gently on the lips. Quickly, and a bit awkwardly. Letting go, leaning away, it was difficult to tell if the red on his face was a blush or something from one of the windows.

"Why don't we go sailing?" he said. "The two of us."

"Seriously?"

"Am I being rude, inviting myself? If I am, please don't take it that way. I'm sorry."

"You're not being rude."

"Obviously, I'll stay at my house, but we can still maybe go to a movie or something, along with the sailing, of course!"

Lexie was tongue-tied.

"If you want to do something like a movie," James said. "No pressure."

"Of course I do! I'll check with my mom! Leave here Friday or Saturday?"

"After basketball. I can arrange for our driver to take us."

Lexie just stared.

"You'll check?"

"I'll call right away. I'll call tonight!" Her eyes flashed excitedly in the blending colors.

"You really are pretty," James said. "I meant it."

She craned forward like a bird and pecked him on the cheek. "Get moving! I want to call my parents before curfew!"

Lexie pushed him off the pew, the two of them laughing like preschoolers.

CHAPTER 22

THE THIRD WEEKEND OF WINTER SESSION, THE
last weekend of January, was the first weekend students were allowed to leave campus.

Sherlock's ugly bruises had mostly healed. The
three stitches had been removed and his sling dis-
carded. He'd been rude to teachers and classmates
alike, requiring a visit to Headmaster Crudgeon's
office. Sherlock had appealed for permission to
leave campus over the weekend, but could feel
Crudgeon resisting the idea.

"We are all worried about you, Mr. Holmes."

"I can't help that, nor will I try to. I'm British.

We can handle a good thrashing, believe me. Why is it you don't want me visiting the Moriartys, Headmaster?" Sherlock's lack of filters surfaced at the most inappropriate times.

"I didn't say that!"

"So," Sherlock said, "if I was requesting a weekend in Hartford, you would have the same concerns?"

"Of course I would! Be careful, young man, you're treading on thin ice."

"I expect more of you than clichés," Sherlock said.

"Do not consider yourself my equal, Mr. Holmes. It would prove a grave mistake."

"Oh, I do not. Believe me." Sherlock's unflinching resolve put a magnetic charge between the two men. North and south. Repulsing.

"The change of location will do me good," Sherlock continued. "A walk along the Charles. The cinema. A museum or two. What could be better for the soul?"

"Supervision is my concern. You're in a fragile state whether you recognize it or not."

"Not."

"You see? All the more reason to keep an eye on you."

"To what end? Am I a bit low? I am. But not

emotionally, Headmaster. Physically. I have hurt for the past few weeks. Physically hurt! As you may know, some teeth were loosened. It made it difficult to talk for some time. I'm better now. Improving. I get along splendidly with Moria. We're chums. Good chums, at that. I'm told Miss Delphine's cooking is 'to die for'—an expression I loathe, let it be known, but just the same, it would be a welcome change to this slop."

"Be careful, Mr. Holmes."

"The choice is yours, sir. Of that, we are both aware. Moria offered, and I accepted. The poor girl has lost her father. At the very least, can't we allow her a chum to brighten up a weekend?"

James informed me—he did not ask—that since Ralph was coming to fetch me and Sherlock that he and Lexie Carlisle would be riding with us and that we'd have to wait until after basketball practice. He also told me that he would ride in the front seat with Ralph and that our guests deserved both windows, so I was to ride in the middle. I had learned to pick my battles with James. This one, I let slide.

Ralph picked us up from school in the same big black car I had once loved but had since come to think of as Father's car, a remembrance that made me sad. The evening was frightfully cold, the roads slick, and the going slow.

Ralph stayed out of our four-way conversation. James talked over the seat to Lexie while Sherlock and I said a few words to each other. Lexie was kind enough to try to include me in the conversation but James just as quickly steered things to a topic familiar only to freshmen. In short: my older brother was being a jerk.

James had always seen the worst first. Once into his teens he'd complained even more, seeing the bad in everything. He could pick at any topic like it was a scab, scratch until those around him could no longer ignore it.

I didn't like being reminded of my (few and small) imperfections, but I could tolerate it. It was his complaints about others I found disturbing— his withering criticism of every meal, television show, and film; the personal attacks on people he barely knew. The one benefit to me was that my brother, by being such an intolerable and insufferable critic, helped me to see that perfection was not worth striving for. It didn't exist; there would always be a James out there to remind me of my flaws. My strategy, my goal, became to manage my shortcomings, ticks, and abnormalities. To work for a balance and avoid extremes. I began to appreciate my friends as much for what they weren't as for what they were.

Prior to Baskerville, living with James had been like living on a volcanic island with smoke and steam and lava threatening to blow. Since the initiation, if anything, he'd only gotten worse.

"So, sailing, huh?" I said into the car.

"Yes," Lexie said.

James glowered at me, wanting me to keep my nose out of it.

Sherlock came out of his trance. "I've never been."

"Oh! You must come sometime," Lexie said.

"Yes!" I agreed.

James went even more sour toward me, if that were possible.

"Winter sailing," Lexie said. "Not that I'd recommend it as a first try!"

"Scary," I said. I heard the next words coming out of my mouth before I understood my motivation behind them. I suppose I felt pushed to the side and diminished, so I was trying to prove myself. "James met up with a winter sailor the morning we were heading back from Christmas break on the Cape."

No matter my motivation, I reveled in seeing his reaction. I might as well have thrown him out of the car or punched him squarely in the nose.

With the knife in, why not twist it? I wondered. "You took the whaler out to a sloop on the morning we left the Cape house, James. Remember? Who was that you were visiting? A girlfriend?" Seeing a speechless James Moriarty was as rare as catching sight of an Attwater's prairie chicken.

Lexie looked surprised as well.

Ralph broke the tension by offering to stop for French fries, as long as we wouldn't let it wreck our appetites. We voted unanimously in favor.

James bumped me with his shoulder on the way into the fast-food place. Lexie and I used the washroom. When we were at the sinks she spoke to me in the mirror.

"James seemed upset about that."

I didn't have to ask what she was talking about. "He didn't know I knew. Brothers."

"Why was he so mad about it?"

"Brothers," I repeated.

"Does he have a girlfriend?"

And now I knew the source of her anguish.

I laughed and left that as my answer.

"No one?" she asked.

"Oh, please," I said. "Truthfully, I didn't think he knew girls existed. Lord knows he's never treated me like one."

She laughed. She had a deep, full-throated laugh that made me like her right away. The way a person laughed told me a lot about them.

"Are you and him . . . ?" I said.

"Us? No!!" But her eyes told me otherwise.

"Uh-huh," I said.

"Don't tell him! Please!" She looked terrified.

"Of course not! Besides, he won't speak to me for another few years at this point."

"The sailboat thing?"

"Exactly."

"Why's he so weird about it?" Lexie asked.

I arched my eyebrows. That was as much as I'd give her.

The car's backseat windows fogged. Our fries, I suppose. Or our body heat from the tension that hung in the air along with the smell of catsup.

A gloom filled the car. Ralph fiddled with the defrost. James scribbled into a small notebook, the kind with a black elastic band around it. It wasn't his diary. Not the one I knew of. This was a new notebook. One he kept on his person at all times. Hid on his person at all times.

A notebook I was suddenly desperate to read.

CHAPTER 23

LEXIE CARLISLE LIVED ON AN EXCLUSIVE PENIN-
sula at the end of a half-mile-long causeway for
residents only. The home, one of maybe a hundred
on the peninsula, was roughly the size of an airport
terminal, with its own dock where an eighty-foot
yacht was tied up to one side, and a forty-eight-
foot schooner to the other. At the end of the dock,
a boathouse, bigger than most homes, accom-
modated smaller sailboats, rowboats, a Boston
Whaler, kayaks, and two Jet Skis.

James and I had lived in and around wealth, but
among people who chose not to display it openly.

Other than clothing and a fancy car or two, old money liked to hide under mattresses and in safe deposit boxes. It didn't distinguish itself by attracting attention. It was there to serve the purpose of longevity, education, and benevolence. The Carlisle wealth was more the billboard variety. Trumpets, fanfare, and fireworks.

Lexie seemed overly excited, slightly nervous, and possibly embarrassed by her parents. James didn't have to ask to know that a boy visiting their home was not a common occurrence. Her mother, good-looking in a tennis player kind of way, seemed more delighted than her daughter. She knew of the Moriartys and, as she told James in a bit of a flutter, "your family's been so generous to the city."

He joined Lexie on one of the four sofas with a half-dozen television remotes in front of her. They talked through the sail that would follow the next day. James had been invited to eat before going home to Beacon Hill.

The kitchen table was set formally. Dinner was a spicy chicken with rice. Mrs. Carlisle called it a Cuban dish.

James understood it was socially unacceptable to discuss politics with strangers. But what about when it was a person's job? "What's it like being a city councilman?"

"Boring," Mr. Carlisle said, laughing at his own joke. A fit and tanned man—even in winter—Mr. Carlisle had salt-and-pepper hair, thick eyebrows, and a jutting brow that lent him an intensity countered only by his soft blue eyes. "No, no . . . it's actually quite interesting. Working with the public to explore the common good is fascinating, James. You get kooks, criminals, cops, doctors, gangs, the poor, the dispossessed, and the obscenely wealthy." He said this as if the last group excluded the Carlisles. "It's never the same, which keeps it exciting."

"I'll bet. Anything big at the moment?" James wondered if he could figure out what interested Lowry about the man.

"So much of it's 'big.' Right now, I'm working on securing approvals for new high-rises that will cost nearly a billion dollars to develop. There's a great deal at stake in any such deal. You make friends and enemies. It's tricky." He chewed and swallowed. "We're also considering the construction of a floating casino north of the city; we're dealing with a lawsuit concerning the Big Dig, approving some vending changes in Fenway, and battling the taxi union on ride sharing. That's this week!" He laughed again, sipped whatever was in his glass, and seemed to get lost in thought for a few moments. Mrs. Carlisle picked up the slack, asking about school.

James answered most of her questions with lies, since she couldn't handle the truth. *I've been led through a ritual and initiated into a secret society. I'm going to run the society, a society of criminals if I'm right. I'm here to trick your daughter into allowing me to spy on your husband, and I have no idea why I'm doing any of this.*

The more he thought about it later, he probably should have just said what he was thinking at the time. He likely would have won a laugh and nothing more.

After dinner, he and Lexie toured the main level of the home before heading outside, without coats, for a trip to the boathouse and a preliminary look at the tiny boat they were to sail.

On the way back to the house, James saw what looked like an office through lower-level plate-glass windows that faced out to the water. At his request, Lexie showed him this level as well: a weight room, a yoga room, a sauna, a heated indoor-outdoor pool with a lockable glass divider, and her father's office.

Bingo!

"It warms up midafternoon. Best part of the day for us. My dad will take the boat out to the buoy and back to make sure it's good."

"I'm psyched," James said. "Will your parents be around after?"

"Saturday? My mom should be. Later, not so much. They always have some kind of fancy dinner they attend. If you want to hang around I think my cousin's coming over." James gave her a strange look. "I know that's kinda weird. She's not like a babysitter or anything. Well, a chaperone, I guess. But you mentioned a movie, and she can drive."

"That's cool," James said. "No problem. Who knows how we'll feel. You may hate me by then."

"Doubtful," she said, giving him a look he didn't fully understand.

If she caught him breaking into her father's office, he thought, she would most certainly hate him. Of that, James had little doubt.

CHAPTER 24

At 2:00 a.m., Friday night, James entered my room on tiptoe.

"Come on. It's time," he said. A bleary-eyed Sherlock stood behind him.

By agreement, we wore pajamas in case a quick dash back into bed was in order.

Lois was a light sleeper. She had tended to prowl the house like a ghost since Father's death, checking windows and doors just as Father had done in the months before his accident.

Father's office was chillier than the rest of the house. At least I hoped that was why I shivered.

Sherlock took control, moving toward the key buried in the ashes. Surprisingly, James didn't protest. Within seconds, Sherlock stood behind the desk. He opened the blotter, working to restrain it to avoid the loud pop. There was the gun wrapped in the oily cloth. The manila envelope. The Bible verse and the word "Nevermore" burned into the wood. Sherlock felt around inside the drawer.

"That's disappointing," he said, though not specifically to us. He seemed to just be thinking aloud. "No trigger, no trip, no switch. I thought we'd probably missed one the first time."

"That's what you were expecting to find?" James asked. "Are you kidding me?"

Sherlock fished a folded sheet of paper from his front pocket. "A hundred and forty-four square feet are unaccounted for in the measurements Mo took. It's somewhere behind the wall."

He handed the sheet of paper to James, who unfolded it.

"There is only one possible location for the missing space," Sherlock continued as James scanned the floor plan. "It's simple geometry."

"Geometry is not simple," James said, "but I see what you mean."

Sherlock said to me, "He is very good at math, my roommate. A logical mind capable of grasping the point of things quickly."

I'd never heard Sherlock compliment anyone, much less James. Judging by his expression, it was new territory for James as well.

"I think that bump to your head messed with you," James said.

"Let's not go there," Sherlock said. "It was not a simple bump to the head, and we both know it."

Studying the sketch, James pointed to the wall opposite the hearth.

"That's where it would be," he said.

"And that is where the water was," I said.

Sherlock laid out the plan. We were to search Father's library for any other Bibles, because of the verse burned into the drawer. He also wanted us to mark the location of any books written by someone with the name "Timothy," first or last. Finally, he put great emphasis on looking for the title "Nevermore."

I took the lower shelves, Sherlock the highest, and James the four between. We would save the library ladder for last, a device that ran on a brass rail on the north side of the room, the side with the most books.

Sherlock referenced both an unabridged dictionary and a fifteen-volume encyclopedia for the word "nevermore," but found little of interest.

Forty-five minutes later and bleary-eyed, the three of us sat down on the rug together in defeat.

"I don't understand it," Sherlock said.

"Mo was probably right," James said. "The missing space must just be under the stairs or for the chimney."

"But the numbers tell us it's right there," Sherlock said, pointing at the shelving. "The water that came down tells us it's right there."

"There's something else," I said, "isn't there, Jamie?"

"Such as?"

"That sound we heard when we were in there." I pointed to the wardrobe to the right of the fireplace. I told Sherlock about me being chased by James, because I'd "borrowed" his journal, and that we'd both ended up inside the wardrobe because Father had come home early. We'd heard a tremendous clunk while in there, a sound that in no way matched the softer click of the desk mat opening.

James nodded. He didn't fight me for bringing up what we'd heard, but, like me, he didn't have an answer for it either.

"Nevermore," Sherlock said. "That has to be our answer."

"I'll get my phone," I said. I was off through the silence of the house before either boy could stop me, through the foyer with the ancient Moriartys looking down on me from their oil paintings, up the staircase like a cat in pursuit, into my room. Both excited and scared, I found the experience electric. I felt more alive, more present than at any time since Father's death. I felt a connection to something bigger.

I returned to the boys, quietly closed and locked the office door, and addressed them. "'Quoth the raven, "Nevermore."' 'The Raven,' by—"

"Edgar Allan Poe." Sherlock sprang for me. "Brilliant!"

I nearly screamed, I was so startled by Sherlock's sudden movement. He was not one I thought of as agile or light-footed. Jumping at me, he was all flailing limbs and eyes the size of Ping-Pong balls.

He kissed me.

On the lips.

He kissed me on the lips.

HE KISSED ME ON THE LIPS!

It was just a peck, the kind of kiss Mother would give for my getting a good grade. Mistaken aim, no doubt; he was probably going for my cheek and I turned my head too fast. But none of that mattered. Not to me.

"Edgar Allan Poe." He aimed that sharp nose

of his high in the air like a hound on a scent. "Of course!"

Again, I started for the lower shelves, James for the middle. Sherlock stopped us. We turned to him. I didn't care for his imperious posturing and high opinion of himself. He lacked all degree of modesty, which could be as off-putting as the cologne he wore.

"Give your father some credit!" he said. "It most certainly will not be at a height where a child could latch onto it. Well?"

James and I were unmoving.

"The ladder, you sillies!"

"What the helicopter are you talking about?" asked James.

"The book is how to open the missing space," I said to James, filling in for Sherlock as he scrambled up the library ladder.

"The hidden space," Sherlock said, pulling himself and the ladder along the wall of books, his long, manicured thumbnail clicking along the spines, with me helping push the ladder behind him. "Raven . . . raven . . . raven," he muttered. He stopped the ladder abruptly.

"There!" he said, tugging on a volume. "I've got you!"

CHAPTER 25

SHERLOCK PULLED THE BOOK BY THE TOP OF ITS spine.

Nothing happened.

He removed it from the shelf. Turned the book fully around. Opened its pages carefully, as if expecting something to fall out.

"Brilliant," James said, mocking Sherlock's British accent. It was rude and uncalled for, and spoken behind glossy eyes and wet lips. This was the new James, the James who put himself at the center of the universe. No wonder these two boys didn't get along.

"I could have sworn . . ." Sherlock said, crestfallen.

"It makes total sense," I said. "And it's so much like Father, isn't it, James?"

"I suppose." James teetered between Brother James and Scowerer James. James the Old and James the New.

Sherlock stretched down to hand James the work of poetry. He slid his bony hand into the narrow gap left between the books. "No button or— Hold on!"

A pronounced sound, a *clunk* like a car's hood coming released, resulted in a section of the bookshelf popping open.

James and I both recognized the sound. We'd heard it from inside the wardrobe.

"No way," said James.

CHAPTER 26

THE UNUSUAL THUMP AWAKENED LOIS LIKE A gunshot. She spilled out of bed, into her slippers, and was pulling her robe around her as she raced down the back stairs. She rattled the kitchen door, checking that it was locked; it was. She hurried to the front door; the same. She grabbed a fire iron from the parlor and continued her methodical search, throwing back window drapes, peering behind couches. She headed upstairs to see if one of us had rolled out of bed in our sleep.

Empty beds.

She touched the sheets to measure warmth.

Cold. We'd been gone for a while. She checked for our clothes—James would just put on whatever he'd worn the day before. His clothes remained in a pile. She felt more at ease. More comforting, his running shoes were under the pile. James had not left the house.

My room was perfectly tidy, leaving Lois no way to measure if clothes were missing.

She checked the windows, grateful to find them locked. In her mind, the three of us had likely sneaked off to the home theater in the built-out basement. The possibility of any malfeasance or kidnapping seemed slim. She would not wake Ralph without checking herself. Ralph knew who wrote his paycheck. He might report the darlings to Mr. Lowry.

Downstairs again, on her way to the kitchen and the door to the basement, she looked down the short hallway toward the study. Something grabbed her. She took a moment to explore.

The pocket door to the library remained closed, as it had been earlier. The washroom door hung partially open. Perfectly normal. Lois wasn't taking any chances. She threw open the door sharply, lost her hold, and slammed it against the interior wall. She threw on the light. Empty.

That left only the office.

CHAPTER 27

JAMES PULLED OPEN THE SECTION OF LIBRARY
wall as Sherlock descended the bookcase ladder.
The three of us faced a dark but cluttered space.
We stepped inside.

I used my phone as a flashlight, revealing a
room that looked like a magician's lair might look.
Sherlock found a light switch.

We stood in the workshop of a mad professor,
a space only a third the size of Father's office. One
hundred and forty-four square feet, I was thinking. It was much cooler inside, the air significantly
drier.

Part museum, part library, with books of every sort: fat books, tall books, all of them ancient books. But there was sculpture and statuary, large portfolios tied shut with strips of black ribbon, framed postage stamps, framed paintings standing in groups leaned against each other. There were stacks of wide, four-inch-high mahogany drawers.

"You've got to be kidding me," James whispered. "Look at it all!"

"Certainly not what I expected," Sherlock sighed. He caught my eye, and silently directed me to look at the desk and, as it turned out, the small dark oil painting that hung over it: James Ashlyn Wilford with his gold cross and rainbow of light. I suppose I must have made an alarming sound because James snapped his head toward me.

"What?" he asked in a coarse whisper.

I tried to think what to say. "Jewels!" I pointed out the small stands littered with diamond and pearl necklaces, earrings, gold and silver brooches. "Look at all the jewels." I slid open one of the drawers. It was lined with velvet and strewn with more jewels. I wondered if we might find the necklace from the painting in one of these drawers. I could tell Sherlock was of the same mind. He started pulling open drawers a little too enthusiastically.

He discovered a stash of freeze-dried food and a small sink hidden into the complex woodwork.

"It's a safe room," James said, seeing it. "A place to hide where no one can get you."

"It's a vault," I said. The second drawer I opened required a good hearty pull. I counted twenty-four gold bars, each eight inches long. "Oh my gosh . . ."

Sherlock looked through the framed art. "That's a van Gogh," he said. "If that's an original . . ." He continued through the stack. "Titian. Cezanne. This can't be."

"Because?" I asked.

"If these are originals, do you have any idea how much even one of these paintings is worth?" Sherlock gasped. "Tens of millions of dollars. Each painting."

"W-what?" I stammered. I touched a gold bar and tried to pick it up. It was so heavy. "I think these are real, too."

I didn't know if the room had run out of air, but I had. I couldn't find my breath. Couldn't catch it. Maybe the room was airtight despite the two grates in the ceiling and what looked like a complicated control panel on the wall. Climate controlled to protect the art, I was guessing.

"What's going on?" I asked.

"Father wanted you to find this," James said. "You, not me. I don't belong here."

"Don't be ridiculous," I said, taking in the elaborately carved antique desk. Alongside it an equally ancient lectern held a small book, leather-bound with gilded edges. I opened the journal, recognizing Father's handwriting immediately, but not the language. "Anybody?" I asked.

It took Sherlock one look. "Greek. Ancient Greek, to be exact. Like the paper in the drawer. The language of scholars. Greek Orthodox priests. Coptic Christians. Odd."

"Because?" I asked, drawing my fingers along Father's handwriting and feeling him in the room with me.

"I doubt there's more than a few scholars who can still read it, much less write it. All at university, I would think. Your father was apparently one of them."

Sherlock pointed out what James and I had missed: a plaque over the moveable section of library shelving that served as the door.

It was the same verse that was burned into the drawer. This time, attributed.

For the love of money is a root of all sorts of evil, and some by longing for it have wandered away from the faith and pierced themselves with many griefs.

— I Timothy 6:10

The loud bang startled us.

"Quick," Sherlock whispered. I hurried out of the secret room and carefully unlocked the office door from the inside. It had been a stupid idea to lock it in the first place. Slipping back through the open bookshelf I helped pull the shelving shut. Sherlock wouldn't allow it to be closed all the way. "We don't know how to open it," he whispered, fighting against James, who continued to pull.

"How hard can it be?" James quipped.

"How loud can it be?" Sherlock asked.

James relaxed his pull, leaving the deep door open with only a fraction of an inch to go before being fully closed.

"We need to hold it," James whispered incredibly softly. "In case someone pulls."

The boys took hold.

CHAPTER 28

I DROPPED TO THE FLOOR AND CHECKED IF ONE could see below the bookcase. In fact, there was a space of a quarter inch or so. I saw the office door swing open, saw what I knew to be Lois's slippers as the office light came on.

Lois crossed toward Father's desk and I lost sight of her. I heard the drapes rustle, Father's office chair move.

From my prone position, I looked up my brother's exaggeratedly long leg. He was looking down at me. I hand-signaled something opening, while I silently mouthed, "The desk!"

We'd left the desk mat open! I could feel Lois staring at it: a gun and envelope. What must she be thinking?

Click. She'd shut it.

On the way back across the office her slippers stopped exactly in front of us. I wondered if she felt a pocket of this hidden room's colder air. Had it made her skin crawl?

Did she sense us?

Seeing only her slippers and pale ankles, I could picture her looking around the office more carefully. Maybe she felt something she couldn't explain to herself.

A moment later, she hurried from the room, catching the light switch. Hurried like the house was on fire.

CHAPTER 29

"SHE'S GONE," I said.

"We are so busted," James said.

"Upstairs," Sherlock said, grabbing Father's journal from the lectern and stuffing it into the small of his back.

"We'll tell her we were in the basement," I said.

"What if she's already checked?" James asked.

"Hurry!" I said.

We left the hidden room dark. Eased the section of bookshelf back into place. It made very little sound closing.

Sherlock had kept hold of the key. He returned

it to the left side of the fireplace ash.

"We are soooo busted," James repeated.

We slipped out and took off running, crossing the foyer and flying upstairs for our rooms.

We had no idea what to expect.

CHAPTER 30

"Nice try," Lois said, from the doorway into my room. "I said, nice try, Moria. Playing asleep like that. I was in here not five minutes ago." She switched on the lights. "Where were you?" Arms crossed, eyes squinting.

"Downstairs, watching a movie."

"You're lying. The television is cold. Hasn't been on for hours."

I hadn't thought of that.

"Your father's desk. Tell me about that."

"What about his desk?"

"Don't play games with me, Moria."

"You mean the gun? You weren't supposed to see that."

"You are in a world of trouble, young lady. You and your brother and your friend."

"They don't know anything about it," I said, somewhat honestly. "Father showed it only to me."

Lois wouldn't think to look under the covers for my phone. James and I had agreed on this while on our way up the stairs as he dialed me and opened up the connection. Whoever heard Lois speaking to the other would mute his or her phone, preventing Lois from hearing anything through the device. It would allow the other to monitor exactly what was being said, so Lois couldn't try to trip up the other.

"I couldn't sleep. I went back down there just to look at it. I still haven't touched it." That much was the truth.

"And brought the boys with you," Lois said.

"No, I did not."

"Moria!"

"I can't speak for them, Lois. Maybe they heard me? Maybe they checked on me and I wasn't here in my room? How should I know? Maybe they were creeping around the house trying to find me or spook me or whatever. If they were, you know James, you never would have seen him. He's like a chameleon the way he can hide." The truth again. I watched her process my explanation.

The trick now was to move her thought. "He showed me how to open it. Showed me the gun and how to use it. He showed me a couple of other things as well, all of them secrets I was supposed to keep. Secrets I plan to keep. You should have checked the wardrobe first. That's where I was hiding when you came in. I got out before you ever reached the desk." I had watched the slow and careful movement of her slippers.

"You expect me to believe your father showed you where he hid a gun?"

"Did you know about it?" I asked.

"I most certainly did not!"

"Ralph?"

"How would I know? No! I'm sure of it. No, no, no."

"He was worried, Lois. You know how he'd been over the summer. He told me if I didn't hear from him at least once every three weeks I was to check that hideaway for a message from him. If no message, I was to take the gun and keep it with me."

"You're lying. He would never have said such a thing."

"I think you underestimate my father's love for

his children. If he went missing, then he feared for us. But he didn't go missing, did he, Lois?"

"And you disobeyed him," she said, pointing out a fault in my argument. "You didn't keep the gun with you."

"I hate guns. Was I supposed to take it to school with me? I left it. But I check every now and then like I did tonight, just to make sure it's still there." I wondered if she knew about the other secret hiding place. I got nothing. She was unreadable. I conjured up my best frail voice. "For what it's worth, I don't like being called a liar. It's hurtful." The truth once more.

James wasn't the only one changing. At twelve, I had two grown-up employees. They worked for my legal guardian but I suspected if James and I complained enough, Lowry would fire either of them. It would never happen. They were both like family to us. But the possibility existed and charged me with a sense of responsibility. Seeing all that gold—gold and jewels that belonged to me and James—didn't exactly hurt things. I felt rich and in control.

I also had a sinking feeling I was mistaken on all counts.

CHAPTER 31

The Boston Public Library's Central Library opened at nine on Saturday mornings, giving us time to do our research before James was to go sailing. The older of the two buildings, built of Milford granite, stood like a Grecian temple.

"Trying to translate that was painful," Sherlock said. He wore the same clothes as the day before. None of us had slept more than a couple hours. Sherlock looked it. I hoped I didn't.

"Translate what?" James asked. "The journal?"

"That one's impossible. I'm hoping someone here can help us with that. No, the page of what

Moria called gibberish from the gun drawer."

"But," I said. "I hear the 'but' coming."

"I could make a joke about that," James said, "but I won't."

"Thank goodness," I said.

"But," Sherlock said, "I managed to figure it out. It was numbers, random numbers at first glance."

"Let's not play Twenty Questions," James said as we climbed the steps toward the towering doors.

"I suppose I can spare you my agony. It's dates. I've got six dates for us to research. There are probably many more on there. For today we have six."

"You're thinking news stories," James said. "You brought us here to research news stories."

"Perceptive of you, James. Correct. One wonders why someone would encrypt a list of dates. Looking back at those dates seemed a logical place to start. And your father left them to be found."

"What if they're just business stuff or something?" I asked.

"There may be a story even so," James said, teaming up with Lock. The pair of these boys working together was a little hard to take.

"Agreed. And while you and Moria are digging up articles, I'll try to see if someone knows of a scholar of Ancient Greek who might transcribe your father's journal and maybe even this sheet of scrambled dates."

"I don't know," I said, "Father was an intensely private man."

"And he's dead," James said coldly. "And his killer could easily be mentioned in that journal, Mo. Sherlock's right. We need someone to help us."

The grandeur of the library stole my breath. I hadn't been here in several years, and I appreciated it more from the moment I entered. We stood in an ornately decorated chamber with a vaulted ceiling and an echoing, cathedral-like resonance that demanded reverence—in this case, to the written word.

James and I hunkered down in the second-floor reference area. Only then did I realize our mistake.

"James, why is it the least socially capable of the three of us is attempting to interact with the librarians?"

"That is strange," James admitted, typing on a computer terminal. He was cross-referencing the six dates with *The Boston Globe*. I had been assigned the *Boston Herald*. "Do you realize," he said, "they've digitized all the *Globe* newspapers from 1872 to the present? How awesome is that?"

"The earliest date we have is 1972," I reminded him. "Four in the 1990s and one in 2008."

James muttered, annoyed with me. When he said something was awesome, I was supposed to agree.

"Awesome," I said.

"Shut up," he said, "I'm trying to concentrate."

In a different area code than us, near the front entrance, Sherlock waited at an information desk. When his turn came, he stepped up, fully prepared to make his inquiry.

The librarian beat him to it, an older, gray-skinned woman, with kind eyes.

"Those were the Moriarty children you came in with, weren't they?"

Sherlock said nothing.

"He—Mr. Moriarty, their father—the family in general, have been such wonderful benefactors of this library. Such a tragic loss. Such a fine man. And the children. Moria, isn't it? Jimmy?"

"James."

"My, how they've grown."

"I wonder if you might be able to help me, to help James and Moria. It seems their father fancied himself something of a Greek scholar. He left some writings behind explicitly for them but they're written in Ancient Greek. I've considered calling the universities for them, but thought it more prudent to begin here, where ancient text is part of your business."

"Such an interesting and unusual request."

"I try," said Sherlock, going for humor. She regarded him curiously. "Never mind," he said.

A morbid-looking fellow behind the counter, possibly a few years out of college, had twitched at the librarian's mention of the Moriarty name. Taken by itself, that wouldn't have won much consideration from Sherlock, but it was the boy reaching for his mobile phone a little too quickly that seemed more than coincidental. Especially given that a library desk phone sat within reach. The boy's pallor and unkempt appearance influenced Sherlock as well, though he knew it should not. He, Sherlock, was not much better at presentation.

More to the point, the boy didn't send a text; he made a call. As Sherlock juggled conversation with the matron he kept watch on her assistant. How much weight could be put on an odd-looking college-aged boy making a phone call? Sherlock wondered. The call began, ended, and the boy went back to work on his computer terminal.

But Sherlock was put off by it. He considered

paranoia an affectation for others. He wouldn't allow himself emotional response. He reacted to visual and audible stimuli and believed himself clinical and analytical in his assessments. The boy was a problem.

Partially tuned in to the matron, Sherlock heard a name and wrote it down. A lawyer by the name of Thomas Lehman who visited the rare book room with regularity to read Ancient Greek.

"Self-taught," she said, "as I understand it. A delightful man. A true gentleman. I'm sure if he can't help you, he will be able to point you in the right direction."

Sherlock thanked her and moved on. Joining us, he told James and me how correct he'd been in assuming the library was the place to check. Neither of us fed him the gratification he was fishing for. Overtired and somewhat irritable, I found his pretentiousness taxing.

"Anything?" Sherlock asked us, sounding disappointed. "Do the dates mean anything?"

"There's so much that happens on any given day," I said. "It's overwhelming. Strikes. Governments in turmoil. Sports. Natural disasters. Crimes of every kind."

"Nothing much in *The Globe*," James said.

I heard what only a sister, or maybe a parent,

could hear: James was lying.

"Check out November first, 1967," I said, more interested in James's response than what he might find.

I saw once again the unseen: my brother didn't want to revisit that date, but under pressure, he typed anyway.

"It's not a headline, but a mention," I said, "at least in the *Herald*. The real story is the evening edition of November sixth."

Sherlock may have felt the tension between brother and sister. But whatever the case, a boy who loved to meddle stayed out of it, his head pivoting between the two of us.

"It'll be front-page news on the sixth, I promise," I said. I gave James no choice. He brought up the front page to November 6, 1967. I couldn't help but question his resistance.

I addressed Sherlock, the neutral party. "Get this . . . one of the dates you gave us is August fourteenth, 1962. The only news, the biggest news on the fifteenth, was a robbery from a mail truck on Cape Cod the day before. One and a half million dollars stolen! Six guys. All with guns. *Revolvers*, it says."

James snorted. He wanted me to shut up.

"On the first day of the trial, November sixth,

1967, the key witness is said to have gone missing five days earlier. The guys arrested are let off because there's no witness. Five days earlier is November first, another of the six dates you gave us."

"A crime," Sherlock said. "You should start again, looking only at crimes on the dates in question."

"It's a waste," James said emphatically. "Do you know how many crime stories there are every day? It's practically all they wrote about back then."

"Big crimes," Sherlock said. "Notable. Unusual."

"Father was not a criminal," I said, though I suspected otherwise, given all I'd learned in the past few months. My stomach sank.

"Of course not!" James barked. "I don't believe there's a connection. Not for a second!"

"What about all the stuff in the room?" I asked, my voice quavering. I knew the truth. Why wouldn't James admit it? But I had my answer: the initiation.

"Look, we would need to connect the stuff in that room to one of these stories," James said. "I didn't find that. You didn't find that. That stuff in the room, it's all investments."

"But why hide it?" I asked.

James blanched. "Shut up."

"It's just too much stuff, James. Too valuable. You know that. I know that." I felt so absurdly cold. "Sherlock knows that."

"It's vast wealth," Sherlock said. "But I suppose, given the heritage, the longevity of your family, it's possible such goods had been accumulated over a very long time."

"There! You see?" James said. "The accumulation of wealth. Exactly!"

"It looked more like a pirate's cave to me," I said.

"This isn't Narnia!" James complained. "It's not *Pirates of the Caribbean*. Get real."

Sherlock twitched noticeably. "Listen, you two," he said so softly I nearly missed it. *"Do not look!* But to James's right is a pale creature I saw earlier at one of the librarian desks. He's with two others. Unsavory, if you ask me. If I'm right—and when aren't I?—they are looking for you two. So I think it best we split you up. Moria, you will please keep your face in the direction it's aimed. Stand up slowly and head into those stacks. James, behind us is an elevator. It will be arriving in . . . five seconds. You will take it to the garage while Moria and I will take the stairs to the ground floor. We will keep them guessing. We shall rendezvous at the Dartmouth Street entrance. Nod if you understand."

James and I nodded gently, barely a tuck of the chin.

James said, "See you there. Good luck." He touched my arm fondly, more the gesture of the James of a year ago. I treasured the contact.

"Off we go," Sherlock said. "Nice and easy."

The elevator toned behind us exactly when Sherlock had said it would. It was one of those things I wouldn't forget about Sherlock, a moment like that. He possessed the ability to know more, understand more, see more than five people put together.

As I reached the end of the short aisle between bookshelves Sherlock appeared, in stride. "Follow me," he said. "Look straight ahead, not so much as a glance to your left, not even if someone calls out to you."

"You're scaring me, Lock."

"Good, then maybe you'll walk faster."

CHAPTER 32

J AMES RODE THE LIBRARY'S ELEVATOR ALONG
with a white-haired couple who stood in silence.
The couple left at the ground floor. Others joined
him. He arrived to the garage and calmly walked in
the direction of the exit signs.

Once outside, he stopped, placing his back
against the cold wall, waiting to see if anyone had
followed.

He counted to sixty and headed toward the
Dartmouth Street entrance.

CHAPTER 33

"Company," I said, leading Sherlock through the glorious Bates Hall. My memory of the library had come back slowly, like awakening from a dream. Father was in that dream. Sherlock and I hurried, hand in hand, through the stacks.

A woman in her late twenties kept pace with us. She looked so casual that it was hard to believe she might be following. But I trusted Sherlock. My heart beat a bit faster now, my feet moved more quickly.

"Do you suppose she's—" I choked out. I needed a better workout program.

"Most certainly," Sherlock said.

We passed through the mezzanine. Sherlock let go of my hand and sped up to pull alongside me. "I'll take care of her," he said. "You find us a cab, or plot a route back to your house. You know the city. I do not."

"Got it!"

Sherlock turned an about-face. The sound of a collision echoed through the grand space.

I never looked back.

As I crossed the entrance chamber, there was Lois, of all people, looking like a schoolteacher awaiting us after a field trip.

Sherlock, his hair ruffled, his face beet red, appeared unexpectedly beside me. I let out a yip.

"Don't do that!" I said to him. "Warn me. Say something. But don't spook me."

"You're welcome," he said.

"This way," Lois said calmly, as if we'd arranged to meet her. She led us through the library's hallways.

"Lois," I said. She and Ralph had dropped us off. "I thought you had errands to run? That we were meeting back at the house?"

"We were in the neighborhood," she said.

I glanced at Sherlock to suggest I didn't believe her. There was nowhere to do errands in this neighborhood. It was all high-end shopping. Had she been spying on us?

We followed Lois into the Newsfeed Café. She lowered her voice. "Where's James?"

"Dartmouth Street entrance," I answered.

"Why?"

"Never mind that," I said. "We need to keep moving, Lois. There are some people here who weren't very nice to us." I couldn't think of a better excuse.

"Ralph is just outside. Text James and let him know."

In my two years of owning a smartphone, two years of enduring endless complaints and criticism about texting, Instagram, and Snapchat, this was a first. Lois telling me to use my phone! "Ah . . . OK."

"I wouldn't mention the trouble inside. Not in front of Ralph."

"Ralph?" I said, objecting. "He's family."

"And he feels incredibly protective of you two. You mention something like that and he's likely to drag you inside and have you point them out to him, and we don't want that."

"No! Of course not." I heard what she was saying, but it felt like there was a different message swimming just below the surface.

Lois opened the café door out to the sidewalk.

Our black car idled at the curb, Ralph behind the wheel. We took only a few strides in that direction before a man called out from behind us.

My first instinct was to run. Sherlock followed me into the car's backseat. Lock was pulling the door shut as the voice, a foreign voice filled with authority, stopped him.

"Might I have a word, please?" He stood tall and wore a dark, calf-length belted overcoat. His nose and ears red from the cold, he stepped closer, training his flinty gray eyes past Lois and onto me. Me, not Sherlock.

He allowed a small wallet to fall open from his right hand. It contained a gold badge.

CHAPTER 34

"Detective Superintendent Colander," the man said. He wasn't French or German or Spanish. Scandinavian, maybe. His badge read: INTERPOL. International Police. "Where is James Moriarty? He went inside with you. Are we to meet up with him?"

How, I wondered, did this man, an international police officer, know that Sherlock was not my brother?

"He's . . . busy," I said. "He won't be home until later." I carefully covered my mobile. If no one took it away from me I could text James to hightail it away from here.

"There are individuals inside the library identified as international criminals. Those same individuals arrived after a phone call was placed from within the library mentioning you and your brother." He didn't bother to explain how his people had intercepted the phone call. I wasn't sure I wanted to know.

"The librarian's assistant," Sherlock said so only I could hear him. "I knew it!"

Detective Colander addressed Lois. "I wonder if I might ride along?" He unfastened his coat, apparently to show us he wasn't armed. It seemed a strange thing to do.

Sherlock opened his mouth to speak but I squeezed his arm. This was grown-up stuff.

"You'll sit in the front," Lois said. "I'm with the children in the back."

I hated being called a child. Mr. Lowry was working for Father's estate—James's and my estate—and Lois worked for Mr. Lowry. Therefore, Lois worked for me.

She opened the front door and gave Ralph a wary look. I caught a faint drop of the chin by Ralph. He'd agreed to something. I didn't know exactly what, but it had to do with the detective.

I texted without looking at my phone.

cops. stay away. follow my phone.

I hit Send. James and I were following-friends on our smartphones.

Lois joined Sherlock and me in the backseat. The detective superintendent sat alongside Ralph. He rattled off an address then leaned around the headrest. "Once we get to our destination, I'd like to speak with just the two young people, if that wouldn't upset things too horribly."

"They are both minors. He," she said, referencing Sherlock, "is not one of us. Currently I am in the service of Moria's legal guardian, Mr. Lowry. He must be notified before there's any of this nonsense."

"I cannot stop you from involving Mr. Lowry, nor would I try to. But I can and should advise you that my relationship with these two will grow far more formal should you elect to involve attorneys. That said, the decision is entirely yours."

Ralph's eyes flashed at Lois in the rearview mirror.

"All the same," Lois said, "it's a call I have to make." She worked her mobile phone and spoke softly with her hand cupped over her lips.

"And you are?" Colander asked Sherlock softly.

"James's roommate at boarding school. We're in the city for the weekend."

"Your name?"

"Sherlock Holmes."

"And you will be seeing James in the near future?"

"This evening," I said.

Lois handed her phone to Detective Colander. "The children's legal guardian."

"Very well," said Colander. Another clandestine discussion that ended with Colander thanking Lowry and passing the phone back to Lois.

"OK," Lois said. "Yes. I understand." She ended the call and pocketed the phone.

"I will visit with Moria and Sherlock here," Colander said, pointing for Ralph to slow the car. We pulled to the curb in front of a large reflecting pond surrounded by office towers. In the distance, an old stone church. "You may accompany us, if you wish."

"Oh, yes, I wish," said Lois. "And, as you are very much aware, Mr. Lowry will be on speakerphone."

Colander's face puckered, one part smile, one part snarl, one part consternation.

Ten minutes later, we gathered in a small, unmarked conference room. I was happy to see Ralph along with us as well. Just in terms of his sheer size, when Ralph was nearby I felt safer.

Outside, the reflecting pond reflected, stretching the office towers taller.

"My title makes me sound more important than I am," Colander said, clearly trying to break the ice. "The fact is, for some time now—years, a decade or more—our international police agency has been aware of, and has been tracking, an Irish criminal gang. Sophisticated crime. No swat-and-grab burglaries or that kind of thing. Computer crimes. Blackmail. Identity theft. Immigration violations. Money laundering."

"Irish mafia," Sherlock said.

"You could think of it that way, certainly. Let's call it the Irish Mafia. Fine! Why are they interested in one or both of you?" Colander studied us both.

I said nothing. Sherlock said nothing.

"You spent over an hour referencing older periodicals. Newspapers, mostly. Tell me about that."

I found myself aghast. Who could possibly know what we'd been doing in the library?

"History papers for school," Sherlock said, not missing a beat. "You know the kind. Citations and such. A better library than we have at Baskerville, our school."

"Of course," Colander said. "Reference."

"Newspapers," I said, supporting Sherlock.

"So, what you're telling me is that the Meirleach—that's the name they've taken for the past eighty years or so—are interested in high school students who are doing their homework." He made it a statement.

"Who are they?" I said.

Lowry jumped in over the speakerphone to protest. The two men entered a discussion. It was agreed Colander could continue.

"The Meirleach are usually busy slitting throats and pulling museum heists."

"Slitting throats?" I blurted out.

Lowry again, telling Colander to back down on the sensationalism.

Sherlock couldn't resist playing detective. He said, "So you intercepted this call, or maybe you followed these Meirleach people to the library. They led you to us, Detective Superintendent. You're asking us to believe that you then abandoned your surveillance of international criminals in order to talk to a couple of teenagers?"

"Detective work is rarely simple, young man. My explanation of what I may or may not undertake is, frankly, not relevant."

I cleared my throat. "Our father passed away recently." The detective nodded; I had reason to believe this was not news to him. "I don't mean to sound all Inspector Gadget, but there were events before and after, as well as some curiosities. As his daughter, I have a right to know. My brother and I have the right to know what's going on. Exactly. Precisely what's going on. The truth, Detective, if possible."

"I make a living of the truth, Moria. What I can advise, if you would allow, is this: Go back to your school. Stick to your studies. The three of you. Leave the investigating to those of us in the business. It's a dangerous world out there. You shouldn't go around poking animals at the zoo."

"Are you investigating Mr. Moriarty's death?" Sherlock asked. "How curious that is!"

"I'm not at liberty to say," the detective answered.

"But you don't deny it."

"I'm not in a position, Mr. Holmes, to confirm or deny such an accusation."

"So you're a politician," Sherlock said condescendingly.

Colander laughed privately. "Appointed by them, to be sure."

"What would an international agency like Interpol be doing investigating an accidental death in the USA?" Sherlock said.

"I would not jump to conclusions, Mr. Holmes.

Answer me this: What were you after in the periodicals archives? I can and will interview the
librarians if needed."

"Do that," Sherlock said.

I worried Sherlock's defensive attitude might
be hurting James and me. "Dates," I said, irritat-
ing Sherlock greatly. "We were researching some
dates that Father left me. We didn't find much, but
there was some mention of the family in the society pages." My English teacher at Baskerville, Mr.
Cummings, had told us that details sell the story.
So, I added, "I recognized the names of some Beacon Hill families. Nothing more important than
that. I suppose he wanted me to know who the
family friends were. To whom my brother and I
could turn if in need of help."

"You have us for that," Ralph said. I loved him
for it.

"May I see those dates, please?"

"No," I said, "you may not."

"Young lady—" Lois said.

I paid little attention to Lois. "My father left
them for me, Detective. He made a point of it. Not
my brother, but me. Not you, but me."

"The dates may be of value to my investigation," Colander said.

I didn't want him seeing the story about the

robbery. I felt confused and horrified by our dis-
coveries, and I was not about to share them.

"You think we're lying about something," Sherlock said. "We're not lying."

"I think that there are the lies we speak, and
the lies we keep."

"A philosopher."

"I have scads of free time," Colander said.

"Good on you," Sherlock said. "We don't." He
grabbed my arm and pulled me to my feet. "We'll
be going now."

Lowry spoke up, confirming Sherlock's wishes
and supporting the end of the discussion.

Colander stood. In a way I felt sorry for the
man. He seemed to be doing what he was supposed
to be doing. His mistake was, it involved our family.

"My advice," he said, "keep your eyes open and
your wits about you, you two. Tell James to do the
same." He passed us both his business card from
under the badge in the wallet. "Funny thing about
the truth. When you keep it from me, men like me,
us from it, we can't help you. As much as we'd like
to." He appealed to me more than Sherlock.

I nodded.

"Think about it, Moria. And listen, the next

time you're scared, really scared, don't hesitate to call me."

I nodded again. "Yes, sir."

"You'll catch them? Arrest them?" Sherlock said.

"Yes, but only after they've committed a crime, and by then, I fear, it'll be too late."

CHAPTER 35

Aᴛ ʜɪꜱ ʀᴇǫᴜᴇꜱᴛ, I ɢᴀᴠᴇ ᴍʏ ꜱᴍᴀʀᴛᴘʜᴏɴᴇ ᴛᴏ Sherlock the moment we'd pulled away from the curb. He returned it a few minutes later with an article open in the web browser. I couldn't believe what I read.

This could not wait.

"Before we go home, could you drop us at a museum?" I asked from the backseat. Lois turned around and looked at me as if I were crazy.

"Haven't we had quite enough for one day?" Lois asked incredulously. "You want to go to a museum after what we just went through?"

"Yes, please." I had to think what would convince her. "We're going to meet up with James, if it's all right with you and Ralph?"

"Of course! Why didn't you say so?"

"Sherlock and I will meet him inside. It could take him a while." My fingers were already texting. "We could take a cab home or—"

"Don't be silly! Of course, we'll wait."

"Thank you." I wished they wouldn't.

"Which museum?" said Ralph, as if giving his OK. And he was driving.

"The Fordham Fashion Museum," I said.

"Why there?" Lois said, somewhat accusatory.

Having read Sherlock's magazine article, I lied, to gauge Lois's reaction. "Father mentioned it a couple of times. James and I have always used it as our secret meeting place, a place no one would think to look for us."

"Hmm," she said.

"Are you okay with that, Sherlock?" Ralph asked.

"It wouldn't be my first choice," Sherlock said. "But I'm game."

The front seat laughed at that.

Ralph dropped us in front of the Fordham

Fashion Museum with its stately gray granite edifice, Corinthian columns, and a black rubber welcome mat carrying its name.

The museum's lobby rose three stories to a set of spectacular chandeliers. On the walls hung framed dresses and uniforms, outfits of every kind. Signs marked exhibit halls. Rope lines were in place to keep things organized, but they seemed optimistic. Even on a Saturday, it wasn't crowded.

The tickets were expensive. Sherlock made me pay. Once inside, I pulled him onto a bench.

"Whatever are you doing?" Sherlock asked, resisting.

"Waiting for James and looking to see if anyone's following us."

"I can't imagine we were followed from that conference room at Interpol headquarters."

"How did you find that article?" I asked.

"It was something the librarian said about your family's generosity. You know the saying, 'The best place to hide something is out in the open?' It was that, too. And your mentioning the society pages to Colander. That did it for me. If your father didn't have the necklace locked away somewhere—which in fact, he might—then why not place it somewhere for safekeeping?"

"But this, of all places?" I said.

"I tried to put myself into your father's shoes."

"Don't ever do that. Don't ever say something like that again."

"Sorry," he said. "But, listen, a house can burn down. A safe deposit box only has two keys and a person must be an adult and a signature is kept on file."

"Lowry," I said.

"Perhaps, but a lawyer is not family. The necklace is part of your family's legacy. A man like your father"—I glared at him—"might, just might leave it where his children could get it without much fuss. He could leave a document allowing privileges for you, or any future Moriartys, for that matter."

It bothered me that Sherlock could come up with such stuff so quickly. We'd both just read the article. It referenced a 1978 major renovation to the Fordham Fashion Museum funded by our family foundation. In 1986 we had financed a show of Russian gowns from the tsars. But it was a "personal bequest" exactly seven years earlier that had me reading each word carefully. It was said to be "a significant collection of personal jewelry, contemporary ball gowns, and swimming/yachting attire."

Mother had left the family seven years earlier.

"It's my mother's stuff," I said. "Her jewelry." I could barely speak the words.

"That was my presumption," Sherlock said. "I'm sorry if that's insensitive of me."

I waved my hand trying to let him know I was OK with it. I couldn't speak. Not just yet.

"Maybe some items from your grandmother. But yes. Your family had a connection here for decades. It was that connection . . . Then your father made a sizeable donation of personal items."

"Why give away the cross if it's the only way to read the Bible?" I asked.

"Why indeed?" Sherlock said. "As I said, it could be so others, like you and James, could get to it without a lot of legal-smegal. Or, I suppose, your father may have just needed a place to hide it for a while."

"Because he was afraid of the Meirleach!" I thought back to how Father had become so para- noid in the months before his "accident."

Sherlock picked at his prominent nose. I looked away.

"You're saying he hid it in Mother's jewelry. Why not his secret room?" I asked. "Why not there?"

"We may yet find it is in there, Moria. We didn't have much time to look around. We can look again tonight."

"But you think it's here?"

"I find it interesting that your father made the donation. I don't think there's a flea's chance in a fire that anyone would ever think to look in the Fordham Fashion Museum for it. He knew it would be safe here, even left on a hook in the hallway." He had me laughing. It felt good. "This place isn't open tomorrow. It was kind of now or never. Worth a try. Worth asking someone about."

"I agree completely. I just hope James shows up."

On cue, my brother walked through the door. The three of us shared an awkward hug moment. We caught him up on Detective Colander and Sherlock's theory about the Moriarty cross.

"OK then," James said cheerfully. "I'll ask."

He crossed to the information desk, with me and Sherlock close behind. James introduced himself by name and spoke to a woman with white hair, from whom he accepted a brochure.

"Jewelry, second floor. Two galleries, nineteenth and twentieth century. I asked about diamond necklaces. She said they have many."

I preferred the stairs, from where we could see ahead and below. The stone staircase was wide and regal. I felt like a princess and imagined Sherlock my prince, an image that didn't quite work but I went with it anyway.

The moment the three of us entered the nine-teenth-century jewelry exhibit we saw it. James approached the pedestal in the center of the room. A glass box on top held a gold cross on a heavy silver chain. A large jewel hung from the bottom of the cross. There was no question about its compari-son to the painting of James Wilford.

"Just what you said," I told Sherlock. "Out in the open."

"Where no one can find it," said he.

I watched as he appraised the room strategi-cally: another door to the side to a third exhibit hall, the entrance to the exhibit behind us. He dis-appeared for several minutes, leaving me to stare at this necklace, the sight of which cut me to my core. It had been in the family since before the Mori-artys. It was in my blood. I could tell James was thinking the same things, feeling the same things. Whether he'd meant to or not, Father was teaching us our family history.

I wasn't sure when Sherlock had returned. I found him by my side, studying the necklace intensely.

Without looking at me he said, "Nothing you can do about it today, it being a Saturday. The ear-liest we could ask someone—you two could ask someone—about your right to it," he said, "would be Monday, and we'll be back at school."

"It's so beautiful," I said.

"Yes, it is," Sherlock agreed.

"You're saying we have to wait until the next time we come to Boston?" James asked testily. "That's unacceptable."

"I asked," Sherlock said, "just now, if the director or any of the administrative staff were in today. They are not. Regular business hours."

"But it could be weeks," James said.

Sherlock studied the cross and jewel with his nose practically touching the glass box that secured the heirloom.

"I wonder," he said. When I asked later he refused to explain what he'd meant by that.

CHAPTER 36

James felt apprehensive about sailing with Lexie. He didn't want to like her—he had an assignment to take care of—but he kinda couldn't help it. She was not at all the girl he'd assumed her to be. Everyone at school who mocked her were idiots. Judging by their assessment, it was apparently some kind of crime to be quiet, smart, and wanting nothing to do with the boarding school brats who dominated the social structure at Baskerville.

Turned out, she was the opposite of them, in all the good ways. The opposite of some stupid nickname that had stuck simply because the words sounded so good in combination. Lexie the Loser. If she'd been Jamala the Impala or Ruby the Beauty her fate would have been entirely different. As it was, she was victim of a catchy nickname, and nothing more.

Liking her made sailing together all the trickier. They were about to have fun together. How could he have fun with her and then spy on her father? He felt dirty.

Mr. Carlisle picked him up at the train station and made small talk on the way back to the peninsula. James had dozed during the short train ride, already exhausted from the busy morning. As Lexie had predicted, her father had taken the sailboat out for a trial, during which he tested the rigging in the cold conditions. James heard all about it.

The house had been built to impress. It succeeded. Its size and remote location made it look to James like something from an X-Men movie. James was led downstairs to a guest room where a microfleece wet suit, long underwear, neoprene boots, and other clothes, including a Windbreaker, awaited him. The outfit was slightly clumsy but warm.

Mr. Carlisle, having no need to remind his daughter, an expert sailor, about the hazards they faced, did so anyway. He made her and her crew promise not only to wear the life vests but to cinch them down tightly.

James had sailed for years from the Cape house in all weather, and in all different sailboats, large and small. He felt tempted to mention this, to do a little boasting in front of Mr. Carlisle, but he resisted. James and Lexie boarded the sailboat and pushed off. Nearly instantly, they moved at high speed.

The 470, Lexie's boat, performed well when close-hauled. The skipper and her crew hiked out over the windward edge to level and stabilize the craft, increasing its speed. In strong wind, the act amounted to standing with one's feet on the side rail, your body extended a matter of a few feet over the foaming white wake that broke from the bow. With the boat ripping atop the water at breakneck speed, the maneuver of tacking charged James with both adrenaline and terror, a mixture he found intoxicating.

Shouting over the roar of wind and sail, he called triumphantly, "I . . . LOVE . . . THIS!"

"IT'S . . . THE . . . BEST!" Lexie answered, sea spray wetting her face.

She handled the small boat well, her decisions sharp and crisp. James found her lack of hesitation impressive and comforting. No loser was Lexie.

Here, in her element, she proved herself mentally strong and courageous.

"Ready about . . . !" she called. In this maneuver that altered the course of the boat, the two of them needed to duck under the boom in unison and scurry to the other side in order to be in place for when the sails caught the wind. It was like a complicated and thrilling dance move. The slightest mistake, or missed timing, and the wet, slippery surface of the fiberglass boat was likely to send at least one of them into the water.

". . . hard to lee!" Lexie pushed the tiller. The sail roared as it luffed. The two of them ducked and worked lines—releasing one, tightening another—as they scrambled into position. The sail filled. The boat jumped up onto its rail, water coursing across the top. Lexie and James moved from a crouch into a full standing position as counterbalance to the force of the sail. They sailed like this for thirty minutes. It felt more like five.

"Not good!" she shouted.

"It's great!" James countered, wiping spray from his eyes.

"There!" she said, jerking her head feverishly.

"Oh . . . no . . ." In front of them, between them and the shore, a thick, guncotton gray squall appeared as if out of nowhere. It came from the north, barreling down the coast as a curtain of gray-black threat.

"That's snow," she said. "And ice."

"Can we outrun it?" James shouted.

"You do the math!"

She was right: the front moved with excessive speed, eating into the dull blue sky and hiding the shoreline as if a curtain were closing. The peninsula and the Carlisle home looked toylike.

"It's not likely, but if the rigging ices . . ." Lexie said. She didn't complete the thought.

"Yeah!" James said.

"We'll capsize."

"I said I know!"

The speed with which the boat moved heightened every word, every flex of James's muscles. The water beneath them begged for a mistake.

Her voice hoarse from shouting, Lexie said, "If we run for shore, my dad will have an easier time finding us. The moment he sees the snow, he'll come for us. But it's coming from the north, the far side of the peninsula, and by the time it hits, he'll have had no warning."

"The city? Someplace south?"

"Puts us farther out to sea than Dad will expect. We might possibly outrun it if this wind direction holds. But if we're made to run downwind we'll slow down, we're less stable, and we're much farther than where they'll search for us."

"Don't talk like that! No one is going to have to search for us."

"James, if that's a wet snow . . . and when aren't they at this temperature? . . . we're going in."

"Don't . . . say . . . that!"

"Remember what Dad said about holding on to the boat. We hold on to the boat and we don't let go."

"I am not playing Jack in *Titanic* for you, Lexie!"

She bellowed laughter. "Thank you for that. I needed it!" She looked toward the peninsula and then toward shore. James could feel her calculating wind speed, distance, and the changes the storm might bring.

"You know how satellites and spacecraft get a slingshot effect using a planet's gravity?" she shouted.

James did not like the sound of this.

"I have an idea," she said.

"Run for home?" James asked hopefully. She didn't answer him. "For shore?" No answer.

They sailed a minute longer, still aimed toward the peninsula. "I think there's a third option," she said.

"How did I know you were going to say that?"

Her face tightened, the wind suddenly colder, the first tiny flakes of snow blown in advance of the storm. "Let's find out!"

CHAPTER 37

For James, it was like entering a cave or a big gray mouth. The closer they sailed toward the island, the lower and wider grew the cloud generating the snow and wind. Rapidly, it bore down on them, enveloped them from all sides, spraying a cold white ice in advance like rice at a wedding. Lexie's theory involved putting the sailboat into the throat of the blow. She tacked toward shore once inside the gray, as the ice gave way to snowflakes the size of fireplace ash.

The snow adhered to the aluminum, glommed onto the sailcloth and fiberglass in gooey clumps.

It stuck to their faces, and had they not been wearing swim goggles as part of their survival skins, it would have stuck to their eyelashes as it did their exposed hair. It would have blinded Lexie, and they'd have gone off course.

She moved the tiller in faint degrees, while holding to it strongly, and navigated out of the ash into the ice flakes, the wind fiercer than any they'd faced. All but blind, they could see no more than a foot in front of the bow.

They hit the mooring buoy without ever seeing it. Its line, tethered to a deep anchor and therefore stationary, tangled in the sailboat's centerboard. It acted as a trip line: one moment the sailboat was ripping along, the next its speed cut in half, the bow giving way to the pull and turning them downwind.

James fell.

His feet popped off the edge and he slid on his back across the sailboat's deck, grabbing frantically for the tangled rigging and, finally, the edge of the hull. Three fingers were all that held him. Inverted fingers because of his being on his back.

"HOLD . . . ON!" cried Lexie, who had somehow managed not to fall.

Then, a splash as the boat righted and the sail luffed, clapping. Lexie had fallen off, her harness tangled. The rigging whipped the aluminum with sharp cracks. James slid like a bar of soap. As he slid, he rolled and, as he rolled, he slapped into the water where Lexie had vanished. His gloved hand caught hold of webbing. The force threatened to tear his arm out of its shoulder socket.

He had hold of Lexie's belt.

Coiling line around his right arm to hold on, he tugged with his left on the belt. Her head appeared out of the ice and foam. She wrapped her hands around his forearm as the boat slowed behind a windless sail.

Together, they moved her to the edge rail, where Lexie switched her grip to a line. Then, "Look out! Jibe ho!" she hollered.

The boat had come around just far enough for the wind to find the sail again. This time, it filled it like a boxer's punch. It screamed to starboard side. The lines went taut. At once the boat was going ten, twelve, fifteen knots, its port side elevated, James dangling once again, Lexie folded over the edge, half on, half off.

His face pressed to the fiberglass, James didn't see what she did, or how she did it. Over the roar and the pitch, he heard her unclasping her safety belt, and he shouted for her to stop. It was a reckless and absurdly dangerous gesture, a cocky, outlandish thing to do in the face of such natural power. The boat continued to sail along. James lifted his head. Lexie was back in her harness, the lines untangled.

"Put your leg through that line!" she shouted, hand on the tiller, having solved the tangle of James's rigging and simplified it down to a single move.

"There!" she called, as he managed the move. "You're good."

A moment later, he climbed to her side and they were sailing again.

"All good?" she cried.

"I don't even know what that means!"

"You're alive!"

"All good," he confirmed. "You saved my life."

"Maybe. Maybe not. And you, mine, I think. But we'll never know, will we? And that's a good thing!"

"You're . . . out . . . of . . . your . . . mind!" James bellowed above the raging wind.

"Yes! Absolutely. One hundred percent!"

"We could be home in front of a fire!"

"Pathetic, isn't it? Who would want that?"

"I'd raise my hand but we might capsize."

"Don't you dare!"

She had the boat hauling with the wind, charging

like a bull. Ice was building on the pulleys, collecting on the boom, but he knew somehow they were through the worst of it.

"That jibe," she cried.

"Oh, man! I thought it was going to break apart."

"The best thing that could have happened. It broke all the old ice off. I've got five times the control I had."

"We're cooking!" he said. In fact, they were standing prone to the water, perhaps eighteen inches above its surface. Flying.

And then, no ice, no cloud. They were a matter of only yards from large rocks stationed as a break to prevent shore erosion. Lexie called for James to trim the sail as she heaved the tiller, the rocks growing larger, coming closer.

At what to James seemed like the last possible second, she called to come about. They switched sides as deftly as synchronized swimmers. Ballet partners. A thing of beauty.

There, not a half mile away, stood the causeway, the two-lane road from shore to the private island. They were in a pocket of clean air, just behind the torrent of the squall.

"We would have hit the rocks!" James called, piecing together the evidence. "If the storm had stretched to here, this far, we would have hit the rocks! You could have killed us!"

"It was either me or the storm," she said, barking out another of those dark laughs. She eased up on their speed. "It'll blow out in a few minutes. It's turning south-southwest. Dad will be half crazed by now."

James felt the bumps and bruises, the strains and aches. He looked over at her as she called out for him to give more line and she tweaked the tiller. She caught him staring, looked at him until he had the nerve to look her in the eyes. They sailed like this, eye to eye, for a few hundred yards. She never looked forward, nor to the sail, nor to the stays at the top of the mast. She looked at James. Unrelentingly. And he, at her.

CHAPTER 38

LEXIE AND JAMES RECOUNTED THEIR ORDEAL over tea served in the living room with an amazing view of the sound.

Mr. Carlisle focused his attention on James while his wife served freshly baked chocolate-chip cookies and poured strong black tea, offered with milk and sugar. It was part celebration, part ritual to thank Poseidon the sea had not claimed the two.

Mr. Carlisle leaned into their every word. He thanked James for rescuing his daughter. James no longer felt like a guest, his connection to the family now warmer. Lexie was enjoying herself immensely.

James wasn't sure he could go through with the spying.

Mr. Carlisle informed everyone—he did not offer—that he would be driving James to the Beacon Hill home. No train ride for the boy who saved his daughter. James smiled, having no idea how to respond.

"Should I go now?" he said, feeling awkward and wondering if Mr. Carlisle was trying to drop a hint.

"No, no! Not at all!" Mr. Carlisle said.

"Have another cookie," Lexie said.

"More tea?" her mother offered everyone.

"I don't mind the train at all," James said.

"After what you just did, James . . . Well, I'm indebted. We're all indebted!"

"I think I caused the problem as much as anything I did to help things," James said honestly, though it came off as false modesty.

Mr. Carlisle grinned, clasped his hands together, and again leaned forward. "Those moments . . . they define us to ourselves and to others. Whether you know it or not, you learned something about yourself today, James. Both of you did," he said, looking at Lexie. "And people like me learned something about you as well. I knew your father, James. He put his money where his mouth was, where his heart was. He didn't do it to be noticed, he did it to make a difference. Charter schools, outdoor education. I'm in city politics and I saw things firsthand. It's a tough, sometimes brutal thing to try to have a real effect in a city like Boston. Some of us do it by getting elected or appointed. Some of us, like your father, by being rich and uncompromising. I didn't always agree with his methods, but the man had passion, real passion to make a difference. Thank you for what you did out there today."

"We were wearing our vests. She'd have been fine."

"Again, thank you, James. Learn to take a compliment, boy."

"You're welcome," said James.

"That's better."

Another cup of tea, more small talk. All James could think about was Mr. Carlisle's office downstairs.

When the conversation died and not even Lexie could think how to restart it, Mr. Carlisle made his decision.

"Good! What a pleasure. Collect your things, James. I'll bring the car around."

James patted his pockets. "Oh, dang. I think I left my earplugs. Is it OK if I check in the guest room?"

"Of course!" Mrs. Carlisle said.

James stood, wondering what he'd say if Lexie tried to join him. She moved forward in her over-stuffed chair, but her mother placed her hand on her knees, stopping her. Thank goodness for mothers, James thought.

He hurried down the spiral staircase from the family room. On the way to the guest room, he passed the home office. He listened to ensure Lexie wasn't following. Hurried into the office.

"Carlisle keeps an appointment book in his study. The contents of that appointment book are not online in any manner," Lowry had explained during the meeting in the house.

James headed to the large, cluttered desk. Despite the glass wall looking out to the water, the lighting was dim, the overcast sky mimicking dusk. James divided his attention between the office door with a partial view of the spiral staircase and the contents of the desk. He pushed papers aside, try-ing to remember exactly how he'd found them so he could return them to their proper place.

The appointment book appeared. Larger than he'd expected, it opened on a spiral binding, each side showing a full week.

Door . . . desk . . . door . . . His attention shifted continually.

James phone-photographed the current pages. Turned the page. Another photo. Two more weeks. Turned the page again. Another photo, another two weeks.

Door . . .

Lexie's bare feet coming down the spiral stairs. He moved the papers back into place while stuffing his phone into his pocket.

What to do? he wondered.

Only then did he realize he hadn't returned the appointment book to the current week. Instead, he'd buried it with the paperwork that had been covering it.

He remembered Sherlock and me talking about things hiding in plain sight. As Lexie passed the office, rather than be caught, he called out.

"Lex! In here!"

She stopped. "Did you find them?"

James couldn't think.

"Your earplugs."

"Oh! No, not yet. I got sidetracked. My phone's being stupid and Mo—Moria—was going to forward this email . . . she wants me to stop at some bath store on the way home. That's why I told your dad I could just take the train. You think I could check my email? I know that's kind of random."

"Just have her text you."

James stood still. Duh! He didn't hesitate. "I know, right? Moria does things her own way, that's for sure."

"Well, sure . . . Hang on . . ." She sat down and logged into her father's computer. James went through the unnecessary step of logging into his email.

"Nope!" he said. "All good."

He stood to leave. Lexie turned.

James looked down at the desk, trying to use his X-ray vision to see the appointment book. He needed a matter of seconds to set it straight.

"You coming?" she said.

"Yeah," he said, feeling the desk like a noose around his neck as he left the office.

They searched the floor of the guest room for swimming earplugs he knew weren't there. While crawling around on his knees, James said, "So, Lexie, I've never had a girlfriend."

"Girlfriend?" Shock.

"Well, you know?" He felt foolish.

"No," she said, "I don't know."

"Ah . . . I'm an idiot."

"No, you're not. That's just . . . that's a big word."

"We kissed. The chapel." James sounded like a

lawyer defending his case. He meant for something warmer.

"I remember, believe me. That doesn't mean . . . you know?"

"You kiss a lot of guys?"

"No! Gross! I do not! Not . . . no."

"Then . . ."

"But, I don't know. Boyfriend-girlfriend? I mean, I guess. I just hadn't thought about it."

"You hadn't thought about it? Seriously? Because . . ."

"Because what?"

"Because I think about it a lot. OK?"

"You."

"Yeah," James said.

"And me."

"Well, yeah. I guess."

"You guess or you know? Because this is a big deal, James. To me it is. Too big a deal, given that my dad's waiting for you." She looked around frantically. "No earplugs."

"What?" James said, forgetting himself.

"Your earplugs?"

"Oh. My earplugs! Right! No problem."

"If I find them, I'll bring them to school."

"OK. Sure. Thanks."

"Before you go," she said shyly. Or maybe she was just acting. If so, he didn't know what that meant, nor how to respond. "What were you going to say about you never having a girlfriend?"

"I didn't say 'never.'"

"Yes, you did. You said, 'So, Lexie, I've never had a girlfriend.'"

"I might have," James said.

"Oh, that's exactly what you said. Believe me, we girls remember things like that."

"I was . . . I don't know. I was going to say I don't know exactly . . . you know?"

"How to act?"

"Yeah."

"What it means?"

"Yeah."

"If we tell others?"

"Yeah."

"Well," she said, touching his nose like a fairy princess working her wand. "I guess we'll just have to find out."

CHAPTER 39

I DIDN'T APPRECIATE BEING SHAKEN AWAKE. I preferred being whispered to from across the room. As a result, I slapped the hand that touched my shoulder.

"Hey!" The voice of a boy. With a British accent. Sherlock!!

IN MY ROOM!

I pulled the bedding with me as I sat up, my mind lagging quite a bit behind my physical reaction.

"What are you—"

"Shh! James just sneaked out."

I blinked. Relaxed some, if telling the truth. Checked the clock. Just past midnight. "What?"

"Just now. Thought I was asleep. I heard him changing in the hall. Followed him downstairs, not so he'd know it. He went out a dining room window."

"Not the balcony?"

"What? No! Window!"

I knew exactly what he was talking about. The only window in the house that wasn't alarmed was in the dining room. Last Easter, beef gravy from the buffet had splashed onto the window magnet that connected to the house alarm. Our dog London had not only consumed the entire magnet, screws and all, but a piece of the window frame as well. Ralph had installed a wood brace to keep the window from opening.

"Lexie? You think?"

"No! All black. He dressed in all black. I know where he's going! We have to go, right now."

"Go?"

"Moria, if I'm right, he's going to try to steal the necklace."

CHAPTER 40

"WHY AREN'T WE GOING INSIDE?" I ASKED
Sherlock, trying to keep my nerves under control.
My teeth chattered so fast I sounded like a keyboard. My hands shook. I didn't want Sherlock to
see any of this. He'd insisted I dress warmly, but of
course I'd dressed so I looked better.

Idiot!

The alley behind the fashion museum reeked
thanks to the six Dumpsters, one of which hid us.
We had a view both to the street behind and the
museum's alley door, which now was blocked open
an inch.

"Because I don't like surprises. If he's going to steal the necklace, then why not let him steal it for us?"

"He's not a thief!"

"He's not alone."

"What?" I said.

"Consider all the evidence, Moria. Trust the evidence."

"Dumpsters?"

"The hot chocolate."

"What are you talking about?"

"Return, if you will, to your unfortunate situation in the bathtub."

I was glad it was too dark for him to see me blush. This boy had pulled me out of the tub. My embarrassment added to my sense of cold.

"I'd rather not," I said.

"Are we to think someone meant you harm? We'd be fools if we did. No. You received the hot chocolate from Ralph, who would never harm a hair on your body." Another chill on my part. "So, let's back up. If someone drugged the hot chocolate, we have three suspects: Mr. Lowry, doubtful as he remained in the library that evening; Headmaster Crudgeon, a possibility since James said the man left the library for a few minutes; and our dear Lois, again unlikely."

"I'm fascinated, really. But could you speed this up a bit and maybe find someplace warm?"

"The hot chocolate had to be meant for either Lois or Ralph, as neither guest had ordered some. You may recall we heard later that Lois had asked Ralph to check the car for her purse."

"So?"

"This is me, Moria. Please. When I entered the house, being the curious and observant fellow I am, I saw in the reflection off a mirror in that office a piece of a lady's purse tucked under a jumper—"

"A what?"

"A sweater—a horrible word if there was one." He closed his eyes. "Navy blue, possibly cashmere jumper, black leather strap handle on the purse with gold hardware."

I gasped aloud. It was Lois's purse and sweater!

"Ergo: she had not misplaced her purse." Sherlock drew a breath. "Let us consider then that the hot chocolate was intended for Lois. If so, why is she sending Ralph on a wild-goose chase for her purse? Makes no sense. If, on the other hand, the choco was intended for Ralph . . . think about it. Takes a sip. Trundles off in search of the purse. Falls weary somewhere along the way."

"But why?" I asked, not daring to contradict his logic.

"The only possible reason: information. I suggest the dose rendered you unconscious only because it was intended for a bigger person. It had the same effect on Bath as you." I didn't appreciate being compared to our dog. "But Ralph . . . They only wanted him slowed. They wanted him pliable. They are looking for something. Answers."

"They?"

"The Scowerers, of course. Do you think the visit by Crudgeon and Lowry was coincidental? Moria! It was to keep James, maybe you and James, occupied while all this went down."

"But Ralph and Lois were—are—loyal!"

"Yes, and possibly to a fault. Think about it. If James told either Lowry or Crudgeon anything about what the three of us were up to and they suspected Ralph, during his years of service, may have learned about certain aspects of your father's business, including secret hiding places, then Ralph needed to be questioned before a couple kids messed everything up! Look, this Irish gang is after something. I think it is your father's journal, and quite possibly the discovery of how to decrypt the Bible. The Scowerers want to protect it. The Meirleach want to possess it. Interrogating Ralph, even though one of their own, would only make sense."

"You have a devious mind, you know that?"

"Tell me I'm not right!"

Oh, how I wanted to! How I wanted to catch him in the wrong, this conceited, opinionated boy. But I also had something of a crush on him, and had no desire to make an enemy.

"James betrayed us?" I was crushed over that as well, but a different kind of crush.

"I'm afraid so. It's possible that James informed Lowry of the necklace, that Lowry has provided some Scowerers to help him steal it."

"But why include James?"

"Honestly? I believe it's for experience. James is being rewarded with excitement and offered a chance to do something he hasn't done before."

"I want my brother back!"

"Yes. I imagine so."

"What's your plan?" I asked.

He mulled that over. "First and foremost, I am not a criminal. You are not a criminal. If caught, I would be sent back to England. You would be expelled and sent home. On the other hand, taking what is rightfully yours from your brother is hardly stealing. Especially if he's just stolen it himself."

"So we let him break the law for us. Isn't that cowardly?"

"Not devious?"

"You're tangling up my words. That's not fair."

"I am, and it is," he said.

"It's freezing."

"Here." He put his arm around me and pulled me into him. My eyes shut for a moment while I wondered about his motives in doing so. Of the many things I could picture Sherlock doing, comforting others was not one of them. He was far from warm and cuddly. Skin and bones, and cold at that. But I enjoyed being held. "Patience," he said in a whisper. I felt as if I could doze off and fall asleep.

I must have done just that. Sherlock squeezed my shoulder. I awoke to the sound of running. I was already starting to think like Sherlock: more than one; fewer than five. I had my answer as they passed us: four.

They hurried through the door as silently as a light breeze.

"Who? What?" I whispered.

"Dash it all!" Sherlock said, his voice a knot of frustration. "Irish! You can smell them for kilometers! I'm afraid, dear girl, we must call in reinforcements. This is for Superintendent Colander now."

"What?" I tugged on his sleeve to stop his hand from going for his phone. "No! James can't get arrested."

"You'd rather he be hurt? Those men didn't go in there to have a chat or a spot of tea, you know. James and his fellows are outflanked."

Fellows? "Not if we outflank the outflankers," I said.

"Reckless, irresponsible, and ultimately dangerous for all concerned."

"Are you afraid?"

"Nice try, Moria." He broke loose of my hold and withdrew his phone. He dialed.

While his attention was on the phone, I stood and rushed past him for the door, entering an emergency exit staircase. Concrete, a metal handrail. Sterile, unflattering lighting on each landing. A narrow hallway connecting the backs of several of the exhibit halls. I eased open the first I encountered: wedding dresses, eighteenth century. The next, knives! Three men—all holding knives in gloved hands.

Meirleach! Irishmen. Sherlock was right.

James was himself in the company of three men. One held a nunchaku—two lengths of wood connected by chain; the second, a knife of his own; and the third, a bola, three small balls connected by string. This man started the balls whipping over his head like helicopter blades.

"Continue," the thickest and shortest of the

Meirleach said, his back to me. He was speaking to one of James's men, who held a strange saw and was in the process of cutting into the glass case that held the cross necklace.

"I don't think so," the Scowerer said. They just had to be Scowerers.

"You finish it, or we'll finish it for you."

I saw two other Meirleach blocking the doorway from the exhibit hall into the hallway.

The short man said, "Boy, you're going to tell me how to use this trinket, and if I suspect you're lying, it won't be pretty."

We had a major problem: James didn't know what purpose the necklace served.

I witnessed a silent exchange between the man with the saw and James. He indicated a small wire attached to the box.

James offered him a faint nod.

The man carefully broke the wire and grinned slightly. He seemed immensely pleased with himself.

I nearly squealed as Sherlock pulled me away from the door and into shadow.

"I heard a car skid just now, with my own ears," he whispered, his hand cupped to my ear. "Thing is, a fraction of a second later, I heard it through the phone connection with the superintendent." I said nothing, having no idea what he was talking about. "You see?" I did not. "Colander's phone heard what I heard! He's close by! Can't be more than a block or two."

"But—"

"The Meirleach. He must have tailed the Meirleach."

James interrupted from the other room. "You know," he said, "we can't just let you take it."

"You're just a lad! Let the men speak. Is there to be blood here tonight, mates?"

"He speaks for us," a deep voice said.

"I don't know what the necklace is for," James confessed. "I just know it's important."

"Too bad for you, lad," said the Meirleach. "Seems you'll be coming with us."

"I wouldn't count on that," another voice said.

"Our fight doesn't involve you boys. We have a treaty, your kin and ours. It's the necklace and lad we want, nothing more. No blood to be shed."

"Oh, but it will," the other voice said, "and it'll be yours, friend."

I looked over my shoulder for Sherlock, to see what he made of it all.

He was gone.

What a coward! I thought. First calling the police, then running off. No wonder he'd been so badly beaten up; the boy had no fight in him!

That was when the overhead lights came on. I leaned forward to get a look into the exhibit hall.

Nearly all the men were looking up at the ceiling. As the Meirleach raised their heads, two of the Scowerers did not.

The Scowerer with the bola released it. The string device flew across, wrapped around the throat of the Meirleach leader, and all three pieces of metal struck his head. He fell.

The Scowerer with the nunchaku unleashed it on the Meirleach closest to him. One clip, and this man fell, too. The remaining two Meirleach charged, knife blades glinting. James slid into third base and tripped one. The man holding the saw caught this man's forehead with his knee. Grunts and cries as blows flew. Drops of blood sprayed the floor.

I watched James spin, prepared to throw a punch, only to hold off.

It was Sherlock by his side.

"Holmes?"

"At your service." Sherlock was in the process of pulling his belt from his pants.

"What are you—?"

One of the fallen Meirleach jumped up and reached for James. Using his belt as a whip,

Sherlock strapped the man across the outstretched wrist. The belt looped around several times and, as it did, Sherlock pulled, twisting the surprised Meirleach. He kicked him in the back of the knees and the man went down for a second time as the belt loosened and fell free.

"Improvisation," Sherlock said to a stunned James.

"The lights? You?" James asked.

"But of course. Distraction is the better part of valor."

"James!" I shouted in warning as a scruffy, thuggish man with the bola still wrapped around his neck attacked James.

I shouldn't have shouted.

In James's mind, my voice didn't belong here. I caused him a moment of brain freeze. In doing so, I gave an attacking Meirleach a fraction-of-a-second advantage. That proved to be all the man needed. He seized my brother and raised a knife to his throat. "All right, mates, that'll be all!"

Sherlock, belt held up as a whip, froze.

The commotion in the room stopped as if a switch had been thrown.

At the same moment, a crash was heard below, and the thundering of a good many boots.

The police? Colander? I wondered.

The Meirleach Sherlock had briefly defeated struck him with the butt end of his knife. I'd never witnessed brazen violence like that. Nor had I experienced such an instant reflex. As Sherlock sagged, I ran to him.

The thug half dragged James toward the back of the exhibit hall, where I'd entered.

Men who were down came to their knees slowly, both Scowerers and Meirleach.

A dazed Sherlock shoved me away as I reached him. "Run!" he said. I staggered back into the arms of a Scowerer.

Everyone scattered, the sound of boots hurrying toward the room.

The last I saw of Sherlock, he was holding his hand to his bleeding temple, his eyes dazed, his legs weak.

CHAPTER 41

COLANDER FOLLOWED THE BOSTON POLICE Department SWAT squad inside the fashion museum.

They walked together to the second floor and into the exhibit hall.

"Silent alarm," the police sergeant explained, pointing to the saw lodged in the partially cut glass box containing the cross. "Private firm. Conducted a drive-by. Found the alley door ajar. Called us. It all took a few minutes."

Colander shook his head. "I don't like it. My call was from a minor. Your boys see any kids?"

The sergeant called out and asked. Heads shook.

"We'll button it up tonight. The lab boys will be here first thing in the morning. I don't expect much."

"It can't be tonight?" Colander pointed out the blood on the floor. "There's certainly at least one victim."

"Budget cuts," the sergeant said. "We'll notify the local hospitals and clinics. If we turn up the vic, then yes, we might be able to press the lab boys out of bed. If I may ask, what brought you here in the first place?"

"A tip."

"This kid you mentioned."

"Right."

"You got here fast."

"I was out for a walk," Colander said.

"Sure you were," the sergeant said, "on account of it being such a nice night and all."

"I'm Danish, Sergeant. In Denmark, this is spring weather." The two men shared a distrustful and awkward laugh. They moved into the exhibit's adjacent room, where a statuette and its stand had toppled. "Must have been quite the scuffle. How many do you figure?"

"Hard to say," Colander answered. "I'd only be guessing, but one on the saw. The one doing the bleeding over there. The knife man. Three at least. You?"

"Don't know. More, I think." The sergeant continued to study the look of the scene, the scuff marks on the floor.

"Gangs?" Colander asked.

"A fashion museum?" the sergeant proposed. "Too classy. Feels more like our other museum heists: organized, planned."

"So, one or two got greedy?"

"Something like that. Though the necklace is still in the case. Doesn't add up."

"You'll put a man on the door downstairs?" Colander asked.

"Of course."

Colander passed him his card. "Let me know if you turn up a stabbing victim or anything else?"

"I'll check with my lieutenant first, but if she says it's okay I've got no problem."

"That would be grand." The two men shook hands firmly.

"Interpol?" the sergeant said, sounding impressed. "Working a case here in Boston?"

"Yeah. I get that a lot."

An hour and twelve minutes later, Sherlock finally took an audible breath. He had waited for all sound of the police to end. Then he'd waited thirty minutes longer. He carefully—oh, so carefully—eased his long, well-manicured fingernails into the crack between the acoustic ceiling tile and the suspended metal frame, and lifted the piece from its resting place.

The pedestal he'd used to climb up into the hung ceiling had fallen over, statue and all, as he'd reached for a pipe. With all the police milling about, he'd thought for sure they would find him out and bust him. He did not take it as a sign of good luck; for Sherlock Holmes, "luck" was another word for preparation. He attributed his avoiding arrest to his quick thinking, supreme decision making, and the proper physical execution of the climbing itself. That the pedestal had fallen over was not bad luck either. He should have thought to kick it over, for a statuette sitting on the floor next to an empty pedestal could have raised eyebrows.

The drop to the floor without the pedestal in place was a long one. Sherlock landed with his feet straddling both sides of the fallen column. Despite his reputation for clumsiness and for not having grown into his lanky body, he landed with grace and therefore quietly.

Ten minutes of sneaking around left him aware of a police car with frosted windows claiming the curb outside the museum's main door. He returned to the exhibit hall, prepared to use his right sock as a glove to avoid leaving fingerprints. He stepped up to restart the sawing of the glass box holding the necklace when he studied the cross and jewel more carefully. He leaned in, closer still.

He let go of the saw, realizing he didn't need it after all.

CHAPTER 42

"WHAT DO WE DO?" I SAT AT MY VANITY, FAC-
ing a fast-pacing Ralph, my bedroom door
closed—a first for all the years Ralph had been in
my life. My beside clock read 2:22 a.m.

I looked at the door. "Are you telling me you
don't trust Lois?"

He stopped pacing, threw me a sharp look, and
muttered, "Another time for that."

"Can Mr. Lowry help?"

That stopped him again. "What did you say,
young lady?"

"He's a lawyer, right?" I said as innocently as

possible. I wasn't supposed to know anything about the Scowerers, but James's abduction had jarred me so much I couldn't remember what I was supposed to forget.

"I don't think an attorney will help much in this instance." But I could see in his eyes that Ralph believed otherwise. Involving Lowry was a good idea, and he knew it.

A tap on my window made me flinch so involuntarily that my chair went over backward. Ralph reached to catch me but missed. He quickly helped me up before hurrying to my window and throwing back the curtain.

Sherlock, wet from a continuing freezing drizzle, peered through the streaked pane. Ralph let him in, after, in typical Ralph fashion, laying down a towel for him to stand on. Sherlock removed that strange cape of his and shivered from the cold.

"Hello, sir," Sherlock said to Ralph. Sherlock flashed me a look that told me he wanted to be alone with me. Nothing I could do about that.

"We do have a front door," Ralph said.

"That could easily be being watched. Any word from James?" Sherlock inquired.

"Nothing." I shook my head and fought off tears. I was so sick of showing my emotions, but found it impossible to control.

"We must rescue him," Sherlock said as if discussing something routine, like shopping at the supermarket.

"One thing saying it," Ralph complained. "Quite another doing it."

"No ransom or anything like that," I said, showing him I was holding my phone close.

"Computer or smartphone please," Sherlock said in a demanding voice. I dug out my laptop from under my bedcovers. He sat on the edge of the bed, wet enough to leave a mark, and started typing, then paused to pinch the bridge of his nose while squinting his eyes shut. "Two of the knives brandished had black plastic handles, with curved blades showing signs of having been sharpened multiple times. Filet knives." He pronounced it "fill-ette," so it took me a moment to realize he meant fish knives. "Third man from the jewel box had fish scales on the left leg of his denim trousers." He opened his eyes and punched a key on my laptop. Studied the screen. "I believe the term is 'scrod,' meaning 'cod or other whitefish.'" Closed his eyes again. "The one doing all the yapping had a piece of blue paper adhered to his left boot. A torn corner. A label, perhaps. We must keep that in mind. It may or may not hold significance. Two of the men had fresh cuts on their left hands. Multiple cuts on and near the knuckle of the index finger. One had a light blue bracelet like a rubber band on the left wrist, the remnants of a torn surgical glove, I should think. But the kicker was the black gravel along the seams of the soles of the boots of two of them. Not gravel at all, of course."

"Of course," said Ralph, openly sarcastic, obviously bewildered by this boy. "Because?"

"Crushed seashells. *Mytilus edulis,* I believe. The so-called blue mussel."

"Fishmongers? Are you telling me these boys are fishmongers?"

Another stab at my laptop. I nearly warned him not to break it.

"Two . . . I repeat, a total of two companies process both scrod and blue mussel within the radius of Boston's public transit, the city bus routes."

"What do buses have to do with anything?" asked Ralph.

"Did I fail to mention it?" Sherlock looked up at Ralph for the first time. Squinted again. "Coin pocket of the man wearing the blue rubber band on his wrist: bus receipt sticking out. Sorry to say I couldn't read it, or perhaps we'd know more. Shoddy of me." A few more punches of the keyboard. He was horrible with computers! "There!" He spun the laptop around, showing an image of a shipping box. "The blue label, you sillies! Camden Cod and Shellfish. Cold processing, frozen foods. Of the two companies, I'd say we start there. The piece of blue paper on the man's boot. Did I mention that? Say what?"

"Incredible," Ralph muttered.

"And do what?" I asked.

"Use our powers of observation, Moria! Do the workers wear surgical gloves? If so, blue or white? Any activity at the facility after hours? Any familiar faces? Or clothing? The coming and going?"

"There's three of us!" I said, reminding him.

"And James makes four," Sherlock said. "Never discount the hostage in situations like this."

I heard the mirth in my own voice as I repeated, "And James makes four."

CHAPTER 43

James found himself locked in a smelly room with a mattress and smelly blanket. The window was taped over with newsprint from the outside, clearly the inside of a noisy, smelly facility. There was a smelly bucket and a roll of toilet paper, and they'd delivered fast-food hamburgers for breakfast, if it was even morning. He had no way of knowing the time.

Despite terrifying him with their knives and threats of violence, his kidnappers were also idiots: the hinges were on the inside of the door. If he could figure out a way to remove the three hinge pins, he could pry the door open. For that, he would need tools, and it was not exactly as if they'd left him with a toolbox. They'd stripped the room bare— probably a small office before it had become his prison cell.

A bucket. A roll of toilet paper. An air mattress. A blanket. He needed some oil, a hammer, and a screwdriver, or a hammer and something like a nail or ice pick, something to drive the hinge pin up from the bottom.

No hammer. No ice picks. No nails. But the hamburgers had been good and oily.

A thin pen might work, if it was metal instead of plastic. Pencils were surprisingly strong end to end.

Wouldn't they give him something to write with if he asked? If not, maybe he could request a cross-word puzzle or Sudoku from the morning paper?

Would they refuse him that?

Only one way to find out.

He started banging on the door.

CHAPTER 44

FISHERMEN FISH WHEN THE FISH ARE RUNNING. That meant Camden Cod and Shellfish ran seven days a week, or least they did on the Sunday morning we pulled to within sight of a rambling, waterfront structure that might have been mistaken for an old mill or warehouse. It appeared to have been renovated or enlarged at least three different times, some of it one story, some two story. A tall brick smokestack carried the company sign but the *h* was missing, making it "Cod and S ellfish." The parking lot teemed with old-model cars and pickup trucks with bumper stickers that had no place being read on a Sunday.

"What do we do now?" I complained, having been roused from bed far too early.

"We wait for the eight a.m. shift change," Sherlock said, stifling a yawn.

"You don't have any idea when there's a shift change!" I protested. "What if it doesn't happen at eight?" I had visions of my brother being tortured, or starved, or hanging upside down like in James Bond movies.

"We wait until nine, obviously. And yes . . . et cetera, et cetera."

Ralph's shoulders suggested he was tense. He had dictated the plan. Sherlock was only rehashing it, and as he sipped coffee from a travel mug Ralph appeared to be reconsidering some or all. He wore a knit cap, blue jeans, a brown plaid shirt, and a hoodie under a canvas jacket. I rarely saw Ralph in work clothes, certainly none like these, but I understood it was all part of a disguise intended to get him inside while other workers poured out.

"We saw the door as we drove past."

"Yes, Mr. Holmes."

"You're bothered."

"It's daylight, isn't it? The plant is up and running. This is not a game. You and Miss Moria will need to take *great care*."

"Yes, of course. In our favor: it being daytime, there's no night watchmen," Sherlock said. "No suspicion of an attempted breakout."

"Once inside, Moria will go to the right. You, Mr. Holmes, to the left."

"We keep our heads down," Lock said, looking at me. "We make no attempt to rescue James unless the odds appear heavily in our favor."

"And, you will recall, that decision is left to me," Ralph said. "Let's not forget that, Mr. Holmes!"

"You will find, sir, that I forget very little. In fact, nothing. Forgetfulness is the sign of a weak mind."

Twenty minutes later, cars of all sorts began arriving. Clumps of workers formed in the parking lot, cigarette smoke rising between them like fog.

Sherlock sat back confidently as, at 8:00 a.m. sharp, the exchange of workers began, with our dear Ralph among those entering. Sherlock and I entered the chain-link perimeter and worked our way to the bay side of the building and a door where we could expect to be greeted by Ralph.

"Over here!" I called to Sherlock. We hid behind a large truck backed up to the loading dock. A dozen garage doors were pulled down to the dock. No shipping on Sundays. This altered our plans somewhat.

His eyes danced, his fingers twitched. Sherlock looked like someone had poked him with a Taser. "That's going to be our entrance. Over there." He pointed to a line of black flaps that served as a barrier between the truck bay and the warehouse.

"That's not what we told Ralph."

"We're improvising, aren't we." It wasn't a question, but a statement.

"And if we're caught?" I said.

"Such pessimism. You really must work on that, you know?"

He was right—of course! I'd lost my sense of happy endings and fairy-tale existence. I worried this was what it meant to be grown-up, in which case I wanted nothing to do with it. Father's death, that sense of irretrievable loss, hung on my shoulders like a wet wool coat. I didn't know if I would ever be able to shake off the cold of that tragedy, but I'd been rewarded with a small but noticeable glow of warmth at the thought Mother might not be a lost cause. A trickle of hope had seeped under the door of my absolute abandonment. I was not about to mop it up; nor was I intending to drink of it. But secretly I longed for the hope to spread, forming a bigger pool, and from that other tributaries: possibility, plausibility, predictability, inevitability. In essence, I hoped for hope.

The loading dock being quite elevated, Sherlock offered me a leg up. He lunged me over rubber bumpers made of cut-up truck tires, and I rolled, and rolled, and rolled until passing under and through the barrier of insulating strips. The far side was chilly, five times more smelly, and extremely noisy. I ducked behind some kind of rolling cart. Sherlock arrived a few seconds later.

The processing plant conveyors carried dead fish in various stages of decapitation and disembowelment. Slimy fish guts filled gigantic rolling tubs while men and women in blood-covered rubber aprons, gloves, and paper hairnets wielded razor-sharp knives.

I threw up, spontaneously. Not much in quantity, but enough to make me retch a second time. Sherlock once again patted me on the back—not the reaction I'd expected from him. He took off to our left.

I hurried to the right, scurrying post to post for cover. I admit, I copied Sherlock's moves nearly to the step. I took care to get a decent view of the work area, doing my best to make sure no one was looking my way before I moved on; thankfully, cutting a fish with a knife sharp enough to take off your fingers required concentration.

Across the warehouse, up a metal staircase, I

saw a string of small office spaces atop a platform that jutted over the plant floor. One of the four had newspaper taped over the window. It was as if I wore a charmed necklace that warmed when in the presence of great good or great evil—James was in that room. James was behind that newspaper. James was within my reach.

Maybe sisters just knew these things; maybe James and I weren't like normal brothers and sisters; maybe I was wrong, my heart taking the place of my brain.

I'd lost contact with Sherlock, now a good distance away. I searched for Ralph among the aproned workers in their hairnets. The noise in the room competed with the horrendous odor. I literally bumped into opportunity. Several of the thick rubber aprons hung on a hook fixed to a steel strut column behind which I was hiding. On a scummy shelf sat a box of latex gloves and another of the paper hairnets. The apron hung below my knees, the hairnet made me blush, but I moved across the plant floor without anyone taking a second look.

Coming around the third set of conveyor belts, I spotted Ralph at the foot of the metal stairs. I walked past him slowly.

"Newspaper on windows upstairs," I said, moving on.

"Got it," he said immediately, looking like a foreman surveying his workers. Sherlock wasn't to be seen. I'm not sure why, but I glanced up.

There, in the crisscrossed tangle of steel rafters, a thin shadow of a boy held to a riser. Nearly invisible. Wraithlike. Sherlock. The steel beam upon which he stood connected to another and another in uniform fashion, like a mapped grid of city streets. Two blocks up, and one block to the right would take him along an avenue that connected to the balcony outside the office cubicles.

"You! Back on the line!" called a man's voice from up above. It took me a moment to look, a moment longer to realize he meant me. I acknowledged with a lift of the hand and headed for the nearest conveyor. A group of men and women stood side by side. Knives were held in a slot between two pieces of wood attached to the conveyor equipment. I withdrew a knife, then pulled a dead fish off the conveyor and onto a well-worn plastic cutting board that ran the length of the line. The woman next to me caught the fish just behind the forward fin, sliced toward the head, then down with a crunch. Her left hand swept the cut parts into a bin while her right nudged the fish onto the belt. She grabbed another.

I did the same, feeling light-headed and ready

to toss my cookies onto the moving belt. I severed the head. It wasn't so hard. Swept it into the bin, pushed the fish back onto the conveyor, and grabbed another. The woman next to me shot me a glance, no doubt wondering at how slowly I'd accomplished the task. She had done four fish to my one.

"You new?" she asked in a heavy accent.

"Very."

"Faster, or they put you on guts and grime. You don't want that job."

"Got it! Thanks!" I remained pathetically slow compared to the others. When I thought I'd reached blinding speed, I counted her five to my two. She handled a knife well. I'd have wanted her on my side in a street fight. Desperate to turn around or look behind me, I resisted. Not only would I give myself away, I might reveal Sherlock or Ralph as well. Instead, I looked across the busy plant floor, taking note of possible routes and exits to get James out of here.

"Do you think he's watching us?" I asked the kind woman next to me.

"No. None of 'em stay out here so long. Bobby, he's Sundays. He bosses some and goes back to his online poker. He won't be coming out until he needs more coffee or the toilet. Keep going, you're doing fine."

"I'm pathetic."

She laughed, her hands moving automatically. I had the feeling she could do this job blindfolded.

"Irish?" I asked. "Is Bobby Irish?"

"Irish? All them is Irish! Can't hardly understand some of them," said a woman with an impossibly thick Eastern European accent. "Friends. Family. Who knows. I just do my work."

Meirleach? I wondered. Scowerers? I couldn't tell one side from the other. My brother caught in the middle. Why did Father have to leave us? We needed him now more than ever.

Sherlock hugged a vertical beam only a few yards from the balcony. His head hung as he stared down at Ralph, who was apparently blissfully unaware of his location. Look at me! Sherlock willed.

Nothing.

An idea! Sherlock spotted some welding slag, scabs of metal that had rested atop the beam for generations, just awaiting a boy's curious fingers. Carefully balancing, he squatted and picked up one of the many lumps. Aiming at Ralph, he swung his arm and dropped the chunk. It landed and broke into pieces at Ralph's feet.

Ralph was apparently not new to such spying, for instead of immediately looking up, he did not react in the slightest. Five seconds passed. Ten. Sherlock was about to throw a second chunk of weld when Ralph moved a few feet and glanced up.

Sherlock twisted his wrist, fingers clasped as if holding keys.

Ralph nodded. Message received.

Sherlock looked on as Ralph crossed to Moria on the conveyor line. He reached past her, withdrawing a knife he then cupped so that it hid behind his forearm as he returned to the stairs. He climbed.

Sherlock moved, tightroping his way across the narrow beam until reaching the balcony. He climbed over the railing just as Ralph arrived at the top of the stairs. As if they'd carefully rehearsed, the two met at the door to the room blocked with newspaper. Ralph broke the tip off the knife on his first attempt to pry open the door. The second attempt worked as he drove the knife handle into the latch with a throw of his hip. The door came open, but from the opposite side. Unpinned from the hinges, the door fell inward, slamming to the floor.

"Oops," Ralph said.

James jumped over the fallen door, was caught by Ralph, and swung onto the balcony.

"Ralph!" Sherlock said, ducking behind James, seizing hold of the fallen knife, somersaulting, and planting the broken blade into the toe of a large shoe.

A man screamed. We all turned to look.

A gun fired into the ceiling. Sherlock had just saved Ralph from being shot. The knife driven into the man's foot had caused him to raise his arms just as he was going to fire.

Half the workers dove onto the floor.

Sherlock and Ralph, with James between them, rushed down the stairs, where I signaled them to use the back of the building—the way Sherlock and I had entered—and then followed in lockstep. Call it woman's intuition, sixth sense, luck, I somehow knew trouble was coming through the door to the parking lot.

It came, not in the form of police responding to a gunshot, or a well-wishing civilian playing Sunday Hero, but a man who may or may not have been in the building already. Whoever it was, the man, a knife thrower, possessed keen eyesight, a steady arm, and remarkable accuracy.

Having pushed the workers out of his way, he had dozens of blades at his disposal, all dirty with fish guts and blood, the first of which came so close to my nose that I smelled it. A second knife caught Ralph in the forearm, opening a nasty wound. A third might have killed one of us had Sherlock not appeared from the shadows holding a trash can lid out as a warrior's shield. Three knives in a row collided with the shield and fell to the concrete. The next hit a steel post as we passed behind it. Another, and another, Sherlock somehow adroitly intercepting them, his reactions as fast a swordsman's.

"I took fencing, you know?" he said, utterly calmly, as if reading my thoughts—again! "The foil, for me. Fifteens as often as not."

Clank, clank! More knives fell to Sherlock's shield. He pushed us back through the insulating curtain of rubber. Outside now, we jumped down from the dock—Sherlock helping me, which I greatly resented—and we ran, which was no contest. I beat them both by a good deal.

Ralph's forearm was bleeding badly as he climbed behind the wheel. I pulled off my paper hairnet and tried to tie it around the wound.

"Compress it instead!" Sherlock instructed.

Ralph drove one-handed.

"You . . . How? . . ." James's throat caught. "Thank you! Thank you so much."

"You're welcome, dear boy. Know you'd do the same!"

For once, James didn't complain about the use of the nickname.

CHAPTER 45

James, Sherlock, and I all napped until lunch. I looked out my window to see men trying to look casual on the sidewalk by our townhouse's front door. Scowerers. Of that I had little doubt.

We were under guard.

Lois prepared a lunch of tomato soup, a choice of grilled peanut butter and jelly or grilled cheese sandwiches with ham, and a heaping bowl of potato chips. Heaven.

We were scheduled to leave with Ralph for Baskerville Academy around four o'clock. It would be safer there, we all felt sure. We were told to head upstairs and do our homework and rest. Ralph had a nasty line of stitches on the underside of his left forearm that James demanded to study close up, inspecting like a surgeon.

"Does it hurt?" James asked.

"Never mind that."

Sherlock, whose shoulder was bothering him again, and who wore a lump on his right temple that looked like a golf ball sawed in half, knocked lightly on my door a few minutes past one.

I admitted him and offered him my vanity stool while I sat on my bed, legs tucked under, Cucumber and Ellie sprawled on my pillow.

"Remember the library gave me the name of that man?"

"The Greek scholar," I said.

"Exactly! Very good, Moria!"

"I'm not a moron, you know! That was only yesterday."

"Feels like a fortnight," Sherlock said. "He rang me back. A voicemail. Offered for me—us—to pay him a visit."

"What? Today?"

"I think, maybe. Before I ring him back, I wanted to check with you. Are you up for it?"

"Translating Father's journal? Of course! What do you think?"

"I think we've had quite a weekend, and perhaps this should wait."

"You do?" I gasped.

"No. But I wanted to give you an out, if you wanted."

"I don't want," I said. "To wait!"

We both grinned, coconspirators once again!

"Who do you trust more, Lois or Ralph?"

"That's a horrible thing to ask, after the way you made up all that stuff about my bathtub night."

"I made up nothing!"

"You have no evidence! You, who insists on only following the evidence."

"It's what the circumstances of the evening suggest, Moria. Ergo: circumstantial evidence."

"It's conjunctive," I said harshly.

"I think you mean conjecture, as in 'a conclusion from incomplete evidence.'"

"You know perfectly well what I mean," I spit out, humiliated.

"You have to pick one of them, Mo. I can't do it for you."

"I hate you!"

"No doubt."

"Ralph. Why, I don't know, but—"

"Fine. We can work with that." Sherlock

sounded so cold and unsympathetic to what he'd just asked me to do.

"Work how?"

"Someone has to help us get out of this house. We're prisoners, Moria, or hadn't you noticed?"

CHAPTER 46

RIDING IN THE DARK OF THE TRUNK OF THE family car, an ungainly tall boy beside me—his feet to my head, and vice versa—proved an unsettling and uncomfortable solution to escape my own home.

"If the Scowerers are protecting us," I said into the pitch black and the smell of rubber, "why do we have to hide from them?"

"Don't make the mistake of thinking of them as private bodyguards. They are protecting James first, and you second," Sherlock said, speaking softly. "They are protecting what's of value to them. Why, we don't know. Who they are, exactly, we don't know. Only that they are secretive, organized in a somewhat military way, and they have enemies."

"The Meirleach."

"The same."

"Ralph is taking a risk," I said.

"He is. If my theory is correct—and when am I wrong?—he was himself a target: the hot chocolate. I'm confident he has figured that out as well. There would appear to be a fine line between allies and enemies, and it does us no good to speculate on how everything fits together and where we stand. And by 'we' I mean you and James."

"You, too."

"Sadly, no. There is every evidence I don't matter a hoot to either side. Perhaps that may help us at some point, Moria. Perhaps we gain a little something from that."

"My hip hurts," I said. "That pointy bone. I need to roll over."

"Don't even think about it. That is not going to happen."

I knew he was right. "OK, but on the way home I vote we hide under a blanket in the backseat."

"Is there a blanket?" Sherlock asked.

"Don't go getting technical on me," I said,

amusing him. I enjoyed making him laugh. It was like finding the right place for a jigsaw piece that had confounded everyone else at the table.

Thomas Lehman, a short man in his late seventies, with thick glasses, gray hair, and heavy eyebrows, admitted Sherlock and me into his penthouse apartment atop a brick condominium tower that overlooked the bay. It was filled with marble busts and statuettes, many chipped or missing noses, as well as parchment scrolls and 1960s-era contemporary art, and I felt as if we'd visited our second museum of the weekend. There was a cluttered, professorial feel to the sitting room. The man walked sturdily, had a clear voice and hearty chuckle. A man easily self-amused. Sherlock and I sat where he told us to, facing him with a view out the windows.

We waited for him to speak. He was that kind of man.

"You're Moria Elise."

"Moriarty. Yes."

"And you are James?"

"No. A friend of hers. A school chum. I'm the one who called you." Sherlock scribbled down his cell phone number and email address and passed them to the man. "In case . . . well, I don't know." Sherlock untucked his shirt and withdrew Father's journal from the small of his back. I wondered how long he'd been hiding it there.

The lawyer turned amateur scholar flipped pages, reading. "How did you come by this?"

"It was my father's. He . . . passed."

"Yes, I'm sorry about that. I knew him. Socially. Did I tell you?" He addressed Sherlock.

"I should have thought to have asked," Sherlock said.

"This can be a small town at times. Functions. Some art auctions."

"Buying or selling?" Sherlock asked.

"I beg your pardon?"

"You and Mr. Moriarty. The art auctions. Were you buying or selling?"

Sherlock was thinking about the stacks of paintings, the busts, rare stamps, and other collectibles in Father's secret room.

"That's confidential information, I'm afraid. I don't feel comfortable discussing that."

"Apologies."

The man's good humor was gone, the lawyer present. "Do you mind?" He didn't wait for our answer. He sat back and read the dead language, turning pages regularly. Five minutes passed. Ten. Sherlock's eyes told me he didn't want me interrupting the man.

"His handwriting isn't easy," Lehman said without looking up. The single sheet recovered from the gun drawer dropped out of the journal and into the man's lap. "What's this?"

"Numbers," Sherlock said.

"I can see that."

"I tried . . . that is . . ." Sherlock said, "I was able to get the first three lines. We'd like the rest, if possible."

The man set it aside.

"I have poor eyesight, and I tire easily," Lehman said, not that we'd asked. "Aging is horrible, unless you consider the alternative." A glint to his eye. I liked Thomas Lehman, Esq. "From what I just read, it's an . . . accounting. Part business diary, part personal journal. I'm sorry to say that on first glance I don't believe its content is proper for persons your age. This is grown-up stuff."

"We are investigating Mr. Moriarty's death," Sherlock said.

The lawyer managed not to break a smile, though his eyes filled with mirth. "Are you now? Is that so?"

"It's thirty-seven pages. How long for you to read it and give us a general idea of what we've got?"

Lehman regarded Sherlock. He seemed to be

considering handing the journal back.

Please no! I spoke mentally.

"Thirty minutes."

"Can we wait?" I asked.

"May we?" Sherlock said, correcting my gram-mar. He could be such a snob.

"How are you getting home?" he asked.

"We have a car waiting."

"Of course you would." The man sounded dis-turbed by the thought. "Very well. If I doze off I urge you to wake me. Gently, for heaven's sake, but wake me just the same."

We woke him twice.

I sent Ralph a text at the thirty-minute mark. He wrote back, reminding me of our 4:00 p.m. departure time for school and that we had to return for bags and James.

At quarter past three, the man turned the last page and sighed deeply enough he might have been snoring again.

"As I thought: not for your age." He closed the journal and reached to hand it back to Sherlock. But Sherlock wouldn't take it from him.

"That won't do," Sherlock said defiantly. "That won't do at all."

"Young man, this is personal, private, sensi-tive information. I'm stunned you have it, quite honestly. I would find someplace safe, extremely safe, to lock this away, and Moria could return to it in five years' time."

"We had an agreement!" Sherlock said.

"We had an understanding," Lehman corrected. "I have done as you asked. I have read the document. Far too quickly. Nowhere near what could properly be called a translation. Could I transcribe it? Yes, I believe quite sincerely I could. But it would be hurtful to Miss Moriarty and her brother, James. Again: let's put this on mothballs for a few years."

"We'll only find someone else," I said, sounding a little too bratty. My inner brat revealed itself when I was denied what I was rightfully due. Without a mother, I'd suffered my brother's heavy-handedness and Father's deferring to James for way too long. I wasn't about to allow some stranger to emphasize "Miss Moriarty" and get away with it.

I had my limits.

Thankfully, I could see Mr. Lehman reconsidering. "That would be unwise. You might find the next person inclined toward taking advantage of your father's journaling."

"Blackmail," Sherlock said.

"Consider yourselves lucky you came to me first," Mr. Lehman said.

"Tell us," I said, wondering whether to add "please" or "you old buzzard!"

"Some of it," he began, without further argument, "is of a personal nature, as I've said. An adult, personal nature. I skimmed over a good deal of this, as it's none of my business. A full transcription will, of course, reveal these moments in their entirety. I repeat: I have my reservations about the wisdom in sharing such intimate details with persons your age. I doubt seriously I would do so."

"'Some of it,'" Sherlock said, echoing the man. "What about the rest?"

"Indeed." Mr. Lehman looked up at the ceiling for guidance, or perhaps to organize his thoughts. His expressive eyebrows lifted and fell, his eyes themselves looking enormous behind the lenses. "There are elements of . . . suggested impropriety, frankly. Again, that is something I believe beyond the purview of any young woman, any daughter." He focused on me. I cowered, looking down while trying to find my breath.

"It is not my desire to continue," Mr. Lehman said, "but I will respect your request, Miss Moriarty, and leave it up to you how much to share. Honestly, I'd be far more comfortable sharing the contents first with your priest or minister or family lawyers in order—"

"No!" I reacted too harshly, sitting him up straight.

"That certainly hit home," he said, wearing his curiosity as pursed lips and wide eyes. "Why that reaction, Moria?"

I looked to Sherlock and back to Mr. Lehman. "I don't trust our lawyer, Mr. Lehman. Not fully. Yes, I know I'm considered just a child. I understand he's a highly respected lawyer. But I don't trust him. Why is it, do you think, I shared this with you, a complete stranger, rather than him?"

"You are how old?" he asked.

I swallowed. "Twelve and a half."

He shook his head. "I'm sorry, young lady. It's just—"

"My mother left us seven years ago. My father looked after us with a full-time governess of sorts and a wonderful man who's more like an uncle. My father died less than three months ago under . . ." I beseeched Sherlock to jump in.

"Suspicious circumstances," Sherlock said.

"'Suspicious' according to whom?" Mr. Lehman asked. "The police?"

I glanced at Sherlock again provocatively. Help! My throat had constricted. I couldn't get out a word.

"Should we tell you what's in that journal?" Sherlock said.

"I thought you couldn't read it! What's going on here?"

"We can't," Sherlock said. "But it is our . . . belief . . . that Moria's father was involved with a criminal element." This wasn't my belief at the time, but I let Sherlock speak, for I felt I might learn more from him in the current setting than I had from our prior discussions. There was something about his defiance I felt reluctant to challenge. "That his interests extend internationally. That for such . . . business arrangements to exist over generations of the family's shipping business . . . the family would need to exert influence over bankers, possibly dock workers, possibly even police or politicians." I wondered if Sherlock could see me losing color, for I felt fainter the more he spoke.

"I can confirm," said Mr. Lehman, "that some of the passages I read more carefully than others, seemed—only seemed, mind you—to suggest some of the same."

It was my turn. "Please," I implored him.

He opened Father's journal and turned pages once again. This time, a casual observer. "It's public knowledge that your father inherited the responsibility to manage the shipping company at a young age. Absolutely. He wasn't much older than your brother at the time. James must be sixteen? Seventeen?"

"Fourteen."

"Well, your father was in his early twenties. It had to have come as a heavy burden, as one can only imagine. Your family's business is indeed international and extensive. A lot to grasp for such a young man. According to this document, it is also well diversified—a great deal of assets, the wealth spread into many other businesses—although there are few details concerning specifics. According to this, your father was all about divestiture—that is, spreading out the money. The journal is more your father's internal thoughts, private thoughts, about various meetings and strategies over which he has agreed or disagreed with his board and associates."

"Within the company?" I asked.

"So one would assume. It doesn't mention company names so much as people. Negotiations. Those who angered him, mostly.

"Your father," he said, again directly to me, "faced challenges, burdens really, that few men could face alone. I will do my best to provide a written transcript. That should take a week, possibly less."

"At the end of the journal," Sherlock said, "how close are we to the present?"

"No way to tell. I expect there are likely many more of these journals. This particular one concludes with mention of a political struggle within the organization. A vying for power, a disagreement over the true policy and direction of the corporation. Your father had rivals. It's fairly clear he took actions that may have resulted in division rather than reconciliation."

"The organization split?" Sherlock said.

I didn't like hearing Father talked about this way, as if he might be in the next room, or waiting for me back home. I'd attended his funeral, and it was still too fresh in my memory.

"Ideologically, yes. Corporate direction. Perhaps at the very top, yes." Mr. Lehman removed his glasses nervously and squinted as he cleaned them with a tissue. "There are passages concerning you and your brother, Moria. Clearly, your father loved you both very much and was working to construct what I could call a more legitimate platform upon which to do business."

"Diversifying," Sherlock said. "Improprieties?"

"Yes. Away from same. Correct."

"Allies were turning against him, or rivals?"

"Honestly, it's vaguer than that. There are

initials, only. Greek letters do not translate exactly to the Roman alphabet. If I knew the names and roles of the various players, perhaps I could tell you more. Then again, he may have used some kind of code in case the journal fell out of his hands. As it has."

"His most obvious rival?" Sherlock the investigator asked.

Mr. Lehman twitched an uncomfortable grin. "Heth," he said, sounding as if he sneezed. "'Eta' is the English pronunciation. *H* is the English letter representation."

"Eta," Sherlock said softly.

"The struggle was in great part with this man."

"Not *L* or *C*?"

"There is no direct correlation to our letter *C*. Lamedh is the closest to *L*, written as an inverted *V*."

"My mother," I choked out. "Did he mention Mother?"

Mr. Lehman's lips tightened again, this time to a yellow pallor. His bloodshot eyes hung low like a bloodhound's.

"I'll take that as a yes," I said, starved for air. "Tell me, please."

Sherlock did something extraordinary: he reached over and rubbed me gently on the back. I snapped my head to look at him, and I scared him off. He withdrew his hand. But I hadn't minded it at all.

"Attorneys," Mr. Lehman said, "are trained to be careful with our words."

"Please."

"Yes, there are passages concerning your mother. It is . . . she was . . . one of the conflicts I mentioned. Honestly, this is where I'm terribly uncomfortable, and believe it in all our best interests to leave it at that."

"Seven years, Mr. Lehman," I said, "and I still don't know what happened."

"I can tell you this: your father agonizes over what would be enough to break any man. Several pages' worth. I told you: I skimmed it. None of my business."

"It's my business. Please . . ."

Mr. Lehman and I entered a staring contest of sorts. I was the first to blink, but to my surprise he opened the journal, flipped pages, and read silently, his oversized eyes reminding me of a kitty wall clock I'd once owned.

"He reminisces briefly about the fate of other Moriarty women. Your mother's situation being somewhat comparable. A great-aunt lost at sea during a transatlantic crossing. Another who went mad and was sent off to Australia for treatment."

"Mother was not mental," I said.

"I didn't say any such thing."

"You're saying she didn't choose to leave us? That she was forced to?"

"There's not nearly enough to draw any such conclusions. The last thing I want, Moria, is to put thoughts like that in your head. The details are lacking."

"But it could be," I suggested.

"It could be many things. Anything," Mr. Lehman said.

Sherlock showed no emotion whatsoever, a situation that angered me.

The news confirmed what my heart had always wanted to hear. It set off a torrent of thought and emotion. James and I had considered a thousand different possibilities for Mother's leaving us: disease, abuse, anything to defend the bond a child feels for her parent.

"Maybe," I said, "he told her to leave. For her safety! Maybe that's why he could never tell us."

Mr. Lehman looked sad. I could tell he regretted having said anything.

"Maybe he wanted her back!" I practically shouted. "Maybe they killed him for it!"

Sherlock said, "Moria."

Just my name. Like a slap on the face. Wake up!

"Sorry," I said.

We looked at each other, sharing grave expressions.

"The other sheet?" Sherlock asked.

"I'll work on it. Numbers, mostly. As you've said."

"Take precautions," Sherlock advised the man. "There are some bad men about. We've mentioned you to no one. Any trouble that comes, you will have brought upon yourself."

"Good heavens but you two are interesting," Mr. Lehman said.

Sherlock reached over and took my hand.

"Not terribly," Sherlock said. "But we are interested."

Mr. Lehman liked that. "Even better."

"And we're good friends," I said, moving Sherlock's cold fingers with my own.

Sherlock let go of my hand as if I'd pinched him.

Lehman smiled. "Yes. I can see that."

CHAPTER 47

TUESDAY EVENING, THE COMMON ROOM BUZZED.
Being back at school had begun to feel more normal, the events of the weekend finally left behind.

To the right of the bay window, I saw Sherlock having a curious moment with Ruby Berliner,
his head tilted down nearly into her hair as Ruby
looked straight ahead.

Ruby nodded. A year ahead of me in school,
Ruby ran cross-country and had the figure of a
sixth-form senior. She wore her blond hair long,
rarely in a ponytail, cascading over the soap-ad
complexion of a Swedish fashion model. She had

artistic talent and brains, was president of James's class, and though a quiet girl, could hold her own in a dining room conversation. I didn't hate her, but I didn't have to like her.

Sherlock spoke some more. The way his shoulders moved I would have sworn he'd given her something, but there were too many bodies blocking my vision for me to know for sure.

Ruby looked up—they were far too physically close for my comfort level—and said something, and then he spoke to her again. I wanted badly—so badly!—to march over and interrupt, but I showed the utmost discipline by restraining myself. Gold star for Moria.

James faced a different set of circumstances. Surrounded by his dim-witted friends, Thorndyke, Eisenower, Rubins, and Santos, he was otherwise keeping to himself when in fact everyone in school with half a brain (this excluded the four in his company) knew he was waiting for Alexandria Carlisle to arrive.

Before she did, however, he spotted Headmaster Crudgeon, accompanied by a tall man with slate-gray eyes, a man who fit my description of

Detective Superintendent Colander. They stood just past the coat room, though the visitor kept his coat on, a full-length black raincoat, belted at the waist—again, matching my description. Surveying the room, Crudgeon spotted James just as James picked out Lexie among the arriving students.

Lexie looked as if she'd been crying. Her pace slowed as she entered a room with so many people.

For James, it was like two trains heading for each other on a single track. The detective, Colander, wanted James—of that, there was no doubt. In James's mind, the man's interest had to do either with the fashion museum break-in, or, in some extraordinary twist of reality, with James's spying on Lexie's father. In either case, James had to keep Lexie from any of it, or worse, from becoming part of an investigation. He had to prevent Lexie from being considered guilty by association, something she didn't deserve.

Lexie approached, crying again, but silently. Had Colander and Crudgeon gotten to her first? he wondered.

"I'm so glad to see you," she said, tears welling in her eyes.

Colander and Crudgeon were closing in.

"Why would I want to speak to you?" James said coldly, loudly enough for Crudgeon to hear.

He'd checked with his pals, all of whom laughed at once.

"What?" she said, reeling.

James raised his voice even louder. "Do you honestly think I want to talk to you? As if!" More laughter. James winked at her, trying to signal her, but she dropped her head, sobbing now. She'd missed his clue.

"We . . . talked . . . about . . . this . . ." she groaned, looking up now, while drowning in tears.

"Lex!" he said sharply, under his breath. But too late. Crudgeon was upon him. "Get lost!" he said to her.

Lexie turned, ran directly into the detective, and then slipped past and fled out of the common room at a run, some maids-in-waiting hot on her trail.

"James, Detective Superintendent Colander. Detective, James Moriarty."

The two shook hands, James trying to keep his eyes from following Lexie. It wasn't easy.

"I wonder if I might have a minute," Colander said.

James looked to Crudgeon, hoping for some support. Crudgeon said, "I explained that keeping a boy at Baskerville from his meal was like starving a bear. You never know what you're going to get."

"The cloakroom, perhaps?"

"Sure."

Many eyes, including mine, followed the three of them out of the common room and into the entrance hallway.

The coatroom, a line of racks and hangers, went nearly empty, as none of the students bothered with outerwear, regardless of weather.

Colander made no small talk. "Where is it, James?"

"Sir?" James said.

"Not the answer I'm looking for, son. Where is the necklace? And," he said, "consider your words very carefully. Interpol agents like myself are authorized to, with the cooperation of local authority, detain individuals of all ages in the United States. Especially, specifically, when it comes to acts of terrorism."

"Terrorism?"

"Consider as well the number of closed-circuit security cameras established in this city, footage from which is recognized as prosecutable evidence."

"It's important, James," Crudgeon said, "that you understand the superintendent is not charging you with anything at this time."

James had long assumed Crudgeon was a member of the Directory. If so, was Crudgeon playing headmaster or Scowerer, given that James had gone to the museum under Lowry's direction? Certainly, Crudgeon would not want James arrested. What message was Crudgeon trying to send?

"I'm sorry if I'm being dense," James said to the superintendent, "but I don't know what you're asking. I don't know if you know, but my father died recently. His estate is being handled by our family attorney, Mr. Lowry. I'm supposed to call him when I'm approached by strangers."

Colander did not appreciate any of that. "The fashion museum, son. Saturday night. Last chance."

James swallowed dryly. Crudgeon's face revealed no hint of what he should do.

Dinner was called in the common room.

"I have Mr. Lowry's number in my room. Headmaster, wouldn't the office have it as well?"

"I'm sure we do," Crudgeon said to James. "I'd be happy to provide it," he told Colander.

"I've come a long way to talk to you, James," Colander said. "I've already spoken to your sister and your roommate."

"So I heard."

"Perhaps after the meal—"

"I have homework," James said. "Tons of home-work. You can blame the headmaster for that." He faked a smile, his stomach upside down.

"The video will allow for a probable cause warrant," Colander informed James. "The warrant will necessitate my return and a more formal discussion."

James felt light-headed though he tried not to show it. Gathering his strength, he said, "I'm sure Mr. Lowry will understand what that means, since I don't."

"It means you're in trouble, son. If you don't speak with me now, you're in serious trouble."

James wanted badly to agree to sit down with the man. But he'd been schooled by both Crudgeon and Lowry to never speak to police without Lowry in the room. Not ever. He had said, "We have friends in high places, James, who can work miracles."

"I don't know why I would be," James said as innocently as possible. "But if you say so." He looked over to Crudgeon. "May I be excused, Headmaster?"

"Go on," Crudgeon said.

As famished as he was, James had somehow managed to lose his appetite.

Following the non-meal, James headed for Bricks 2 to try to mend things with Lexie.

Just passing the Main House he saw through the lamp-lit darkness a girl who looked like Lexie being helped toward a waiting car.

The woman helping her took shape as Mrs. Carlisle. But the way Mrs. Carlisle hunched and held Lexie so tightly suggested something was terribly wrong.

"Lex?" James hollered.

Lexie turned her head and seemed to catch sight of James, but hurried away from him.

"Lexie! I'm sorry!" But a chauffeur closed the car door before James got out the apology.

Wanting to find out what was going on, James headed directly to Bricks Middle 2. He swung through the doors, immediately encountering a group of girls, all of whom moved away from him. "LeTona? Annie?" he said.

"How do you feel now?" Annie asked.

James looked at her curiously. "What was Lexie doing with her mom?"

"What do you care after the way you treated her?"

Only then did he begin to understand that Lexie's mother couldn't have possibly made the drive from Boston in the thirty minutes since dinner. "Wait a second," he said. "What exactly's going on here?"

One of the girls called him words she shouldn't have. Ruby Berliner chastised him venomously.

"That's how you treat someone when they're coming to you for comfort?"

"Comfort? I . . . was protecting her! What are you talking about?"

"Her father was hit by a truck. A hit-and-run in Boston."

In his mind's eye, James saw Superintendent Colander. He saw Mr. Carlisle's appointment book open to the wrong week on the man's desk. He saw Tuesday, 4:00 p.m.—one of many appointments that he'd photographed, printed out, and hand-delivered to Lowry. Lowry, who had adamantly refused to allow James to email him any such material.

"Comfort?" he said again. Lexie had come into the common room needing a friend. In his determination to keep her from getting caught by Colander, he'd not only rebuffed her, but made a fool of her.

Of himself, as it turned out.

James stuttered. "D-dead?"

"You didn't know," Ruby said.

"Oh, come on!" Annie complained. "I don't believe that for a second!"

James looked up at the girls, pale and not moving.

"He didn't know," Ruby said.

The foul-mouthed girl chided, "You selfish, rude, horrible tool."

James's mind reeled. He'd done this. He'd caused this. The truck had to have been driven by Scowerers, agents who'd acted on information provided by him.

"Dead?" James repeated the word in between bouts of dizziness. He might have stayed there a few minutes longer. He couldn't remember. He ended up staggering around campus in the cold until finding himself in the Lower 3 hallway, dazed and slightly frostbitten.

He relived how he'd treated Lexie, how without an explanation she must have felt so abandoned.

Could she possibly connect him to her father's death?

They should have told him.

Something else was happening to him. Something he didn't like, but couldn't resist. While regretting the way he'd treated Lexie, he also felt emboldened by the wicked thrill of it all. Remorseful, but excited. Something as simple, as easy, as photographing some pages out of an appointment book had . . .

"Dead?" he muttered aloud.

A boy heading toward the washroom apparently

heard him and moved away from James. Something about the boy's repulsion added to the effect Carlisle's death was having. James sensed both purpose and power, importance and effectiveness. He was a very real part of something big and dark and powerful.

The Scowerers had removed either an obstacle or an untrustworthy ally.

Cause and effect, James thought. He hungered for more, while at the same time wondering if such an order had been placed and resulted in Father's death.

Part of the problem, or part of the solution? he wondered, having little idea of which side he was on.

But, at the same time, he wanted more.

CHAPTER 48

AT MY SUGGESTION, SHERLOCK AND I MET IN one of the soundproofed music practice rooms Thursday night after study hall. Sherlock looked uncomfortable as he pulled the door shut. It took me a moment to remember he'd been beaten up in one of these rooms. I apologized. He told me not to be silly. I told him I wasn't being silly.

Open space on the walls and the inside of the door was covered in egg-carton-shaped foam meant to absorb sound. A small window with a fabric blind looked out into the dark.

I reminded Sherlock that as underclassmen,

and a boy and girl alone in a room like this, we'd receive demerits if caught. The rehearsal studios were notorious make-out rooms and were patrolled vigorously.

"I'm aware of that, Moria." He pulled open a cupboard, withdrew a violin case, and then the instrument. He tuned it poorly and began to play a piece of either improvised or poorly memorized music. Beethoven, I feared. He wasn't bad, but he wasn't good either. Few of his notes were in tune. But when he closed his eyes, I felt sorry for him—he believed himself at one with the instrument. Sadly, his math was off. He wasn't close to "at one."

"What have you got?" he asked, chin to the instrument, notes flying around the space in no exact order.

"Questions."

He continued playing, much worse than before.

"James isn't eating," I said.

"I noticed."

"He isn't talking to me."

"Nor to me."

"He isn't hanging around with Clueless and Brainless."

"Ever since the Colander visit."

"Yes. I saw that," I said. "Do you think there's a connection?"

"Do you think there isn't?" Sherlock asked. He seemed to be trying to make the violin accompany our conversation—the low strings for his voice, the higher notes for me. It didn't work at all.

"Same night Lexie left."

"Indeed." As if he'd made this connection long before anyone else. He could be so obnoxious.

"I also wanted to talk about something else—someone else," I said.

"Is that so?"

"Ruby Berliner."

"Oh," he said. His finger slipped off a high string and twanged against the instrument.

"Can you just stop playing for a minute?"

He stopped. "You don't like it?" He sounded so hurt.

"Lock, I love it. You're very talented."

"If you say so. I studied at the conservatory when but a lad of—"

"You and Ruby," I said.

"If there's anyone you should be worried about—and there is not!—it should be Natalie."

"NATO?" I said, using her nickname. "Why? I don't understand."

"You don't understand." He sounded so condescending.

"No."

"Natalie?" he said. "Your roommate?"

"I know who Natalie is."

"Apparently, you don't. Not really."

"Natalie and you?"

"No! I mean, if you ask her, yes. I think very much yes. From me? No. Not interested. Never was."

I could see how I might have misinterpreted a good deal of Natalie's encouragement for me to pursue Sherlock. She could have been speaking from her own crush on him. I filed it away. "Don't change the subject!" I warned. "Ruby is the subject."

"Ruby is an ally, an employee of Sherlock Investigations, if you will."

"No, I won't," I said. "I have no idea what you mean."

"She is a means to an end. We need her." He started up the violin again, like tugging the cord of a lawn mower until it growled.

"Stop being so abstract, so obtuse, and put that thing down, would you, please?" I couldn't think. He held the violin by the tuning pegs. It looked toy-like in his long fingers.

"I stayed behind," he said. "The fashion museum. I stayed behind."

"Meaning?"

"Just what I said: I hid up in the ceiling. I stayed after all the commotion."

"You did not!"

"I used one of the stands. Was nearly found out by some police, but thankfully, no. They were too dense. When all were gone from the place I . . . well, I kind of fell back out of there. But I was about to saw open the display case holding the cross when I discovered the most unexpected, the most fascinating, the most important fact. One that may, perhaps, solve a good number of problems we face."

"Such as?"

"Procuring the painting of Wilford. Executing the necessary—"

"I mean 'such as' what discovery?" I snapped at him.

"It's not a jewel."

"Excuse me?" I said.

"Hanging from the cross. Transforming the light in the painting. Not a jewel."

"I'm listening." Why he couldn't seem to complete a single thought, I had no idea. My suspicion was that he wanted me to beg, wanted me to celebrate his genius, compliment him at every pause. He had me so wrong.

"Sir Frederick William Herschel . . ."

"Oh, please no!" I wondered if I'd said this

aloud. Another Sherlock history lesson. I didn't have the patience.

". . . in the year 1800," Sherlock said. I exhaled, grateful I'd apparently not complained aloud. "Directed sunlight through a prism and measured the temperature of the spectrum of light. A man named Johann Ritter followed up, measuring the red spectrum. You're bored!"

"Not at all."

"You're somewhere else."

"Nonsense! I'm in Ritter's lab measuring the red spectrum."

"Good!" he said, believing me. I felt cruel. I tried to pay better attention. "It's called a dispersive optical prism. Basically, a triangle of glass. You can look it up."

"No thanks." That I did speak, regrettably.

"Two hundred years ago, your ancestors left a clever visual clue inside the family Bible and a piece of jewelry for their descendants to use in decoding the Bible. One needed the other. You, James, and I pursued the obvious—the jewel. But upon seeing it was nothing but a prism, a specific prism at that, I made an unexpected discovery."

"I'm lost," I admitted.

Sherlock reached into his coat pocket. As his hand came out dragging a string of pearls, it turned out it was a good thing the room was soundproofed, because I let out a scream. In his hand, he held the gold cross necklace.

"Stay calm! This is a fake. This is Ruby's work, but it's darn good work, if you ask me."

"Fake?"

"Just so. Art imitating life, to reverse a cliché. It's what everyone seems to be after, and since neither the Scowerers nor the Meirleach stole it from the museum, I thought a good copy might come in handy."

"But we need the real one," I said, "in order to try it out on the Bible."

"In fact, we don't! But that doesn't mean we aren't curious about who stole it."

"You can be so annoying," I said.

"The necklace is old-school, Moria. Put the prism in sunlight, divide that light into its various colors. Isolate the deepest reds onto the pages of the Bible, and there you have it."

The two of us startled at once. A clap from the window. Sherlock nearly dropped the violin. I jumped up out of my seat. The fabric shade held a batten in its bottom hem as a weight. The wood of the batten had smacked the window casing, driven by a breeze from where the window was open a quarter inch. Reckless of us not to have noticed the window being open like that. Sherlock shut it, ducked under the blind, and locked the window.

"There you have what?" I asked, returning to our conversation.

"Silver nitrate, I imagine!" said Sherlock. "Can't know for certain until we try." He hadn't taken his eyes off the window; something about it bothered him.

"Stop being so Sherlock!"

"Moria, we have ultraviolet lamps—black light—that we can use in place of the archaic methods of using the optical prisms and sunlight. All we need to test my theory is the Bible and a black light from the science lab. Whatever is there, whatever your father wanted you to find, would have been written using the chemical silver nitrate, a long, long time ago. And maybe more recently."

"Note to Sherlock," I said. "We don't have my family's Bible. It happens to be in the headmaster's office!" I screamed.

I looked at his face, still bruised, and tried to imagine what went on in his head.

He raised his solo eyebrow again. "Yes. And I have a plan to . . . borrow it."

"Of course you do." I was blatantly condescending.

"My plan"—the door opened as Sherlock was

speaking—"is to bring our two halves together. It will be fun, I promise."

"Mr. Holmes! What did you just say to her?" Mr. Geissinger, the music teacher, one of tonight's proctors, burned red in the face.

"I . . . ah . . ."

"He's explaining a musical piece to me," I said to Mr. Geissinger. "An improvisational piece."

"Is he?" Geissinger perked up.

Sherlock hadn't played the violin for several minutes. "The first movement with the second," he said to the music teacher.

"I see."

I covered my grin. Sherlock could turn things around on other people, could twist them into knots, could tangle their own words faster than anyone I knew.

"Oh! Yes!" said Geissinger. "Are you a violin man?"

Sherlock ran off a flourish to prove himself. It was better than the earlier music.

"We need a second violin in the pit for the next play. Who's your advisor, Mr. Holmes?"

"I'd rather not, sir. Time constraints."

"I don't give a hangnail if you'd rather not," he said, somewhat confounded by his own words. He looked slightly lost and distraught. "That is, you'll play if I say you'll play."

"Yes, sir."

"And you'll play."

Sherlock didn't acknowledge.

"I'll have the sheet music to you tomorrow. I'll expect a run-through of the first three scenes day after tomorrow." He looked at me. "What the devil are you two up to anyway?"

"Improvisation, sir," Sherlock said. Where his quick answers came from beguiled me. "I'm calling it 'Family Portrait.' It's about the Moriartys, sir. James is my roommate. This is his sister. I'm putting her to music, if that doesn't sound too abstract."

"Abstract? I love abstract! Philip Glass. Steve Reich! Let's hear it, boy."

Geissinger stepped in, allowing the door to shut. He apparently didn't care about delaying his rounds as curfew proctor.

Sherlock played as if I wasn't in the room. His high notes stood my hair on end, and not in a good way but the nails-on-blackboard way. His morose melodies, haunting and aimless, left me thinking of snakes and insects and wiggly, creeping things I wanted no part of. Geissinger called it "inspired."

Ten (agonizing) minutes later, Geissinger provided us both with passes so we could return to our rooms without demerits.

I walked back to my room alone along the western side of the Bricks where an access road separates the Bricks from the JV playing field and a wide expanse of lawn leading to the gym. Bikes were chained up outside shuttered windows, the blinds pulled for privacy. Light from the windows threw pale patterns onto the black asphalt, and I found myself playing step-on-a-crack-and-you'll-break-your-mother's-back. An animal, or car brakes, or something unthinkable cried from the woods beyond the gym, well down the hill from me, and I was reminded of Sherlock's insistence there were strangers in the shadows keeping watch on my brother. Grown men, not kids like us. Perhaps they were out there now, I thought, looking at me.

I walked faster, and the faster I walked, the more frightened I became, the more concerned I was not alone. I found it strange the way fear could take over so quickly. The trickle became a flood, stealing my mood and forcing terror into me only because of the dark, unexplained sounds and things people had told me! I was allowing my imagination to pick and choose among the tidbits Sherlock had shared, and my mind began to paint a picture of my being attacked and dragged off.

I entered my room sweating and out of breath despite the fact I'd never moved faster than a brisk walk.

"You look like you've seen a ghost," Natalie said.

Maybe that was it, I thought. Maybe it wasn't what was there, but wasn't there that had frightened me nearly to peeing myself.

"Or was it Mr. Great, as in Britain?" That was the closest Natalie had come to truthfully expressing a romantic interest in Sherlock.

"Lock the window," I said, "and pull the drapes." I crossed my arms and sat down on the edge of her mattress.

"Where've you been? As if I have to ask."

"Oh . . . a friend."

"Duh! Sherlock. Right?"

"Maybe."

"Forget him, Moria. He's way too nerdy for you. Great accent, but don't be fooled. He's an odd duck."

"Fooled?" I said. "No, NATO, I'm not fooled."

She wouldn't speak to me the rest of the night.

CHAPTER 49

James did not like mice. He did not like the little turd-raisins they left behind. He did not like their squeaking. Their scratching. The way they hopped around and sat up to clean their whiskers. Ick! Eww!

James liked music. He had something of a good "ear," meaning he could keep a tune, could whistle in tune. It also meant he had not just good hearing, but exceptional hearing.

He also heard things while asleep. Things that woke him up.

The sound of a mouse. Being ground-floor

dorms, all the Lower Bricks got an unfair number of rodents, roaches, spiders, and cobwebs.

James awoke. He sat up, his senses on alert. *Not on my bed, please! Please not on my bed!*

More like over on the window, he thought, scratching at the glass. But the drapes were drawn. James would have to open them to confirm his visitor.

James fumbled to switch on the reading light clamped to his bunk frame. He stopped. Light scares mice! Light on, mouse gone. Even with the drapes drawn the light would seep through. He decided against the light. If he scared the mouse, he wouldn't have a chance to—

Screech! His arm hair stood on end. It wasn't anywhere close to the sound a mouse made. It was more mechanical.

James threw his legs up and shoved the overhead mattress to wake Sherlock. By the time Sherlock's eyes popped open, James was standing on his mattress to be close to Sherlock's ear.

"Shh! Not a word!" The room being nearly pitch dark, James imagined Sherlock nodding. "We have visitors. The window!"

Another screech.

"Glass cutter," Sherlock whispered. "Diamond blade. Hand-held."

"You are a freak," James declared.

"They're not after me, dear boy," Sherlock said. "It's the closet or hallway for you. Now!"

"No way!"

"Then your lacrosse stick. Butt end. Now!"

James whisked silently to the closet, slipped open one of its doors.

The blinds ruffled. Wind! Through a hole in the window.

The sound of a hand turning the lock at the top of the double-hung window frame.

Sherlock slipped off the top bunk, grabbed up James's desk chair, and shattered the window through the drape.

"NOW!" Sherlock shouted.

James charged like a knight in a lancing contest, his lacrosse stick held as the lance. He rammed into the drape where the window would have been had Sherlock not broken it. The stick hit something soft, something fleshy. A man's scream. A thump onto the ground.

A burst of cursing.

Sherlock switched on the desk lamp.

James raked back the curtains.

Two sweating faces, obscured by shadows.

James hollered a curse word.

Feet coming down the hall.

"You take the door!" Sherlock said. "Quick."

Distracted by addressing James, Sherlock didn't see the arms reaching for his shoulders. He was grabbed and pulled toward the broken window.

"James!" Sherlock called, half out the window, broken glass cutting him. "I am not James."

Whoever had hold of him released him.

James took Sherlock by the ankles and fell back into the room pulling Sherlock back inside.

"You're bleeding," James said.

"Mmm," Sherlock said, watching the stains spread across his pajama top.

Mr. Cantell entered from the hall. He went gray at the sight of blood.

"Better help him," Sherlock said. Sure enough, Mr. Cantell lost his legs. James caught him and helped him to the floor.

"What . . . just . . . happened?" James shouted too loudly for the small room.

"We can rule out secret admirers," Sherlock said.

"Do . . . not . . . joke! I cannot take your jokes right now. Let's get you out of here." James threw a coat around Sherlock's shoulders. The boys stepped over Cantell.

They hobbled down the hallway, and crossed into Lower 2, staying warm. They would need to cross a field to reach the infirmary.

"Well?" James asked.

"I believe we thwarted an assassination attempt or a kidnapping." Sherlock winced.

"Forget it, don't talk."

"It would appear, dear boy, someone's after you."

James helped Sherlock out into the cold. He looked around, fearing the men were still about. "Once to the infirmary, we say it was a prank. Another dorm attacking ours."

"That's called lying."

"Please!"

"I distort the truth when required, it's true," Sherlock said. "Misrepresent it? Never. It becomes too easy a habit. I will remain silent for you, James. But if asked, if pushed, I'm not going to lie. The question that needs asking is, where were your bodyguards in all this?"

"Who?"

"Please, James, give me at least some credit."

"Yeah, okay," James said. They took off toward the infirmary.

"And for the record," Sherlock said, "you're welcome."

CHAPTER 50

I SAID HELLO TO JAMES AS HE SETTLED INTO THE chair beside me, both of us facing Dr. Crudgeon's desk. We said nothing. The headmaster entered after a few agonizing minutes and sat down across from us. I felt and resented the connection between James and Crudgeon. I was the outsider trying to look in as the man expressed an apology for the attack on James, which was the first I'd heard of it. I looked to my brother with sympathetic eyes, heart pounding, but he looked straight forward at Crudgeon as if I wasn't there. We were told in a cold, calm voice that James and I would have our security tightened, including keeping our dorms under watch. I interrupted several times and was crisply told to listen. James never looked over at me!

His voice filled with impatience, Crudgeon looked tired. He blinked repeatedly. But it was the tension in his voice that revealed his concern. His school was under threat from an outside force. My brother and I were somehow in the middle of it, and Crudgeon intended for it to end now.

I didn't want people watching me. How was I supposed to steal the Bible that was only a matter of a few feet behind me if I was being watched all the time?

"Any questions?" Crudgeon asked, looking at me with a dead stare. I kept my mouth shut. "Good. You two will be allowed to use your mobile phones beyond the one-hour time limit." He gave us a text number, telling us that any message, any character or letter, would be considered a cry for help. We were to always keep our phones unlocked and ready to send to the number. "This is your panic button. Do you understand?" We both nodded. "It is not to be used lightly. But there is no such thing as a false alarm."

I recalled my sense of dread earlier the night before. Had I sensed James's attackers?

On our way out James said, "You OK, Mo?"

"Are you OK? That's the question. And where's Sherlock?"

"I'm fine. Sherlock got cut up by a broken window. Cantell's with him. He took a few stitches, but he's OK."

"Why did you go to the museum without us?" I'd been itching to ask this question.

He didn't answer.

"And what was with that drama with Lexie in the common room?"

"Colander. I didn't want her to have to deal with Colander, but it backfired."

"Did you hear about her father?"

"It's horrible."

"We rescued you, James."

"And for that, I'm grateful."

"You've barely spoken to me since. Is that because you don't want to explain why you sneaked out without us?"

He looked pained. We reached the end of the hall.

"James? Talk to me!" I saw my brother standing there, but I couldn't feel him. "Last night must have scared you. Especially after being kidnapped. Is that what the detective wanted?"

"Colander questioned me about the necklace."

"What about it?" I asked.

"He wanted me to tell him where it is."

"But it's there, in the museum, or it was when we all left."

"Don't you think I know that?" James said.

"That doesn't make sense."

"He thinks I took it, Mo. So someone took it."

He couldn't look at me. I felt ice cold. He opened the door. "Please listen to Crudgeon. Be careful, Mo. If anything were to happen to you . . ."

"It won't."

"Because you're so tough."

"No, because I'm so smart," I said. "You used to be smart too, James. We used to be a team. What happened to that?"

"Things change."

"Not our team. Not you and me. We never change." My eyes stung. "Wherever you've gone, James, please come back."

"What's that supposed to mean?" James asked.

"You might want to think about it."

CHAPTER 51

F<small>RIDAY, AFTER BREAKFAST, S</small>HERLOCK SLIPPED me a note.

art studio study hall

I arrived to the art studio a few minutes before the start of third-period study hall. It smelled sweet, the scent of oil paint a pleasant one. A row of high windows on three of the four walls bathed the room in natural light, canceling out shadows and eliminating the need for the overhead lights.

Sherlock and Ruby Berliner awaited me in the

back. I didn't appreciate seeing Ruby there with him. "My plan is to bring the two halves together," Sherlock had said. Whatever that meant! I didn't care much for Ruby's half.

"You know Ruby."

"Hey," I said.

"It was Ruby's crystals in the window that—"

"I remember," I said, interrupting Sherlock.

"Voila!" said Sherlock, removing a torn piece of drop cloth from atop an object on the worktable.

It was the Moriarty family Bible.

"You stole the Bible? How on earth did you manage that?"

Ruby beamed, grinning so widely I saw something green stuck to her back teeth.

"Impressive, isn't it?" Sherlock said.

"I was there . . . in Crudgeon's office with James. It's in plain sight! Are you crazy? You think he won't miss it?"

Sherlock knocked on the top of the Bible. A hollow sound, like tapping a cardboard box.

I approached it, slipping past Ruby—and yes, feeling slightly jealous of her mature physique and perfect skin—and said, "Do I need gloves?"

A smiling Sherlock shook his head no.

I touched the cover. It was imitation leather, yet it held the exact embossed patterns as did our family Bible. It was blackened at the edges in the same way. The identical family crest and flourish of scrolling calligraphy that had a *W* at its center for "Wilford."

"Good grief. You did this?" I said.

Ruby nodded while blushing.

"It's incredible."

"Thanks."

"It's perfect," I said.

"It is, isn't it?" But Sherlock wasn't looking at the Bible; he was looking at Ruby. I felt a little wobbly. "She is sworn to secrecy, is our Ruby. She knows what I plan to do with this work of hers."

"You could get in trouble," I warned the girl.

Ruby shrugged. "No one saw me working on it. Only you two know."

"Well, we aren't telling," I said.

"My point exactly," said Sherlock.

"I'm happy to help."

"Ruby is friends with Alexandria, and Alexandria with James."

"All the trouble this fall," Ruby said. "Now Lexie's dad. The attack on James. If I can do something to help, I want to."

I worked to contain my rising jealousy. Ruby was far too nice, far too perfect. She and Sherlock seemed meant for each other. The fact that that troubled me so much made me question my true feelings. I was twelve, I reminded myself, hearing Lois's voice in my ear; was I supposed to have true feelings?

"Thank you, Ruby. Moria and I will take it from here."

"It will take three of us," Ruby said.

"Excuse me?" I said.

"To make the switch. My older brother, Sam, dabbles in magic."

Dabbles! Ruby Berliner used words like "dabbles."

"As do I," said Sherlock. This was news to me. "Strictly an amateur magician, myself."

"If you intend to substitute my Bible for your family Bible," Ruby said, looking at me, "you must use redirection and illusion. The three fundamentals are, hide it, move it, never have it there to begin with. If you intend to hide it and move it, it's going to take three of us."

"I was thinking more along the lines of three o'clock in the morning. Dash in. Pluck the thing. Drop off yours. Be done with it," said Sherlock.

"You heard the headmaster," Ruby said. "You really think you're going to get away with that when the campus is in lockdown?"

"Wait a second," I said. "You're saying we

should switch it out when Crudgeon's in his office? Are you insane?"

"Those are two different questions," Ruby said, offering me the most difficult smile to read. "I'm suggesting I call my brother. The rest is up to us."

CHAPTER 52

HAVING SEEN A CHALK MARK ON THE CHAPEL stone before breakfast, James returned to the back side of the chapel after breakfast and again during his fourth-period study hall. It took him several long minutes to identify the man raking leaves.

"Espiranzo," James said, standing casually in case the two were seen.

"I am glad to see you are well," the man said. He favored his right arm slightly.

"You're hurt?" James took a moment to understand. "You're who pulled the guy away from my window!"

Espiranzo was not in the habit of confirming any information.

"You have news for me," James suggested.

"Yes. It is as you said: it is believed your escape from the Meirleach has put increased pressure on those who held you."

"They're going to be fired if they don't recapture me," James said.

"Or worse."

James felt a pang of dread—men hurt or even killed because of him?

"Your having the necklace makes you a—"

"I don't have the necklace."

"It is better when we, as brothers, speak openly and honestly."

"You think I'm lying?"

The leaves spun in a small circle like a cat chasing its tail. James marveled at the perfect symmetry.

"We are told it was stolen that same night."

"It wasn't me. I guess that's obvious. What's so important about the stupid necklace anyway?"

Espiranzo just stood there. "But you were there at the museum."

"Yeah, because—" James didn't want to reveal he could be given orders, that he did what Lowry told him to do. He tried to think how to say it.

"—we had intelligence suggesting we should take possession of it."

"Whoever was the source of this intelligence may have led you into a trap."

"He's reliable."

"Know this, brother. There are those pushing for reform of the worst kind. A change your father resisted. Others, as well. With your father . . . gone, those forces of change are regrouping, strengthening."

"Within the Scow—"

"Brotherhood," Espiranzo said, not allowing James to speak the name of the organization aloud.

"Right."

"Yes. Within us."

A gray squirrel scurried from one tree to another, throwing leaves in its wake, only its fluffy tail visible. It raced straight up the trunk, oblivious to gravity. James thought if he'd been the squirrel he'd have fallen, the weight of Espiranzo's message too great.

"Lowry! Was it Lowry who was against my father?"

"As to that, I wouldn't know. I will not foul my neighbor's well without good reason."

"Who then?"

"It's not for me to say."

"But you know?"

"Believing and knowing are two separate things. Ehh?"

"My roommate, the English kid. He was there at the museum. My sister too. Maybe having a heart-to-heart could tell me something."

"That would be up to you."

James filed that away. "Did the Meirleach kill my father?"

Espiranzo looked down the rake's handle.

"Someone inside the Sc—otherhood?" James asked.

He scratched at the handle's wood grain.

"I'll take that as a yes," James said. "Who? Who killed my father?"

"Lack of solid proof has been the cause of many vile crimes," Espiranzo said.

"Motive?"

"As to that, there are only three motives known to man, James. Power, love, and greed."

"Power and greed then," James said, tormented by the thought of Father having been murdered in our home. "Find out who gained from Father's death, Espiranzo. Get me their names."

CHAPTER 53

The Morning of Mourning arrived painfully for James. He sat across the dining hall at a
table of students he hardly knew. He stabbed at his
food to avoid spilling on his black suit that had
been hand-delivered by Ralph. He'd asked Ralph
again to show him his stitches from the fight at the
fish factory, but instead Ralph pulled and twisted
James's ear as he'd done since James had been a
child.

Lois awaited James in the common room and
joined him after the non-meal.

"Are you all right, James? Can you do this?" Lois asked.

"Why here at Baskerville? Why not in Boston?"

"Mr. Carlisle's family wanted the service here. It's as simple as that."

"It's not simple at all," James said. "Why invite me and not others?"

"Because Miss Carlisle and you are friends, aren't you?"

"I don't even know." James had sent a dozen texts to Lexie apologizing for, and trying to explain, the way he'd treated her. That he didn't want her involved with the headmaster, whom he'd seen coming toward him. Someone later told her about the attack on the dorm, because the only message she'd written James—prior to the invitation to the funeral—had been one of concern for his safety. "I guess so."

Lois wore a plain gray dress, only light red lipstick for makeup, and a look of real sadness. She smelled faintly of gardenias. They walked in the cold, heading nowhere in particular.

"You've worked for Father for as long as I can remember."

"I have."

"You must know a lot of the people he worked with."

"Know of them, yes."

"How'd you end up working with Father in the first place?"

"I knew him a long time ago. I was his assistant at the university. He liked the way I worked, I suppose. That was a long time ago, as I said."

James had heard the story before, even if he didn't believe it. "If I ask you some stuff, will you answer me honestly?"

"I'm not sure how much I can help."

"I think Father—maybe all the Moriartys— kept stuff in the family Bible. I think that's why the school freaked out when it went missing." He thought of Father and how he'd had his accident while the Bible was still missing. He thought of Lowry and Crudgeon and the Scowerers. He thought of betrayal. His own, and the possibility of those who'd been close to Father.

"Are you okay, James?"

A silence settled between them.

"Mo and Sherlock . . . I think they've discovered this way to decode the family Bible. I think I was taken . . . I think those men would have tortured me to find out what I knew."

"James, you really should see someone."

"It's not that. I'm not freaked out by that stuff at all. It's Father, Father's death. We, the three of us, don't think it was an accident."

"Is that so? That's a horrible thought!"

"Greed, maybe power. Someone wanted him dead."

"James . . . "

"I'm certain of it, Lois. I need you to think, to think really hard. Who would have wanted Father out of the way?"

"James! The world doesn't work like that! That's all those videos you play. People don't act like that!"

"Lois, I don't know who else to ask."

"Of course. Well, I'm glad it was me, and not Ralph. You mustn't talk to Ralph about this," she said. "He can't be trusted."

"What's that supposed to mean?" James asked.

"He has a temper. If he made a guess. If he decided on his own that someone had—" Lois pursed her lips. A hundred wrinkles ran from her red lipstick like a bamboo umbrella from a fruit drink. "As to what you ask, I'd be pleased to do what I can."

"I need a name."

"Of course," Lois said.

"And then you and I will forget we had this conversation," James pressed. "You understand?

This never happened."

"Promise," she said, a slight frown interrupting the wrinkles at either side of her tightly pursed lips.

CHAPTER 54

ACCORDING TO SHERLOCK, OUR TIMING WAS perfect: Headmaster Crudgeon would be preparing for Mr. Carlisle's memorial chapel service. He could not, would not, turn me away if I asked to see him. I had no idea if we were up to carrying out Ruby's plan for misdirection and the Bible's substitution, but Sherlock liked the plan and so did I.

"The trick," Sherlock had said, adding to Ruby's plan, "is to interest the headmaster to the point where he can't help himself. To tease him with something he already knows, but would like to know more about. And I believe we have just the tidbit!"

Another trick had been to find a backpack identical to mine and then bribe its owner into loaning it to me. Ruby handled that while Sherlock rode the school shuttle into Putnam, Connecticut, to canvass hardware stores in search of a padlock that matched the one securing the Bible in Crudgeon's office. Meanwhile, I rehearsed my role and line a hundred times. When Lock returned, lock in hand, he demanded we rehearse together. Again, and again.

By the time I walked into Headmaster Crudgeon's office, an appointment arranged by Mrs. Furman, his officious secretary, my hands were sweating. I was having a glandular moment of five-thousand-degree skin and a sense of panic.

"Miss Moriarty. Please, have a seat," Crudgeon said, offering me a chair across the large expanse of his desk.

"Actually, I . . . I know this is bad timing, Headmaster." I opened my backpack—important!—and withdrew a pair of thin knit winter gloves. "I wondered if I might have a look at our Bible?"

Here was the test Sherlock had anticipated. My Bible. But in his office. Would he deny me my right?

"You . . . what? Actually, Moria," I noted the

change to the familiar, "it is bad timing. It's a busy morning, I'm afraid. Perhaps tomor—"

"Now would be great," I said, using the phrase Sherlock and I had practiced. "There's a painting in the Bible," and there came the teaser, "of one of my ancestors. Sherlock Holmes and I think we've figured out why it's in there, the purpose it serves." Nothing new, we assumed, to a man in Crudgeon's position, but information he had to hear for himself.

"I see."

"All I need is a quick look. If you don't mind?"

"I really don't have the time."

"Mrs. Furman, then? Some other adult?" This, Sherlock had said, would put the man into a paradox. His uncertainty would then make him ripe for Ruby's plan.

I tried to lift the glass cover off the Bible, but it was locked. Crudgeon came around his desk, already reaching for the keys in his pocket. "I'll get that!" he said. Phase one complete.

My phone, a phone I was allowed, was on an open call to Sherlock and Ruby, thanks to its conference feature. They were hearing all of this. Sherlock was also recording it all in case Crudgeon offered me anything juicy.

"Gloves on, please," Crudgeon said, donning a pair himself.

"Yes. All set."

"You will work on this table over here." He fiddled with and removed the small padlock that secured the glass case. I had our matching padlock in my school uniform pocket. Carefully lifting the Bible, he carried it to the only table in the room, one away from the door, and therefore an important part of our plan.

I opened the Bible, delicately turning its pages intentionally slowly. "Isn't it beautiful?" I said.

"It is." Crudgeon sounded impatient, and with good reason. The Carlisle service was now less than an hour away—all part of the plan to rattle him.

Crudgeon and I stood shoulder to shoulder.

"Here it is!" I'd arrived at the painting of James Wilford and his sparkling necklace. "He's my many times great-grandfather," I said. "My great-grandmother was a Wilford, but she married Eldridge L. Moriarty and the family business has been run by Moriarty men ever since."

"What exactly are you looking for?" Crudgeon asked. There it was, the question Sherlock had hoped might be asked.

"I'm looking for my mother," I answered, as

practiced. The idea was to knock Headmaster's legs out from under him. And it worked. "My father kept a journal, did you know that?" That was intended to open a trapdoor now that we had Crudgeon on the metaphorical floor. He fell in.

Cue Ruby and Sherlock, who came down the hall and entered Crudgeon's office without permission. Cue Mrs. Furman coming from her post to stop them. Paint a picture of chaos and shouting: Mrs. Furman's objections, Ruby's insistence she was looking for me, Sherlock's stealthy movement past Ruby and into the office.

Cue Crudgeon, turning toward his office door, his mind baked by the mention of my missing mother and Father's journal.

"There you are, Moria!" said Sherlock, having moved far enough to only be a shadow in the corner of Crudgeon's eyes.

Now came the part we'd practiced and practiced.

Two or three steps toward his secretary and Ruby, Crudgeon spoke loudly and with his usual authority. "No interruptions!"

With my back to the door to screen my activity, and trusting Sherlock to signal me if our plan went bust, I slid my backpack into position. I pulled the fake Bible out, replacing it with the heavier original.

Practically before I had it closed inside, Sherlock tossed his backpack toward me, as Ruby physically pushed and rotated Mrs. Furman toward the hall to keep her from seeing us. I caught the throw from Sherlock, swung mine and, as rehearsed, delivered it perfectly into Sherlock's waiting hands, ten feet away from me.

I was already carrying the fake Bible toward the case when Sherlock scurried to leave the office, anticipating Crudgeon's next move.

"Out! Out! This is a private meeting!" Grown-ups can be so predictable.

I lowered the glass case, switched padlocks, and locked the case. I put Crudgeon's keys on the top of the case.

Headmaster turned toward me. It was just him and me in the office now. The Bible back in the case, I indicated his keys.

"Thank you, Headmaster."

"My pleasure," Crudgeon said.

"You found what you wanted?" he asked, his inflection suggesting I answer.

"Oh, yes. Absolutely," I said. "I snapped a photo with my phone." I told the truth. It was just that the photo I'd taken had been of the painting in Father's secret room. "If there's a family secret hiding in that picture, trust me, I'm going to find it."

"I would doubt that very much, Moria."

"That I'm going to find it, or that it's there in the first place?" I asked. "Because as it turns out, my father was full of secrets, Headmaster. And I am intent on uncovering every last one of them."

Sherlock had written those words. I was directed to walk out with confidence. But I stumbled. Perhaps from the weight of the Bible in the backpack, perhaps because my knees had gone all soft on me. Perhaps—even if it did belong to me—because I was stealing something for the first time in my life.

And maybe not for the last.

CHAPTER 55

LEXIE AND HER MOTHER ENTERED THE SCHOOL chapel last. They sat down in the front pew among much murmuring. Sounds reverberated inside the stone church. Cars had begun arriving an hour earlier, amid falling snow. The chapel was packed, holding three hundred guests, every seat filled. The service went on for some time—music, a remembrance by the chaplain, a number of speakers, many of whose names James knew.

He didn't care that much about the service. He wanted Lexie to turn and look for him. She hadn't done so when coming down the aisle with her mom, causing James unexpected heartache.

The shocker came when some guy James didn't know was up there talking about Carlisle's time spent at Baskerville! He and Father could have overlapped here, James thought, or might have been in the same class! Why had no one mentioned that? He and Father were both now dead.

As the service wrapped up, James was looking for Crudgeon, for Lowry, for any face, anyone who connected with the headmaster and attorney. He wanted confirmation the Scowerers had done this to Carlisle.

"You should pay your respects," Lois told James.

"Meaning?"

"The receiving line, just as you and Moria did at your father's service."

"I hated that."

"It's the polite thing to do, James."

"The line will be massive."

"James . . . you are a Moriarty."

"Yeah, okay." James wondered if he, the boy who'd spied on Mr. Carlisle, the boy who'd helped get him killed, could stand in line and shake the hands of his daughter and widow. What was he supposed to say?

The receiving line stretched from the door back toward the nave like a black snake with a thousand arms and a hundred heads. It looked creepy and crawly and sinister. James, somewhere in the middle, had already been greeted by adults he knew from the club and from barbecues on the Cape, but not by their names. One or two of the men seemed to address him with more respect than they might have a year earlier and this made James wonder who these people were, and how he could find out more about them. It also pressured him to stay in line. Leaving now would make him look bad. He shifted uneasily on his feet.

Looked off into the people standing around talking.

And there was Lois. And there was Lowry talking to Lois. Lois and Lowry? Sure, as legal guardian Lowry employed Lois, but the way they talked without looking at each other, both scanning the crowd, seemed off. Not right.

James asked the person behind him to hold his place. He set off toward the two, using other bunches of people to screen him and wondering how such instincts came to him so easily. He identified a direct route to the two down an empty pew. Hunching over and facing away from Lois and

Lowry, he collected programs that had been left behind, as if cleaning up. He inched slowly closer to them.

James heard Lowry say, "Holmes."

Lois nodded.

Was she ratting him out? James wondered. Like had happened with Carlisle, had James tagged Sherlock by telling Lois that Sherlock and I were investigating things?

Lowry head-signaled Lois, and for a moment James felt made of Jell-O, believing he'd been spotted. He shrank lower, collecting more programs from the floor, and he stayed down. Screened by the pew in front of him, he looked in the direction of Lowry's head nod on the desperate hope Lowry might have someone else in mind.

And there was Ralph, who'd driven Lois but had not attended the service as far as James had seen.

And there was a man talking to Ralph.

Short and stocky, this man wore his gray hair long and combed back behind his small ears. It curled up at the back of his neck a few inches off his collar. He had puffy cheeks, feminine eyebrows, wet lips, and an odd-looking, flattened nose. He also had what appeared to be two bodyguards standing within reach, reinforcing James's sense he'd seen the man before. The two kept busy scanning the guests, revealing their purpose.

Ralph spoke to the man intensely. James knew that Irish temper, was surprised to see it, especially in a church. Despite the distance, it was clear the two were disagreeing, if not outright arguing. The smaller man nodded a lot, looked around nervously, worried about eavesdropping. Ralph reached inside his suit jacket, removed an envelope, and passed it to the other, who pocketed it quickly.

James moved toward the two of them, feeling pulled between Lois and Ralph. His place in line was nearing Lexie and her mom. James headed there and waited only a couple of minutes before reaching Mrs. Carlisle.

"James," she said. He couldn't interpret her tone. A mother protecting her hurt daughter, or a widow doing what she had to?

"I'm sorry, Mrs. Carlisle," he said. "For your loss," he added, saying what so many people had said to him not so long ago. "I liked him. He was nice to me." He felt her every muscle tighten.

He moved on to Lexie. She immediately looked hurt and wounded. She lowered her head, refusing to look at him.

"Did you read my texts? I didn't know," James said. He hadn't known they were going to kill him; he hadn't known she was hurting when she'd approached in the common room. It seemed to cover so much.

"Go," she said.

"There was a situation. I didn't want you caught up in it."

Mrs. Carlisle heard that. She turned to James. "Please, leave her be."

James left, wishing he could feel nothing, but aching instead. He could feel him and Lexie locked arm to arm, the freezing water coursing over her, the two of their lives connected.

A few steps away from Lexie, he turned back. "I'm so sorry."

Her head still bowed, she looked toward him out of the sides of her eyes, tear stains on her cheeks.

Ralph approached from within the church, his face as red and blotchy as James had ever seen it. Ralph stormed past James, breathing like he'd finished a long race. James knew well Ralph's intense, uncontrollable anger.

The Irishman stopped next to James and met eyes with him. "We're going to do something about this!" he announced.

He charged on toward the sea of parked cars, having never explained his outburst.

Someone coughed nearby and James looked

in that direction—Espiranzo clearing snow. The Scowerer cocked his head sharply toward the back of the chapel. James hurried to get a view of whatever it was.

The short, familiar-looking man with the small ears and long gray hair, accompanied by the two whom James had seen inside, walked stridently through the falling snow toward a four-wheel-drive SUV, all black, with tinted windows and oversized tires. One of the men held the back door for the short man. A moment later they were off, the SUV backing up but turning to head down the hill, not up to the state highway. The SUV was staying on Baskerville property!

James got within proximity of Espiranzo, neither wanting to appear too chummy with so many people milling about.

"You asked me for a name," said Espiranzo, head down, working a shovel against the light accumulation. "That's him in the fancy SUV."

He might as well have struck James across the face with the shovel, so stunned was the boy standing nearby. James took off, first at a fast walk, then broke into a run, pursuing a lookout spot in order to see where the SUV was headed.

The library terrace offered him a view of the distant varsity football field, the gymnasium, as well as, to the right, the road along the Lower Bricks. This access road connected to another that ran near the tennis center and also accessed the state highway. It seemed likely to James the SUV was merely shortcutting traffic by taking the back way off campus.

So it was a shock when the SUV turned onto the narrow asphalt road leading toward the hockey rink. Woods soon gobbled up the vehicle, but, James thought, there was only the ice rink down there at the bottom of the valley. Why head toward a dead end?

His eyes tracked higher along the treetops and, protruding from the forest, the school observatory alongside the caved-in slate rooftop of a mostly crumbling stone mansion once owned by James's great-grandfather. As far as James knew, "Death March Road"—as hockey players who had to climb its steep hill after practice referred to it— dead-ended into a small parking lot in front of the rink. But there had to be a path that continued to the observatory.

An equally great shock overcame James when he happened to look down at his feet. Engraved into one of the donated terrace bricks, he read three names:

Coop—Ozzie—Dux
1981   .

His heart outpaced his brain, speeding up to where it hurt. Cooper "Coop" Carlisle. Oswyn "Ozzie" Bennett Moriarty. Danny "Dux" Ducksworth. James had heard Father tell stories involving Dux, had known Father had lived in a triple fifth- and six-form years. Had not known the identity of the third roommate until now: Lexie's dad.

Head spinning at the discovery of the connection, his mind struggling with why Mr. Carlisle had made no mention of it at the dinner table. His darker self deciding their friendship had continued long after school, had become a relationship balancing the Scowerers' needs and Mr. Carlisle's military and political achievements. All of it wrapped up in something that now connected one man's death to the other, and all of it to a black SUV disappearing into the woods. James took off at a sprint.

"The name?" James hissed at Espiranzo only seconds later. "You tell me the name right now or so help me—" James didn't know how to end that threat. So help him what? What options did he have?

But Espiranzo answered loyally. "I do not know

his name," the man said, "only that he once was the most powerful cop in America."

"What the heck does that mean?" a red-faced James demanded.

An older couple approached. Espiranzo went back to shoveling, passing James and continuing up the path.

CHAPTER 56

"No need to gloat," I said.

Sherlock was making a sport out of keeping something from me, and I wasn't thrilled with my failure to guess it. The secret had something to do with the notorious Ruby Berliner, who was quickly moving up my list of Least Wanted.

He made the bleating sound of a goat, trying for a play on words. The success with stealing the Bible had made a real jerk out of him. Ruby's attention hadn't hurt anything.

"You see that button on the wall there?" Sherlock said, standing at a lab bench in one of the four science classrooms. "Do us a favor and push the black one."

"I'm not your servant!"

"What in heaven's name has gotten into you?" Sherlock said.

I marched over to the button and did as he said. All the drapes along the windows closed automatically. Blackout drapes rendered the lab nearly pitch-black. Only ghostlike images and shapes remained.

"Stay there for me, please," Sherlock said.

"You're beginning to really annoy me," I said.

"Only just beginning?" he said. "I shall try harder!" He so amused himself he thought it important to chuckle so I wouldn't miss it.

"I think she made something for you," I said, testing an answer to his and Ruby's secret I had yet to voice.

"Warmer," Sherlock said, using a phrase I had taught him only a few months before.

We had history, this boy and I; I needed to be careful and protect my feelings better.

Sherlock switched on a purple tube light that plugged into an outlet at the end of the lab bench. His white shirt collar and cuffs jumped out of the dark; his eyes glowed an eerie yellow. The rest of him wasn't there.

"Well, that's creepy," I said.

When Sherlock spoke, his teeth appeared out of the dark. Only his teeth. "It's working. We won't need the lights. Come on over."

I felt my way and joined him at the high bench.

"Gloves on," he said, handing me a pair of disposable plastic lab gloves. "Ready?" he said.

"Oh, shut up!" We'd only risked expulsion (or worse!) for this moment. Inevitably, the headmaster, intrigued by my visit, would try to open the case containing the Bible. The switched padlock would prevent him from doing so. At first, he would believe it a malfunction. But how long until he figured it out? Our plan was to use Sherlock's master key to return the Bible to the headmaster's office prior to the conclusion of the common room reception following Mr. Carlisle's memorial service. But time was running out, a delay caused, of all things, by Mr. Cantell requiring Sherlock to make his bed and pick up his room. I had berated Sherlock unmercifully that he'd chosen this, of all days, to be a slob. His answer had been, "No, I'm a slob every day," which hadn't helped things any.

"I'll take that as a yes," he said. "You turn the pages. I'll hold the light."

I opened the Bible. Under the black light, the old yellowed pages barely showed at all. "Close your mouth," I told him, "your teeth are blinding me."

"Very funny."

I turned to the illustration of James Wilford, where it was impossible to miss the three characters running down the length of the cross he held.

CC3

"Well, there you have it!" Sherlock said, proud as a peacock. "What did I tell you?"

"You've told me nothing," I said. "I'm a page-turner, that's all. And I resent your treating me this way." I nearly added, "You wouldn't treat Ruby Berliner this way!" but managed not to.

"Caesar Cipher, three," he said. "An ancient cipher, as you can tell by the name. Either the third letter of each highlighted word is moved back three letters in the alphabet, or each highlighted letter receives the same treatment. Web search it, if you like!"

"What letters?"

"You're the one turning pages, so turn."

I wanted to tell him how annoying he could be, but not only would I be repeating myself, but I felt competition from the perfect Ruby Berliner, and I didn't like it one bit. The existence of another girl was keeping me from being me. I didn't know myself! How could I allow that to happen?

"It's not something personal," I said. "Ruby made you something to do with the investigation."

"Positively steaming," Sherlock said, reaching to turn a page himself. I slapped his hand and he withdrew. I began turning pages.

"Something other than the Bible."

"Terribly toasty."

We both fell silent.

GENESIS I

The black light revealed silvery lines on an otherwise dark page. They underlined letters and full words. There had to be twenty of the markings. I turned the page. Another ten to twenty on each of the two pages facing us.

Sherlock chortled, sounding as if someone was tickling his feet. He dragged a camera stand toward us and asked me to place the Bible on its platform. The stand held the camera aimed lens-down to the platform. Sherlock made some quick adjustments to the camera.

"Ready?" he said.

"That's impolite. You haven't told me what to be ready for!"

"You turn the pages. I hold the black light and

take the photographs. I reckon we have twenty-two minutes."

"Could you be more specific?" I asked. It took Sherlock a moment to catch my sarcasm.

"Ha ha," he said caustically. "Five more minutes to reach the Main House makes twenty-seven. Three to replace the Bible and the padlock and be gone."

"Thirty," I said, immediately regretting it.

"Elementary school, my dear Moria? How excelled we are in the way of mathematics."

"The reception's over in a half hour," I said, trying to shore up my defense.

"Correct. We are wasting time. Start turning pages."

I did so.

The camera clicked.

CHAPTER 57

THE NEXT DAY, LATE MONDAY AFTERNOON, before sports, LeTona Heart approached Sherlock outside Studio B in the Writers House, a newish building devoted to language arts. An African American with expressive eyes, a sweet smile, and clear skin, she wore her straightened hair in an asymmetrical side part. A piercing mark on her nostril indicated where a gold hoop hung when not under school rules. LeTona, a varsity volleyball player, had a clutch of close friend-letes who trailed behind her when she wasn't hunkered down in the library working on her honor roll status.

"Hey!" she called.

"Greetings!" Sherlock said. He knew LeTona only by sight.

"Mo asked me to tell you to meet her in the chapel after dinner," LeTona said. "Her photo class is taking a field trip and won't be back until right then."

"Concerning?"

"How should I know?"

"You could have asked," Sherlock said.

"I . . . right . . . yeah. I suppose so." She looked at him strangely. Her eyes said, "Loser."

"So, you did or you didn't? Ask, that is?"

LeTona addressed Sherlock like she was his babysitter. "After dinner. The chapel. It's up to you, weirdo. What do I care?" She hopped down the staircase, her books nearly coming out from under her arm.

Sherlock made eye contact with Natalie, who stood a few feet away, listening in on the exchange.

"That's impolite, you know?" he said.

Natalie giggled to herself. "I happen to care," she said boldly.

Sherlock swallowed dryly. "Is that so?"

"A girl like LeTona eats her young."

"That is foul! Most distasteful."

"It means she'll devour you, Lock."

"Moria calls me that!" Sherlock protested. "No one else!"

"Well, well! Maybe I'll earn that right myself one of these days."

"I didn't mean it the way it came out," he said. "I meant only that it's a private nickname! Gosh! That didn't come out right either! You've tongue-tied me, I'm afraid."

"Well, good!" Natalie said. "At least I've gotten through to you!" She giggled as she walked away, putting some runway model into her stride.

"I can hear you!" Sherlock called.

Natalie raised a hand and waved without looking back.

"I can see you," Sherlock whispered to himself, utterly confused.

Natalie practically cheered when Mrs. Favor, their hall mistress, stopped by the room to say that, "The van carrying Moria's photography group has broken down. Moria will miss dinner. Please collect a box supper for her from the kitchen and bring it back here to the room after dinner."

Natalie nodded, hearing only: will miss dinner.

In Natalie's mind that translated to: will not

meet Sherlock Holmes in the chapel after dinner.

Given that Natalie had a hard time going five minutes in any given day without thinking about Sherlock, given that he'd looked at her this afternoon, had spoken to her, given that Sherlock was going to be stood up by me missing chapel, she felt it her obligation, her duty as my roommate, to pass along the information of my van being late.

If that also happened to offer her a moment alone with the boy, in the beautiful chapel with its colorful windows lit at night, a chance to try to summon her bravery and tell Sherlock—or at least hint!—how she felt about him, then who was going to stop her?

Better yet, she thought, her stomach grinding with excitement, why not skip dinner and get to the chapel in plenty of time to make sure she didn't miss him? She could always run over to the kitchen door after seeing Sherlock and request the box supper they would have prepared ahead of time.

Forced to wear her uniform, she nonetheless spent fifteen minutes adding some color to her cheekbones and filling in her eyebrows, trying to account for the low light in the chapel at night. Added at the last minute—just a slight amount of lipstick, a nice touch.

Natalie veered away from the stragglers who were rushing late to dinner. Butterflies in her stomach. Underarms perspiring. She would have liked to wait for him outside, where the light would be more flattering. But if seen not attending dinner and wandering campus, she'd earn demerits or worse, so she left Sherlock a clue, hanging a heart on the chapel door's oversized doorknob, and then pushed through and inside. Let him try to solve that one, she thought gleefully. She eased the door shut behind her, though it still made a sound like a hammer hitting an anvil as it closed.

She knew better than to turn on the lights and announce herself to anyone outside looking toward the chapel. For now she would find a seat in one of the many inward-facing pews and wait for Sherlock.

The chapel's silence and low light created a creepy environment. Its lofted roof, tall stone walls, and marble floor reflected even the smallest sounds and sent them rumbling throughout the space. After fifteen uncomfortable minutes, Natalie considered abandoning her plan. She had added a good deal of makeup trying to look older and more sophisticated. By doing so, she now realized she'd demeaned herself. To Sherlock, she'd look desperate and somewhat pathetic, and she badly regretted the attempt.

She convinced herself to lose the makeup. She would explain to Sherlock that our photography van had been delayed and she'd not wanted him waiting around for someone who wasn't going to show up. She could play the good friend and hope he might notice her.

Removing the makeup was more problematic. It would take a few minutes. The only bathroom was off the choir room, to the left of the pipe organ in the chancel. She scooted out of the pew, the sound of her feet slapping the marble as loud as hands clapping. She fought to stay calm, hoping she had time to get rid of her (hideous) attempt at fuller eyebrows and higher cheekbones.

Just past Sir Galahad her feet dragged.

"If you see something, say something," Headmaster had told the school.

She didn't exactly see something; she smelled something: human sweat. Body odor. She felt fairly confident the marble statue of the crouching knight was not emitting it, so where was it coming from?

Another step, and the scent was stronger still.

Her skin itched. Her mouth went dry. Her eyes stung.

If it hadn't been for Sherlock coming along any minute she would have taken off. Every inch of her screamed: Get me out of this place!

She stopped, just alongside the large pipe organ.

If you hear something, say something! She heard a whoosh like the flapping of a giant wing.

The smell of "man" suddenly struck as potent as skunk. She turned quickly. She jumped.

CHAPTER 58

"Dr. Crudgeon? I'm Thomas Lehman, professor of antiquities at Wright College, Boston." He
produced his business card.

"Yes? Please, come in." Crudgeon wore a cable-
knit wool cardigan sweater over his shirt and tie,
reading glasses about to fall off the end of his nose.

"Sorry to trouble you this time of night."

"No trouble at all."

"I'm on something of a personal errand
involving one of your students, for whom I seek
permission to visit."

"At this hour? That's an unusual request."

"I came as soon as my schedule allowed. It won't take but a minute, but I'd like to speak with him in private, so rather than apply to his dorm master, I thought it better . . ."

"Him? And yes, I understand completely."

"A young man by the name of Sherlock Holmes."

Crudgeon did not so much as twitch. "Regarding?"

"I'd rather not say."

"I'm afraid without at least a general understanding of the nature of your visit I would be remiss and ill-advised to consent to such a visit, Mr.—"

"Doctor."

"Dr. Lehman." The visitor's face reflected his misgivings.

"The young man, Mr. Holmes, contacted me regarding my expertise in antiquities, sir. And that is as much as I'm willing to share. I will leave it to my client to explain it in more detail should he choose."

"That's scant little."

"I can assure you, it is in no way a personal visit, nor anything more than what I represent to you. It is the conclusion of a business arrangement, and I'm afraid this is the only time in my schedule that allows for such a visit."

"A situation I understand," Crudgeon said, keeping his guest standing in the foyer with his coat on, "but one that continues to leave me feeling uncomfortable at best."

"It is scholarly in nature, Dr. Crudgeon. I would think one would encourage such efforts to expand one's thoughts. Quite extraordinary to have a boy his age reach out to me, honestly. Can't say it's ever happened before."

"Mr. Holmes is an extraordinary young man."

"Indeed he is."

"And one for whom I and this institution are legally charged with guardianship, so you can understand my line of inquiry. I mean it as no reflection of distrust, Doctor. Please don't take it as such."

"Not at all. You're being thorough. I have nothing but the utmost respect for such care."

They stood there. Dead silence. Two men, one in a thick sweater, the other in a winter overcoat and red scarf.

"I'm afraid I need more than you're providing," Crudgeon said.

"Ah! A wasted trip, then. I see."

"You can't be serious! You'd come all this way and turn around?"

"Perfectly serious. Thank you for your time." Professor Lehman turned for the door.

"There must be some line of compromise we can find," Crudgeon said.

Lehman stood with his back to the man, his hand on the doorknob. "There can be a thin line between guardianship and institutional detention, sir. Once crossed, I believe it becomes criminal in nature."

"Now wait just one minute!" Crudgeon bellowed.

But Lehman wasn't waiting. He pushed out into the cold and left the door open behind him for Crudgeon to step forward and close.

Lehman slowed his car at an intersection with a flashing red traffic light. A wood sign declaring "Country Fresh: Eats, Treats, and Take Out" was lit up like Christmas, as were the windows of the establishment.

He parked in the gravel parking lot with three other cars. He'd withheld from contacting Sherlock Holmes directly, feeling it improper to do so given that the boy was a minor. For different reasons he'd avoided mentioning Moria Moriarty to

Dr. Crudgeon. Things were different now. He had, in fact, come all this way, as Dr. Crudgeon had pointed out.

He sent a text message to Lock. There was still time to fix this.

After all, he reasoned, he'd come all this way.

CHAPTER 59

"Chapel's closed for cleaning." The stout man didn't look familiar, was not one of the cleaners whom Natalie saw day in and day out. This guy had a single earbud in his left ear, connected to a phone in his front shirt pocket. A tattoo barely showed above the top button.

"The chapel door was open," Natalie said.

"We're cleaning the floors. You can't be in here."

"I don't see you cleaning the floors."

"We can't start until we've locked the doors."

"We? You, and who else?" Natalie said nastily,

never one to be polite to the help.

His head angled and she looked toward the far end by the entrance where two men stood. If these guys were custodians, she was a nun. "Yeah, okay," she said, the message getting through. "All done praying. I was just leaving."

The janitor touched his finger to the earbud. He whistled by contorting his lips, piercing the air. The two by the door jumped into action while the janitor took Natalie by the arm and slapped his hand over her mouth. He leaned his head into the crook of her neck.

"Listen very carefully," the man said.

CHAPTER 60

Like all other Baskerville students, Sherlock was prohibited from using his mobile phone, and like all other Baskerville students he therefore kept his in his pocket, switched on at all times. His was a flip phone, limited in functions, and he felt something of a twit when it came to operating it.

When Sherlock's pocket buzzed on his way to the chapel to meet up with Moria, he ducked alongside a tree to try to screen himself. He fiddled with the contraption and nearly erased the incoming message before he read it.

tennis court parking lot
i will wait until 8pm
Lehman

Sherlock had fifty minutes. He elected to see Moria first. But reaching the chapel door, he found a handcrafted heart looped over the massive door-knob with a piece of powder blue yarn. He stopped. Considered.

A) Moria was not known for such handiwork
B) The heart implied romance
C) He felt about as ready for romance as
   he did to scale Everest in bare feet and
   underwear
D) Chapels and churches were serious places
   where couples got married
E) See C
F) Moria gave him "that look" every now and
   then
G) See C
H) Stood for "HELP"

Meeting Lehman was a perfectly viable excuse to miss or be late to the chapel. If late, Moria might leave by the time he arrived. All things being equal—which they weren't—taking the meeting with Lehman was clearly his only choice.

Lehman's car was old, in need of a wash, and its engine was running, the driver's window and passenger window cracked open despite the cold, to keep any fumes from suffocating the waiting driver. Sherlock climbed into the car.

"A little cloak-and-dagger, don't you think?" Sherlock said. "We have visiting hours in the Bricks."

"Your headmaster forbade me from seeing you."

"Did he? How undisciplined of him."

"Meaning?"

"He's revealing quite a lot by doing that. Don't you think?"

"I do, but I'm surprised you do."

"Too young?"

"Something like that."

"Nearly every vegetable and fruit must be harvested when young. As it gets older it becomes flavorless and goes to seed."

"I'm supposed to chew on that?"

"Something like that," Sherlock said, aping the man.

Lehman passed the translated journal to Sherlock, setting it in the boy's lap. "I'm done."

"You finished?"

"No. Far from it. But I'm done. And you and Moria should be, too."

"Why?"

"Believe me. Please."

"I do, of course, but I'm the curious sort. It's dangerous?"

"Extremely."

"Because? And don't tell me I'm too young, please. If I, or Moria, am in danger, I have every right to know why and from whom."

"You'd make a good lawyer."

"I'd rather not, thank you. I like puzzles. Mysteries. And don't change the subject."

"I'll say to you what I don't want you telling her: Mr. Moriarty was engaged in criminal activity. There's no doubt whatsoever. That's why I wanted to see only you. The activity is robust in nature and, I believe, dates back to the family's origins in shipping, which still accounts for a great deal of revenue. But the shipping now includes moving oil and other products illegally into countries under sanction. The Middle East. Russia. North Korea.

Vast amounts. To accomplish this, politicians and law enforcement are being corrupted or coerced on an unimaginable scale."

"The person or persons responsible for the death of Mr. Moriarty. Did he speculate on such things in these pages?"

"It's an extremely personal journal. That's one reason I simply could not continue with the transcription."

"Do you or do you not have an answer for my question?"

"You could use some social skills, young man."

"If you're hoping to win a prize for being the first to advise me of such, you've lost. Answer my question, please."

"Some things are better off left in the past."

"And this may be one of them, but that is up to Moria and James—" Sherlock replied.

"Not James!"

"I beg your pardon?"

"James, being the firstborn, and the male heir, is to assume the father's position."

"Ancient."

"But just the same. Control of the trading company has been passed this way since the mid-1500s. Think about that! Think about that kind of wealth and power. Someday, James Moriarty will have no

choice but to be conflicted about such information."

"Up to Moria to decide, then," Sherlock said.

"How old is she?"

"Twelve."

"Call me when she's twenty-one."

"How can she keep her friends close and her
enemies closer if she can't identify her enemies?"

"You have a sharp tongue, young man."

"And a quick wit. I know. I know. And yet
always so lonely," he said in a mocking tone.

Lehman chuckled to himself and shook his
head. "You are different."

"Flattery will get you everywhere."

He chuckled again. "You're forcing me to read
between the lines. I'm loath to do so."

"Then transcribe more of the journal to make
sure you're not giving false testimony."

"No, thank you. I don't want that back. Neither
should you, Mr. Holmes. It's flat-out dangerous for
whoever possesses that journal. It should be locked
up or destroyed."

"Finish translating it, and we'll destroy it
together." Sherlock returned it to the man's side of
the car.

"The attorney, Lowry, pressured Mr. Moriarty
to rid himself of his wife."

The car's air system made a loud effort to keep the car warm.

When Sherlock failed to speak, Lowry continued. "Supposedly it was for her own good. People outside the group, people like you and me, Mr. Holmes, do not end up well. People like Moria. The women of the family, women who ask too many questions, as Mrs. Moriarty did. She took her questions to Mr. Lowry instead of just her husband. She was not the first Moriarty woman to be the architect of her own undoing."

"Alive or dead?"

"Mr. Lowry encouraged Mr. Moriarty to take matters into his own hands. Again, reading between the lines, one gets the impression she may have been sent to something like a convent overseas, or something more practical like an institution here in the States."

"Alive, then?"

"Nothing to indicate otherwise. But a man as brilliant as Mr. Moriarty would not, even in an ancient language, make self-incriminating statements of that nature. It's one thing to write of his feeling about certain business deals, quite another to use such a journal as a confessional."

"Was it Lowry behind his 'accident'?"

"As to that, I would guess quite the opposite."

"I'm waiting."

"There are forces at work within this organization that troubled Mr. Moriarty. A change in direction. Nothing is specified, but as head of the organization he was in the position of making the difficult decisions."

"Someone didn't like his decision."

"Perhaps that. Perhaps he had yet to weigh in and they wanted to put their thumb on the scale ahead of that moment."

"Names."

"There is a board member. Again, reading between—"

"Let's get beyond all that, please."

"Like other board members, a man of enormous influence, wealth, and power. A man who, Mr. Moriarty writes, leveraged his way onto the board, and was most unwelcome."

"A name."

"No. If only it were so easy. Mr. Moriarty names no one, even in ancient Greek."

"Between the lines, then."

"I have my theories. I worked like an historian, using a few interesting references and dates, and working backward. I was looking for CEOs who may have retired on or about the time this person joined the board. Men or women who fit the profile

Mr. Moriarty was describing. An influencer. A judge, perhaps. Organized crime. District attorneys or state attorneys general. The individual possessed the means to demand a spot on the board, and was rewarded. Not killed. But rewarded. That's someone you fear, someone with his own group strong enough to threaten you, even if you kill him. I knew there could be but a handful of such qualified individuals."

"And I am soooooo very impressed with your diligence and reason. But I want a name!" Sherlock allowed his temper to show and regretted it immediately. "I'm sorry. I'm irritable. I'm having girl problems."

"Moria?"

"Maybe you'll translate my journal someday and find out. Really, the name would be most helpful."

"I found a person for whom I could check all the boxes. I tried a dozen times to disqualify him."

"Him."

"I worked back, taking a long hard look at several other contenders."

"The name."

"The one man, the only candidate—as I've said—that makes any sense is the former head of the FBI, a man who retired only weeks before the

board seat was filled. Can you imagine, the former chief detective of the United States signing on
to an international crime syndicate stretching back
three, four, five hundred years?"

"That's rhetorical, I trust," said Sherlock. "Who
else but the head cop to join the head crooks?"

"No, it doesn't work that way. Really, it doesn't.
You're far too cynical."

"Did this man have Mr. Moriarty killed?"

"I am nowhere near to suggesting such a thing.
Did he trouble the waters, absolutely. But it's a long
way between that and the act of violence you're
suggesting."

"The . . . name. The only director of the FBI I've
ever heard of is J. Edgar Hoover," Sherlock said.

"Eleven years as director, nine working his way
up. A reputation for ruthlessness, brilliance, and
hegemony. Do you know what hegemony means?"

"Dominance, but usually by one group over
another." Sherlock considered the man's choice of
words. "You're saying this man, this former FBI
leader, built a loyal group around himself that
questioned Mr. Moriarty's competence."

"His name is Mathias Hildebrandt."

A pair of headlights caught Sherlock's eyes,
coming from an access road that ran between the
tennis courts and the varsity soccer field and led

around to the back of the Bricks, the gym, Alumni House, and other school buildings. A Baskerville school bus returning to campus. Sherlock watched intently as the bus's interior light switched on and students appeared in the seat in profile. The vehicle lumbered past, the students inside in a sudden frenzy to collect their belongings.

Among them, Sherlock spotted Jamala, my other roommate. His deviously quick mind went to work: Jamala was in photography with me, i.e., this was the photography field trip returning—late; i.e., I was not in the chapel; i.e., I had not been the one who'd left the heart on the doorknob; i.e., someone else had left that heart on the door for Sherlock to find.

"Something's wrong," Sherlock said, reaching to open the car door.

"I beg your pardon?" Lehman looked around furiously, concerned over their exposed position. He grabbed for the rearview mirror.

"It was a trap!"

"What was a trap?" Lehman croaked out dryly, looking to the empty passenger seat and the open door beyond it, a dusting of snow and brown leaves dancing in the breeze.

CHAPTER 61

LOCK ARRIVED INTO A CHAPEL SMELLING OF perspiration and a flowery perfume he knew I wore.

He thought to himself: Moria's bus just arrived. She can't be anywhere near here.

His eyes taking time to adjust to what amounted to thousands of stained-glass colors spread across stone and wood and little else, he stepped farther in.

"Hello?" His voice reverberated. He sniffed again, picking up traces of wood oil, damp earth, and the foul smell of men—perspiring men.

Not boys. Not perspiration. Sweat. Man sweat.

Perfume and men. The combination roiled his stomach.

He took several more steps into the chancel before he saw a shape in the pews.

"Who's there?"

"Nat . . . a . . . lie." She sounded so nervous, but Natalie was always twitchy when around him.

"Well, hello! I thought . . . That is . . . I'm confused," he said. Confusion gave way to anger. "Wait just a sec! Did you and LeTona cook this up? I just saw the photography club, you see? There's no way Moria intended—"

Natalie let out a squeal as she was wrestled to standing, her neck suddenly in the crook of a man's elbow.

Two other men cut off the chapel door from Sherlock.

From somewhere deep in shadow near the altar, a hideous-looking thing appeared. It was a man, six feet or taller, wearing a black robe and a papier-mâché mask fashioned into a raven's beak.

Sherlock knew that mask. The Raven had conducted the ceremony at James's secret initiation.

"I'm only going to say this once, Mr. Holmes, so listen up and be careful with your words. A great deal rides on what you say next."

CHAPTER 62

Being called to the lounge in the Bricks could be unsettling or exciting depending on whom you were expecting. Being called to the lounge when you were hungry, having just returned from a trip that went way longer than you wanted, was nothing short of annoying.

I wanted dinner. I had homework to get done. I wanted back the hours I'd lost to the stupid field trip. Funny, I thought, I could plan for the future, but I couldn't do squat about the past. Annoying the way time worked. Or didn't.

I approached the lounge with trepidation. If

Lock or Jamie, I'd send him packing. If a teacher or the headmaster or Lowry, I wasn't sure what I'd do.

Check "D": None of the above.

"Mr. Lehman," I said, stunned to see the man so out of place from where we'd originally met.

"Ms. Moriarty. We haven't much time. I've been denied permission to be here, yet here I am. Do you understand?"

"Not really," I said. But that seemed to trouble him. "I guess." He liked that answer better.

Although typically monitored by the house mistress or an upperclassman, the lounge offered a more private nook away from the craziness of the television in the opposite corner, where five or six girls were gathered in front of a reality TV show involving shopping. There was a lot of snickering going on.

He handed me Father's journal.

"What's going on?" I asked.

"I tried to pass this to our mutual friend. He refused it. I ask you to take it. To protect it." If he spoke any softer I was going to have to put my ear to his lips, which was a nasty option I had no intention of doing.

He looked sickly, sweating the way he was when it was so dang cold outside. Most people ended up with a red nose and bright cheeks when coming inside. He looked gray and pasty.

"Your friend can share with you everything I told him. I warned him, and I'll warn you: lock that up somewhere. Hide it. Don't ever tell a soul what you've done. Not a soul."

"That doesn't sound great."

"It is my opinion that family secrets should remain in the family. Any family. Yours, especially."

"Now you're teasing me."

"Am I? I suppose that's right. Forgive me. Mr. Holmes will catch you up. What I want to make clear . . . why I'm here, with you, Moria . . . what I said to him about your mother—"

"Mother!?" My chest hurt.

"One should not speculate about such sensitive things. I'm ashamed of myself. Perhaps, as Mr. Holmes encouraged, the day will come when I can translate the rest of the journal. When I can feel safe translating the rest of the journal. Perhaps I will be able to better inform you and James at that time. For now, please accept my apologies for interjecting speculation where I should have not. Most unprofessional."

"What . . . about . . . Mother?"

The desk phone rang. Funny, we both looked over at it. Just a phone ringing, but there we were staring.

Mr. Lehman started moving the moment the girl behind the desk looked in our direction. She cupped the phone to call out at him, but too late: Mr. Lehman was already out the door.

Father's journal sat on his chair, along with a few silver pearls of melted snow.

I reached for it.

She was looking at me, now. Far too intensely.

I used a scream from the girls watching the show to make my own move for the door.

CHAPTER 63

WITH EVERY INTENTION TO FIND SHERLOCK, the only real clue I had was a note from NATO, telling me to talk to LeTona if I wanted to find Sherlock. I hated—hated!—having to deal with gorgeous LeTona. Why I should check with her about Sherlock I had no idea, but I wanted the fastest way to Sherlock, and I silently thanked Natalie for leaving the note.

I ducked into the washroom on Bricks Middle 2 to send LeTona a text, hoping like everyone else she kept her phone handy. Otherwise it could take hours of running around to find her.

It turned out she was only a long hallway from me, in the washroom of Bricks Middle 1.

LeTona wore a black leotard top and gray gym pants with WILLIAMS COLLEGE running down the leg. She looked about twenty-four. She was soiling a white facecloth while removing makeup. I'd never known she even wore makeup. She was that good at it.

"What's up?"

"Natalie said I should ask you where to find Sherlock."

She put the cloth down. I saw in the mirror a confused girl. "Did she? Sekulow or Anderson?"

"Sekulow."

"That's weird."

"Why?" I asked. She looked legitimately troubled. "LeTona?"

"She has a mad crush on him, doesn't she?"

"Yes, that sounds about right."

I could see some deep thinking going on. Maybe reliving something. "Listen," she said, "I did a favor for James, okay? I happen to like your brother, a lot. Probably too much. He asked me to deliver a message to Sherlock and I'm thinking maybe Sekulow overheard me or something."

"Because?"

"Because I told Sherlock you'd be waiting for

him in the chapel after dinner."

"You what?"

"Yeah." She shrugged. "That's what James asked me to do."

"So Sherlock's waiting for me in the chapel?"

"I suppose. I mean, dinner ended a while ago, so how should I know?"

"And Natalie overheard you?"

"I don't know! She wrote the note, didn't she?"

"Why would James do that?" It just sort of slipped out.

"He's your brother!" she said. It wasn't just a statement, but an accusation of some sort. "If you want to kind of drop a hint that I like him, I wouldn't mind that at all."

I saw my mouth open in the mirror. I shut it.

James had arranged a meeting with Sherlock in the chapel. But he'd tricked him into it.

That couldn't be good.

CHAPTER 64

I STARTED OUT FROM THE BRICKS ON A BEELINE to the chapel when I caught sight of my brother and his two idiots, Ryan Eisenower and Bret Thorndyke. They, too, appeared to be headed for the chapel.

"Hey!" I called out angrily, stomping toward James. Only then did it register that the trio was not headed for the chapel, but toward Bricks 1, toward me, causing me to wonder if my brother had eyes and ears in every dorm. This was getting creepy.

James took in our public surroundings. It was

almost like a tic, an automatic response, and one I'd never seen before. I shivered as I strode toward him, then regained my composure.

As if that wasn't enough, using some unseen boy code, his two accomplices, looking eerily like bodyguards, stepped back to leave me and James alone as James took me—gently, I was pleased to note—by the arm and led me toward the shadows of the steps leading down into a breezeway connecting Bricks 1 to the Main House.

"What's this with LeTona?" I said in a raspy voice my brother knew only too well.

"Oh, that."

"Yes. That! I have no plans to meet Sherlock in the chapel, so what's that about, Jamie?"

In the dim light of the space I saw only the whites of his eyes. He was deeply troubled, unwilling to make eye contact.

"You two should have included me," he said.

"Included you? We saved you."

"Don't you think I know that!"

"Then what? Why did you want Sher— Oh, Jamie! What's going to happen?" I started off, but he seized my arm, this time not so gently. He held me there.

"Don't," he said. "You can't go there."

"I can, and I will! You coward! What's supposed to happen?"

"You and him . . . keep too many secrets. He doesn't share enough. Now he will."

"They're our secrets, Jamie. Our family. Lock is helping us! What's supposed to happen to him?"

"You can't change that," my brother said.

"But you can, Jamie!" I pulled. I kicked out at him. "Whose secrets are they, anyway?" A hand clasped over my mouth. Arms wrapped around and held me from behind. The two beasts. Where had they come from?

"My boy there behind you saw your little meeting with *Sherlost* in the practice room." I wiggled to be free. I tried to speak, which proved useless. "Oh, yes, Mo, I've been keeping an eye on you— for your own protection. He has things that belong to us, knows things that belong to us."

Again, I struggled. I broke my mouth free of the hand for a precious moment. "This isn't us, James! It isn't Father!" Now I understood Sherlock's long look at the window in the practice room. It had been closed when we'd entered. He'd known that, but didn't want to frighten me. Eisenower or Thorndyke had pried it open, startling us when the shade clapped against the window frame. The spy had missed Sherlock explaining that the necklace in his pocket was Ruby Berliner's artwork. James thought it was the real one!

My brother's expression changed from anger to realization. "Our secrets," James said, as if it had suddenly just occurred to him. He told the goons, "Tie her up. Gag her. Keep her down there." He looked at the pavement. "If I'm not back in an hour, let her go."

I struggled. Eisenower—it must have been Ryan, given the boy's strength—lifted me off my feet, so that I flailed like a spoiled infant in a parent's arms.

"One of you stays with her at all times," James called as he hurried up the brick steps. "You protect her at all costs!"

CHAPTER 65

THE RAVEN STOOD ON THE FAR SIDE OF THE
kneeling Sir Galahad statue, the distant stained-
glass windows fitting his head like a crown of color.

"Costumes," a nervous Sherlock said. "No one
told me!"

Nothing.

"I'd like my friend back, please."

"I warned you, Mr. Holmes. This is a time to
shut up, listen, and cooperate, believe me." The
strange, disturbing bird beak muffled the caped
man's low voice.

"Let her go, and we may have a covenant,"

Sherlock said. "You don't want her hearing this."

"No, it's true."

A man wearing a bandit's handkerchief mask slapped a cloth onto Natalie's face. She struggled and went slack.

"There was no need for that," Sherlock said.

"The necklace you stole from the museum," said the Raven. "We are prepared to win the information in any number of ways, none of which will appeal to you or your friend here."

"I see."

"You will hand it over. One of my associates will accompany you back to the dorm, if necessary. But," the Raven said, preventing Sherlock from speaking, "any games, any attempt on your part to cross me, and there will be Devil's work at play." He raised his arm in a priestly fashion that gave Sherlock misgivings.

"And after we make this exchange, I suppose one of your . . . fledglings . . . here is going to what? Drug me? Beat me silly until I lie to you how to use it?"

"Something like that. More's the pity."

"Just think how I feel?"

"Suffice it to say, you will not be leaving here until I say so."

"Or, more like until I do!" James's voice rose from behind Sherlock.

The Raven's beak lifted slightly. Sherlock could see the man's chin. Who is it? he wondered.

"Leave, now!" crowed the Raven. "We agreed on this."

"I've reconsidered," James told the Raven.

"It's too late," said the Raven.

"Think carefully," said James in a commanding and defiant tone. "We're scrubbing this plan. Think very, very carefully."

"It cannot be reversed," the Raven declared. "What's done is done. You're a moment too late."

Sherlock didn't like the sound of that. "The girl," he said. "She's an innocent victim in all this."

"No one is truly innocent," said the Raven.

"Let's skip the tired philosophy, shall we?" Sherlock proposed. "This is where I offer you this," he said, withdrawing the cross necklace from his pocket, dangling it from the string of pearls, "and you trade me the girl."

"What girl?" James asked. "MORIA!?"

"It's Natalie Sekulow," said Sherlock, correcting. "These beasts—or fowls, or whatever—have chloroformed poor Natalie unconscious."

"What?" James said, astonished and angry.

Two of the bandits approached Sherlock.

"A word of caution," Sherlock said. "The jewel attached is not a jewel at all, but a specially crafted prism of glass. If you approach any closer I shall shatter it." Sherlock spun the necklace.

The Raven was working hard to disguise his voice. Sherlock could not determine his identity.

"Then you'd better set it down gently, boy."

"Of course . . . I will not. Smashed into a thousand pieces, I promise."

"If you put it down, the girl goes free. We give you something to wipe these events from your memory, and we all go on as if nothing happened. Believe me, boy, you want this deal."

"To the contrary. You want this prism. And whether you know it or not, you want my memory, because I know how to use the prism. So trust you, I do not. Nor will I." Sherlock stood his ground. "Natalie, or you are going to be sweeping up glass."

"I don't think so."

The bandits charged.

Sherlock rarely regretted his lack of athleticism, until a moment when he was under attack. He had only the one chance. He spun and threw the necklace underhanded, giving it a great deal of height and arc—right for the stained-glass window, as he'd previously arranged.

A small panel at the bottom of each stained-glass window was opened for ventilation. Sherlock had noticed it earlier in the day, prior to making the arrangement for someone to be out there in the cold.

With everyone watching, the necklace flew in a perfect arc, struck the angled piece of glass, and ricocheted outside.

"Cripes!" the Raven said.

James took off running for the chapel doors.

"No, James!" Not in the plan! he wanted to cry out.

With his attackers distracted, Sherlock hurried deeper into the chapel toward the Raven. He slammed the man into Sir Galahad, sprinting toward the hidden panel behind the altar, a panel that was supposed to have been known only to the Scowerers.

CHAPTER 66

James rounded the corner of the chapel, lost his balance, and slipped. His hand landed on a fist-sized rock. He clutched it, prepared to throw it at the shape of a man bent over while picking up the necklace.

Obviously a Scowerer—or worse, a Meirleach. James suddenly felt an allegiance to Sherlock and Natalie.

"Leave it!" James shouted before hurling the rock like a baseball when the man failed to respond.

James was good at baseball; he had an accurate arm.

The man collapsed lifelessly, the necklace falling in slow motion along with him.

James hurried and slid on his knees, searching the snowy grass for the necklace before the man came to grudgingly and began to fight him for it.

There! James had it!

He kicked out at the fallen man to prove his point, exert his superiority. "See?" he called.

Two men appeared from the back of the chapel. No masks. Meirleach? he wondered.

The two ran toward him. James would need the necklace to free Natalie, just as Sherlock had tried.

The difference was, the Raven would listen to James.

The two drew closer but suddenly James's legs wouldn't move. He scooched back on his bottom away from the body, his eyes adjusting to the dark.

There was something black on the side of the man's head.

A good deal of blood. Blood that was draining from the hole in the man's scalp, oozing really, because the man's heart had stopped.

Out of the dark, a shadow ripped into the two intruders. One of the two smacked headfirst into the chapel and fell unconscious. The other tried a martial arts move of some sort, but had his legs cut out from beneath him.

Espiranzo. He had saved James. "Are you okay?" he asked.

"I . . ." James couldn't speak another word. It wasn't the blood of the man he'd hit with the rock, it was the stitches on his victim's exposed forearm.

He knew the wound, knew the stitches, remembered his own rescue from Camden Cod and Shellfish. The stitches belonged to Ralph.

CHAPTER 67

Sʜᴇʀʟᴏᴄᴋ ᴡᴀѕ ᴄᴀᴜɢʜᴛ, ɴᴏᴛ ʙʏ ᴛʜᴇ Sᴄᴏᴡᴇʀ-
ers outsmarting him or anticipating he might try
to use their underground sanctuary as a means of
escape, but because of a shoelace. He tripped at the
top of the stone steps, tumbled head over heels like
an uncoordinated gymnast, and lay dazed at the
bottom, making him easy prey.

Hauled to his feet by a pair of foul-smelling
Scowerers, he was blindfolded and dragged into
the center of the torch-lit space. It smelled of earth
and kerosene, decaying leaves and campfires. The

flickering yellow flames threw dancing shadows onto his blindfold.

Sherlock was deposited into a chair and tied in place. He heard others enter from the tunnel to the Alumni House basement, a tunnel that he himself had once used. They dragged something heavy and released it.

Someone lumbered down the staircase. The Raven, Sherlock thought. The man was moving painfully because of the shove Sherlock had given him. Sherlock used a memory technique, assigning a particular memory to a place in a room. He used Mr. Moriarty's office as his memory room: the man's desk became the necklace; the fireplace, the chapel; the oil painting, the Raven. He stored these in case he was subjected to the amnesia concoction they'd already threatened him with.

Before they'd blindfolded him, he'd seen Natalie Sekulow, apparently unconscious and tied to a chair.

From behind came the faster feet of someone lighter and more agile hurrying down the stairs from the chapel.

James, Sherlock thought. Confirmed when his roommate spoke a moment later.

"Let him go!" James called.

"The necklace," the Raven said.

"Is mine," James said. "I have it, and I'll keep it."

"You will hand it over." The Raven left a long pause. "And when you do, the boy goes free. The girl, too, though she may take a tad longer to come around."

"I won't. It belongs to me and my family."

"Nrff-rum-de-hmph!" the gagged Sherlock said. James untied the gag. No one stopped him.

"Give it to them," Sherlock said. "On balance it seems a good tradeoff from where I sit."

"Listen to him," the Raven said.

"Think of the necklace like the mouse you heard in our room, my dear boy," Sherlock said. "Just a mouse, after all."

Everyone in the cavern could feel James thinking during the long-harbored silence that followed.

"I told you to shut him up!" the Raven complained.

"Here," James said, "it's yours for the two of them, but it happens now. Right now."

"We're on the same side here," said the Raven.

"I wonder."

"No need for such negotiations," the man said.

"The two outside . . ." James said. "They were Meirleach."

"Yes," Espiranzo said, now following down the stairs behind James. "I'm here for Mr. Moriarty," he added.

"You're assigned to him on my orders," the Raven said.

"No, sir. I'm assigned to him on his orders. And I'll be performing my duties. My brethren here, they took the same oath. Not you to, Director, but to the young man himself. To his line. Eh, boys?"

"Both Sherlock and Natalie for the necklace. That was the deal," James said.

"You'll find the girl in need of a good night's sleep. She won't be coming round for a good twelve hours or more."

"Take her," Espiranzo said, addressing one of the men who'd been with the Raven. The man obeyed. That was when James knew it was going to work out.

Sherlock remained blindfolded as he was led by James through what he knew to be the tunnel to the alumni building. But for once he kept his knowledge to himself.

Once outside, the blindfold was removed and the two boys walked a few paces behind Espiranzo and the Scowerer who carried Natalie in his arms.

"You take her to the infirmary," Espiranzo said to his man. "Ask for Alice. Tell her the girl'll be fine after a night's sleep. She won't question you."

Espiranzo led the boys along the back road

adjacent to the Lower Bricks. Sherlock and James trailed him by several yards.

"The mouse wasn't a mouse," James said quietly. "It was the Meirleach trying to sneak in our window."

"And the necklace isn't the necklace," Sherlock said. "The pearls are poor imitation. The gold is spray paint over a cross from the metal shop. Ruby Berliner fixed it up for me as a special gift."

"What!?"

"In case I needed it. As it turned out, it came in quite handy. Been carrying that thing around for days now. I have no idea where the real necklace is. When I left the museum it was in its case."

"You know what'll happen when that man realizes what you've done?" James said.

"Nothing," Sherlock said, "because I won't be around."

"I don't understand."

"Think about it, James. At this point I know far too much. They would have to kill me or—"

"Expel you."

"There you go," Sherlock said. "I'll be gone by morning, and that necklace won't likely be found out for what it is until some time long after that."

"You can't go!" James objected.

"If it was up to me, I wouldn't. But I will,

because it's not. But don't think you'll be getting rid of me any too soon. Even from a distance, I'll still be working for you."

"I appreciate that, but I don't need you anymore," James said proudly.

"You can't possibly take on Hildebrandt alone," Sherlock said, bringing James to a sudden stop.

"How the crud did you know about him?"

"There is so much I know. One shudders at the thought." Sherlock said nothing of Father's translated journal. Instead, he used some of Ruby's misdirection on his roommate. "It's your mother I can help with."

"Mother? What about Mother?"

"If I'm right—and when am I not?—it's all going to come together. But Hildebrandt will have something to say about that, I'm afraid. If and when we can find him."

"Ah . . . but I already have found him," James said, savoring the one time he'd been able to stun Sherlock Holmes.

CHAPTER 68

I TOOK THE NEWS OF RALPH'S CAR CRASH HARD. New England roads were narrow and twisty, originally horse trails through forest, most of them. The wreck suggested Ralph had been driving southwest from Boston—toward Baskerville Academy, I thought. Why? I wondered. On that, of all nights, why?

The news came the morning after those beasts, Bret and Ryan, had held me for two hours in a dusty, narrow space that smelled of concrete, like a basement. I cried in the chapel. I cried in my room. I cried on walks around campus where no one could see me. Ralph wasn't officially family, so though James and I could return to Boston the following weekend for a service, the faculty didn't cut me any slack when it came to homework. I could be sad on my own time.

But my tears weren't only for dear Ralph, a man whom I loved beyond the limits of love and care. They were for my brother, who hadn't been seen for the past thirty-two hours.

Given that the last time James had disappeared it had been due to unfortunate circumstances, I couldn't help but think he'd been kidnapped again. Mr. Lowry and Headmaster Crudgeon had questioned me for nearly an hour in Crudgeon's office about whether James had contacted me, what he might have told me, blah-blah-blah. No matter how many times I swore I'd heard nothing, they repeated nearly the same questions, suggesting they didn't believe me at all. When, finally, I left, despite their attempts at reassurance to the contrary, I was deathly afraid for my brother.

If my lack of sleep was any indication, James was in trouble. Deep trouble. And Crudgeon and Lowry knew it.

Sherlock would later claim he had acted out of his own curiosity, but I would harbor the suspicions he did it for me, trying to pull me out of my depression and sorrow. At that point, no one in the school, including me, had heard of any events at the chapel, deadly or otherwise. To the student body, and the proctors for all I knew, it had been a Thursday night like any other: unremarkable, cold, and quiet on the hill. The rumors concerned James's disappearance, a good number of which had connected it to his and Lexie's failed relationship. People did not know my brother very well. He would not give an ex-girlfriend more than thirty seconds of consideration.

The only other whiff I got that something strange was going on was when Mrs. Favor visited our room at one in the morning. She didn't need to wake me because I was just lying in the dark staring at the ceiling. She woke Jamala by accident.

After an unneeded apology for waking me, which she had not, Mrs. Favor asked me a string of questions regarding Sherlock. When had I last seen him? Had he contacted me? Answering her questions was not easy given LeTona's involvement, a girl I didn't want to get into trouble, along with Eisenower and Thorndyke holding me hostage, blindfolded—but at my (missing) brother's command. I made up something and tried to memorize my fiction word for word so that I'd be able to repeat it if asked again. Lying wasn't worth the work involved. I wasn't sure why people bothered with it.

Sherlock, meanwhile, was on a mission. A two-fold mission. First, he wanted to avoid anyone in authority at Baskerville, for he feared expulsion. Guessing the Raven had been Crudgeon or, if not, someone close to the headmaster, he knew the Scowerers couldn't allow him to remain on campus. He slept by day beneath the stage in Hard Auditorium. I deposited leftovers from the dining room inside the piano on stage. Second, he wanted to find James, showing that he, Sherlock, had more heart than even I gave him credit for. It wasn't exactly as I'd thought, but nothing ever is.

After dark, nearly a full twenty-four hours following the events in the chapel, Sherlock began his search for my brother in the chapel's bell tower. It was a risky and frightful effort, given that his master key did not unlock the door to the tower, requiring Sherlock to scale the outer wall. He was not a regular at the school's indoor climbing wall, so one can only wonder at the terror that must have possessed the boy as he ascended the stones and grout, toehold by fingerhold. At last, he arrived to the square tower's wood platform and its massive iron bell, rusting and as old as the stars. No James.

Defeated, exhausted, Sherlock looked out onto the Main House and its clock tower. He withdrew his pocket watch. His eyes returned to the clock tower. Of course! he thought.

Sherlock carefully put his weight onto the thick rope that tolled the bell, gently so the clapper wouldn't strike and sound, and slid his way down, opening the locked door from the inside. Let the chaplain figure out that one, he thought.

Next, Sherlock made his way to the rafters and joists above the Main House's third floor and immediately above a former dining hall, turned library, turned extra art studio. Climbing the joists in the dark proved treacherous. Sherlock knew if he fell he would, at the very least, damage the ceiling of the art studio, and at the worst, break through the Sheetrock and plummet twenty feet to its floor, likely breaking most of the bones in his body.

He worked his way up and into the Main House clock tower, having a tricky time of it as he climbed through the clock's gears and inner workings.

"Go away," James said.

"Aren't you impressed in the least that I've found you?"

James was balled up as far from Sherlock as he could get. The single light atop the clock tower found its way through ventilation slats and spread a harsh white light in stripes across the mechanism and both boys.

"Not the least bit curious?" Sherlock asked.

James glared, his skin gray, his eyes unresponsive.

"I've tried a number of places, including the tunnels. I tried the bell tower because I thought if it was me, I'd want a view of what was going on, and a way out in case I didn't like what I saw."

"Shut up."

"You must have leaned against a gear, dear boy. Nodded out, I imagine. Do you remember waking up against the clock's mechanism? It's seven minutes slow, you see? I monitor it carefully against my own timepiece." He withdrew an old-fashioned pocket watch. "It's never as much as a few seconds behind. A perfect piece of timekeeping, this." He slipped it back into his pants pocket. "I measure the two against each other because until your visit up here, they were stroke for stroke. But there I am in the bell tower, and I look across and good lord, seven minutes slow. So I knew, you see? Or was quite confident, I suppose."

"Shut up. Go away."

"You didn't know, James." Sherlock cracked whatever cage held James.

"I thought he was a Meirleach."

"The Raven and his men have made it look like a car crash. Over and done. Not even Moria knows. Never will."

"But you know," James said. "And I know you know. And that makes us enemies. For life."

"I suppose. Ralph would not blame you for trying to protect your family's secrets. I won't use it against you."

"But you could. You're a threat to me. As long as you're alive, you're a threat to me." His slit eyes opened then, revealing true menace. A cornered and caged animal.

"Interesting."

"That's all you've got? Interesting?"

"That's not all I've got," said Sherlock. "I have the stone you threw. It will have your DNA on it, for I promise you were sweating at the time. Some skin, perhaps. I have it put away in a safe place with instructions to recover it should anything untoward happen to me. You don't want to hurt me, James. You had better hope I live a long, productive life. If anything happens to me, that stone will surface. There's no statute of limitations on murder. Did you know that?"

If James was breathing, there was no evidence of it.

"Come down from here. Tell them you were grieving for him. They'll believe you."

"Why would you allow me to do that?"

"Because Moria and I need you, dear boy, and the men you control. The Scowerers. Bringing Hildebrandt to justice will not be easy."

"Why would you care?" James said.

"You and Moria contracted me to help you find your father's killer. That person remains at large."

"We didn't contract you!" James said. "We asked you. Kind of."

"Semantics."

"You think it's Hildebrandt?"

"I do," Sherlock said. "Your father was embroiled in a policy change in the Directory. This, I know, though I can't share how I know it, not yet. That put him at odds with many. Hildebrandt ran the FBI for decades, did you know that? Think of that power, James! Think if a person like that sits on the Directory. How could such a thing happen? Think if he wanted you out of the way! At the very least Hildebrandt's a person of interest to us. He was at odds with your father! Tell me you aren't intrigued, James."

James uncoiled his grip on his shins. "Enemies for life. You understand that?"

"So melodramatic. Give it a rest! I detest such labels. Our paths are currently entwined. Some knots. I'll give you that. But we share a common purpose. And we both care for Moria."

"Leave her out of this."

"Do you think that's up to me?" Sherlock cocked his head like a cat.

"You know too much. The Directory . . . it won't be safe for you."

"Yes. I'm aware. You'll have to control the dogs. You don't want them biting me."

"What's that supposed to mean?"

"Think it through, James. Consider the stone. At all times, consider the stone."

"You assume too much."

"I'll be expelled. We both know that's the only logical step. I'll keep my mouth shut, my head down, but I imagine they will send people for me, or tip off the Meirleach."

"How can you possibly know what you know?"

"It's me, James. Let's not forget it's me."

"You are . . . impossible."

"To the contrary, I'm very much real, my friend. Never underestimate me. I will be your undoing."

"We'll see about that."

"But let's put all that aside until we see Hildebrandt to justice," Sherlock said.

"Indeed." Sherlock waited as the movement of the clock hand made another loud click. "We should set it forward seven minutes before we go so it's available to you as a hideout should you need it."

"It won't be me needing the hideout, pal."

Sherlock smiled nearly ear to ear. "You're better already. Come on, let's get out of here."

CHAPTER 69

SHERLOCK WAS EXPELLED FROM BASKERVILLE for "behavior unsuitable for a student of the academy." He'd been packed up and moved off campus overnight, with no chance to say good-bye to anyone, including me. I kept my phone on around the clock, hoping for a text or an email, even though Headmaster Crudgeon told the student body that, "Mr. Holmes has been forbidden from contacting any student prior to the end of the school year, and if such contact is made, the student in question is to notify any faculty member immediately."

The letter came by mail, in an envelope I nearly trashed without opening. The envelope announced "Your 6 favorite magazines absolutely free!" But a faint image had been used to cancel out the stamp.

It was an image familiar to me, an image I'd heard described by my brother. The letter inside was not from a magazine publisher.

My Dearest Moria:

By now you are aware I was made to leave campus rather unexpectedly. I don't know what you'll be told, but it was not voluntary. I've been expelled and forbidden from getting within two hundred yards of the campus.

What you need to know is this: though I've been sent back to dreary old London, if I have anything to do with it—and when don't I?—it won't be for long!

I have made extraordinary headway in our mutual pursuit—you will know what I'm talking about, of course. I shared some of this, and I believe that is why I've been sent away. You can assume your mail is being watched, that you are being watched, and that your emails and texts are likely being intercepted. So play nice, will you?

Please, Moria: play nice. It will set back our efforts substantially to have you expelled as well. And we are close. I promise you!

You must know this as well—the person who broke a heart cannot, I'm sorry to say, be trusted. He who twists tongues can be and should be so. The lesser of two evils is the more troublesome and even less trustworthy than the aforementioned. The one to blame is known to me. The secret place is no longer, so do something. With these clues I put you on to the path of finishing what we started. But wait for me, please. I am full of surprises.

I plead with you, dear girl, not to forget me. Our task is nowhere near complete, though, I'm pleased to say, we've accomplished what we set out to do.

I have advised our gumshoe of a vessel that should have sailed, but did not. Fingers crossed.

Yours, and I mean that,
Sherlock

My first reaction was sadness. I hadn't considered he might have headed back to England. He was half a world away.

My second reaction was anger. At the headmaster. At my brother. At all those who'd conspired to send Sherlock away. For it had to be a conspiracy.

My third reaction was a combination of paranoia and irritation. Of course, Sherlock would leave me with clues rather than just tell me whatever it was he wanted me to know! But his using clues also signaled he'd feared even my mail would be opened. The less private my life became, the more sleepless and disturbed I became. How was I supposed to live a normal life with the feeling of eyes watching me? I started dressing in my closet with the sliding doors closed. This, despite my having pulled the drapes and turned off the overhead light in the room. I didn't want to speak for fear I was being recorded. I ate less—a good thing. I slept less—a bad thing.

I sat on a toilet seat fully clothed while decoding Sherlock's letter, the stall door bolted shut.

the person who broke a heart cannot, I'm sorry to say, be trusted.

This one was easy. James had broken Lexie's heart. But I didn't want to believe the message. How could Sherlock tell me not to trust my own brother?

*He who twists tongues can be and should
be so.*

No idea who this was or what it meant.

*The lesser of two evils is the more
troublesome and even less trustworthy
than the aforementioned.*

I wasn't sure I could solve this until I solved the
tongue twister. But the lesser of two evils comment
sounded to me like something Sherlock had said
about Ralph and Lois.

The one to blame is known to me.

This one intrigued me. I must have read it
twenty times. No matter how many ways I tried to
interpret it, I believed he meant Father's killer. Your
father's killer is known to me. I couldn't breathe.
How long was I supposed to wait until I found out
if this was true?

*The secret place is no longer, so do
something.*

There were two secret places Sherlock and I

had dealt with: the space beneath the chapel, about which I knew but where I had not visited; Father's secret room off his office.

Sherlock wouldn't ask me to do something about the Scowerers' ceremonial cave. His demand that I take action meant he wanted me to move everything out of Father's hiding place. To where and how, I had no idea. But I knew if he said it had to be done, it was better to act than argue. I could make a plan. I could visit weekends. I had a hunch he would not want me working with Lois. I had my work cut out for me.

we've accomplished what we set out to do.

I took this to mean at least one of two things, maybe both. We'd saved James. Protected him, which was something we'd discussed. We—that is, Sherlock—had identified Father's killer. That meant his death hadn't been an accident. That meant someone was out there who could be held accountable. The fact that Sherlock had not told the police meant he lacked evidence. Was that up to me to find? Was I supposed to wait for him? For how long? Years?

He hadn't included an address where I might

write him. This was supposed to be a one-way conversation, like every other Sherlock conversation. If I hadn't liked him so much, I could have hated him.

CHAPTER 70

NATALIE RETURNED TO CLASSES HAVING MISSED most of a week. She made no mention of her ailment, though something to do with a break-in at the science labs was rumored.

Soon enough everyone would forget the rumors about her, as the students of Baskerville Academy were so good at doing. I didn't forget about her. Natalie and I formed a stronger relationship than ever. Jamala tried hard to crack whatever bonded Natalie and me, and I felt horrible when it didn't work out. I liked Jamala so much, but now I shared something with Natalie, and we both knew it.

Sharing makes for stronger friendship.

James turned even more sullen and dark. He didn't speak to me or anyone else that I could see. Over the following weekend we spent paying our respects to our lost Ralph, I don't think we ever had a meaningful conversation.

We were strangers. James had gone cold. Ralph's crash had clearly upset him to the point that I got the feeling he felt responsible. Maybe he had called Ralph that night. Maybe Ralph wouldn't have been on the road without James. It didn't matter, because James wouldn't speak of it.

Something else struck me: James had aged. It was like he'd gone from fourteen to eighteen or twenty overnight. He focused on his homework and basketball, and nothing else. He no longer worked to appear cool or hang out with the tough guys. He traveled solo.

By spring break nothing had changed. I was frustrated. James was independent. He signed up for a school ski trip out west.

I signed up for the school trip to London. It was supposed to be for fourth form only, but someone made an exception for me. I was playing the sympathy card wherever I could.

James and I headed in opposite directions.

I put great significance in that.

CHAPTER 71

I WAS TRAILING BEHIND THE GROUP OF SOPHO-mores in the National Portrait Gallery as I had been since the start of the London spring break trip. I didn't know any of them. I found the jet lag annoying, the lack of company a relief, and the city of London as wonderful as any place I'd ever visited.

"Edward William Lane," said a boy's low voice over my shoulder. A voice I recognized. A voice that filled me with the flush of excitement.

Two exhibit halls later I found the chance to hang back and let our group of nine go ahead without me.

I had to ask two security guards before locating exhibit hall 15 and a statue of a sitting man wearing a turban. It was a sculpture by Edward William Lane. The only piece by the artist in the museum.

"It's good to see you."

I turned to that voice, but the person wasn't Sherlock, wasn't whom I'd expected. Before me was a puffy-faced college-aged kid with a scruffy moustache, stringy shoulder-length hair, and horrible teeth.

"Do I know you?" I asked, trying to be polite. "Did a friend send you to fetch me?"

The smile gave him away. It was Sherlock, but in such a good disguise I still didn't quite believe it. "Is that really you?"

"That's a question that can only be answered in the affirmative by whomever is asked."

That was when I absolutely knew it was Sherlock. I threw my arms around him and hugged him like my favorite teddy bear. I could feel his arms not hug me back, and realized I shocked him with such a display of affection. I let go and stepped back.

"Good to see you, too," he said.

I wasn't about to apologize.

"First, your father," he said.

"How close are we?"

"Hot as Hades," he said, playing my game of

warm and warmer. "We need Lehman's full translation. It points to a man named Hildebrandt." He
told me all he and James had discussed—a power
struggle within the Directory. One of the most
famous men in law enforcement now helping to
govern a major crime syndicate. It spun my head.

"Knowing and proving," Sherlock said. "Bringing to justice. These must be taken in order. Lowry
isn't a bad guy. I think we saw all that wrong.
Crudgeon, too, for that matter. All the late-night
meetings you and James saw—I'm guessing those
two were trying to advise, not threaten your father.
Ralph was forever in your father's service, your
family's service. I don't doubt Lois's loyalty to your
father, but because of her willingness to sedate
Ralph, I don't think we can fully trust her. There's
a fine line between love and obedience. Lois may
be able to love you and James while being obedi-
ent to her employers. That may prove difficult for
us." Sherlock looked around. "Did you clear out
the secret room?"

"Most of it. Not everything. Lois barely lets
me out of her sight. I've put some in the basement.
Some in the upstairs library."

"And James?" Sherlock asked.

"He sulks. He broods."

"Doesn't surprise me. He carries a great burden."

"Is that a rubber nose?"

"It is! Fantastic, isn't it?"

"And the ears? What little I can see of them."

"Right."

"I miss you." Why would I say such a thing? How could my tongue betray me like that?

"Oh."

"Well, don't get all mushy."

"No, I won't. No time for that." He grunted a Sherlockian grunt. I missed those as well.

"Why can't we just go to Colander?"

"Could do," Sherlock said. "But if I'm right about Hildebrandt—"

"—and when are you not?" I said, brimming with joy.

Sherlock snarled, his beak of a nose pointing down like a hawk's. "He's more powerful than Colander or anyone like him. The strategy might work; it might backfire."

"That's not good enough."

"We must bring Colander proof. Nothing circumstantial—hard-core proof. Even then, it may not be enough. We may have to take matters into our own hands."

"We'll never get the proof without you," I said, another example of speaking before thinking.

"Nice of you to say."

"I didn't mean it!" I stepped back from him. His disguise was so good it disturbed me.

Sherlock said, "I've saved the best for last."

"Would I expect anything less?" I said. "Mother."

"I'm impressed!"

"You should be!"

"We need your father's credit card records. We need to look on the third Thursday of every month."

"Why?"

"His journal. Something murky there. Lehman's full translation may help."

Young voices came from the closest gallery. My group.

We both heard them. Sherlock froze for a moment.

"Third Thursday," I said. "Father taught an evening course every Thursday."

Sherlock looked at me oddly. I hated that know-it-all in him. I loved it too—or liked it a lot.

"Check the university's course book. There's no such class."

"What?"

"I believe we'll find a clue as to your father's activities in his credit card statements. But I shouldn't ask Lois for help with that."

"A difference between love and obedience."

"You do listen!" he said. "The monthly records will likely be in his desk or hers. Someone paid them."

"Noted." I waited for the explanation I could feel coming.

"It's like this," Sherlock said. "If your mother left you, she left you. I don't think there's much we can do about that. But what if that isn't the case? What if she was removed before any harm could come to her? And I don't mean killed! Heavens no! Could your father have handled that alone? Perhaps." He answered himself before allowing me to. "But more likely, he might need a woman's help."

"Lois." I felt as if I had no air left in my lungs, like I was holding my breath underwater and my time had run out. "Obedience over love."

"Or vice versa," Sherlock said. "For once, I think it might have been just the opposite. Love for your mother. Devotion to your father. Look, I don't want to get your hopes up," Sherlock said.

"A little late for that!" I gasped.

He smiled. "Find his credit card statements. We will both need new emails. Email them to me. I can take it from there."

"I do miss you!"

"I'm glad."

"But I find you repulsive."

"Get in line," he said.

I wrapped my arms around him.

Sherlock hugged me back.

"You'll help me find her." I wasn't asking.

"It may not be good news, Moria. You must understand that."

"An answer, some kind of answer, good or bad . . ." I didn't finish my thought. Not immediately. "It'll save James. Sherlock! It'll be just the thing for James to get over losing Ralph!"

"Maybe," Sherlock said. "Though I wouldn't count on it."

"What's that supposed to mean?"

"James is different now, Moria. He's lost the two most important men in his life. He'll never be the same, not ever." He sounded as if he was speaking from experience. Why had I never bothered to ask about Sherlock's life before Baskerville?

"We will bring this man Hildebrandt to justice," I said. "We will find out once and for all what happened to Mother. 'Time heals all wounds,' right?"

Sherlock nodded. We both heard kids approaching. When I looked back Sherlock had taken off, giving me only his back.

But then he turned. The boy I didn't recognize looked at me with sympathetic eyes and I shuddered. He was trying to tell me something about James.

Something I didn't want to hear.

Acknowledgments

Special thanks to David Linker and Lindsey Karl at HarperCollins; Dan Conaway and Amy Berkower at Writers House; Nancy Zastrow, Brett Ellen Keeler, Storey Pearson, and Miranda McVey in my office. Marcelle, my dear wife, who stepped up and took the reins, keeping me organized; Laurel and David Walters, tireless early readers. My three years of boarding at Pomfret School provided the setting.

Author Note

Downward Spiral was outlined and written in its entirety while beta-testing mori, inc.'s collaborative writing and editing platform with the generous help and assistance of Aaron Brady, Lisa Rutherford, Brooke Muschott, and Jennifer Pooley.